"Fairy tales, ballads, riddles and folk s[...] and crimes, love and death, as Oph[...] snatches of them in her madness. Jean Rafferty's *Four Marys* takes up with strong feeling and uncompromising frankness the true histories concealed in these voices from the past; she unfolds their contemporary urgency. These are powerful stories about the lives and deaths of women – and of their children." MARINA WARNER, author of *From the Beast to the Blonde* and *Stranger Magic: Charmed States & the Arabian Nights*

"Through the theme of reproduction, Jean Rafferty unflinchingly reproduces Scottish legends, inscribing them into the contemporary world, so that in sinuous prose the past shimmers to life through the present. *The Four Marys* is a tremendous achievement." ZOË WICOMB, author of *October* and winner of a 2013 Windham Campbell prize

PRAISE AND AWARDS FOR JEAN RAFFERTY'S PREVIOUS WORK:

"Compelling and disturbing in equal measure." DEBORAH ORR, *The Guardian*

"Jean Rafferty is a remarkable writer with the bravery to explore the depths and the talent to take us there." LOUISE WELSH

WINNER of a Rosemary Goodchild Award, Rowntree Foundation Award and Travelex Travel Writing Award

SHORTLISTED for the inaugural Gavin Wallace Fellowship (2013), the Gordon Burn Prize 2013 and a British Press Award

THE
FOUR
MARYS

A QUARTET OF CONTEMPORARY TALES

Jean Rafferty

Saraband

Published by Saraband,
Suite 202, 98 Woodlands Road
Glasgow, G3 6HB, Scotland
www.saraband.net

ISBN: 9781908643575
ebook: 9781908643582

Printed in the EU on sustainably sourced paper.

Editor: Craig Hillsley
Text design: Laura Jones
Cover illustration by Andy Fielding www.andyfielding.co.uk

1 3 5 7 9 10 8 6 4 2

*This book is for the fifth Mary, my dear sister,
who makes my life richer – and funnier.*

CONTENTS

THE
SEALWOMAN

Wishing Night

DOWN, DEEP IN THE GREEN they swam, Mhairi and her sisters, sliding through the currents like silk through a wedding ring. It was dark down there, murky, with the salt sea stippling their skin and the hissing sound of their flippers swishing through the water. All round the north they had swum, and down through the Western Isles, where the beaches were white as bone and the waters turquoise and purple and as green as seas in the warmest corners of the world.

Now they were returning to the flat island out in the middle of the ocean. Not that it was more beautiful here, or the waters clearer, or the fish more plentiful. But it was here that they had started out from and here they always came back to. They had been gone too long and Mhairi wanted to see it. Her head surfaced from the water like a chubby periscope, her brown eyes taking in the rocky bay, the scrubby slope stretching back from the beach and then the distance where she could not see. 'The land beyond', she thought of it, and it held a powerful lure for her. There was a world beyond this watery world of theirs, a world she glimpsed but could not reach.

Mhairi had swum many miles but this island was her home, this and the seas around it.

'Mhairi,' called her sister, and she followed in pursuit of a shoal of fish, dipping her head and allowing the currents to pull her down into the water's depths. They worked fast, searing through the silvery creatures and snatching them in their mouths before swallowing them whole. But later Mhairi came back to the bay. She could not stay away.

The land was dark now. From the water, the beach and the rocks and the slick of green land beyond all merged into one indistinguishable smudge. Brown eyes slowly traversed the landscape. Looking. Longing, on this twilight evening, for the sound the woman made, the sound of human music.

There was none here when they were growing up, but since the woman had come the music had started. She would stand on the rock and coax the music from a curious wooden box for them, just for them. Mhairi's sisters tried to shut their ears to it – they thought it sounded screechy – but Mhairi couldn't. On nights when the woman was happy, the music was fast and gay, tripping out of the instrument the way water bubbled up sometimes across the rocks. On nights when she was sad, the music was low and sweet and plaintive and filled Mhairi with feelings that were too large for their life beneath the water.

The night darkened and the moon grew full, a huge silvery sphere standing solid in the sky, its pellucid light rippling over the land and making it seem as insubstantial as the water.

Morna, the oldest of the sisters, warned Mhairi to stay away from the woman on the rocks. 'It's dangerous tonight,' she said. 'Tonight is the wishing night. Far better to come with us and swim round to the fishing grounds on the other side.'

Wishing night, the scariest and yet the most exciting night of the year, when seals could shed their furry pelts and dance on the beach in the form of humans. Sometimes, in the old days, young men would wait for that night and steal the pelts, hoping to find a seal bride, but nowadays the human people seemed to have forgotten many things they once knew. The seals were never observed in their ritual. When the people looked at them now they saw only animals or economic opportunity, not the people of the water. Some humans even brought whole boatloads of their own kind to watch the seal colonies, without ever understanding who they really were.

Mhairi and her sisters never took part in wishing night. They came from a family famed for centuries for its swimming prowess, and they had no desire to shed their sleek water bodies and take on the clumsy, two-legged carcasses of land people. Many of the seal people shared their distaste and the practice was gradually fading away in a quite natural manner. Many were simply afraid of the humans, with their loud, rackety boats and the scummy oil they left floating on the water. It seeped into the seals' pores and left them feeling dirty and sluggish. Nowadays many seals only felt safe in the company of their own.

But Mhairi was fascinated by the humans. She always went closest to the shore when they swam near a village, and once, oh once, she had even swum away from her sisters and upriver into a big city. She heard the others furiously calling her, but on she swam. 'The water's dirty. Your skin will peel and scab,' Morna screamed at her, but she knew two porpoises had been there the week before and she pressed on.

The city was beautiful, with large, elegant buildings down by the riverside. But there were horrible things there, too. She saw a girl being mounted by a man in a dark, dank spot under one of the bridges. It was a gross and ill-matched coupling, the girl so young, the man so old. Further on, a couple of scruffy men were swigging out of a wine bottle and singing rough songs. They looked so dirty and hopeless Mhairi could hardly bear to look at them. If this was life, human life, perhaps it was wisest not to look at it.

But then a little boy saw her and called out. He was so excited by her that she came half out of the water and looked straight at him with her dark, lustrous eyes. He gawped at her, mouth open in wonder.

'Oh,' he said. 'Look, Mum, look.'

The woman walking with him clicked to a standstill. She had a long black coat and dramatically lined eyes, like some cats Mhairi had seen.

'A seal?' she said, astonished. 'Right in the middle of Glasgow?'

Mhairi preened in the attention. She liked the way the two humans looked at her.

After that she had even more of a fellow feeling for them. She never got the chance to go back into that city, but she had been to many villages and once had even sneaked off to another city in the north. She was such a strong swimmer, even among her legendary family, that none of them could keep up with her. This was a smaller, quieter place and you didn't see the horrible things there, just a lot of people walking calmly around from place to place with their unfathomable sense of purpose. Mhairi wanted to know where they were going and what made them so confident. There was, she thought, something very beautiful about some of them, with their slender bodies and their intelligent heads, not at all like the bulky seal people with their sad, blunt faces.

So as she swam into the bay that night, she was excited at the thought of listening to their strange music. Sometimes as she glided through the water she could hear snatches of it in her head, propelling her on. Sad, prickling with pain, it seemed to insinuate itself into her body, its vibrations rippling through her and merging with the currents of the sea, till she, the water and the music were one.

The woman finally came to stand at the edge of the rock. Beside her was a man, dressed in dark clothes. Usually she was on her own, standing with the violin raised, one of her flowing dresses billowing round her. The one she had on tonight looked like a puff of smoke in the moonlight, made of some soft, drifting material that reminded Mhairi of the angel hair seaweed you found wedged between the rocks.

'Oh, there's my favourite,' said the woman. The man laughed. He turned towards the woman and Mhairi couldn't see his face.

'Don't say you can tell the difference between them, Ursula.' She lifted the violin to her chin. 'Of course I can. Look at her beautiful eyes. You'd almost think she was human.'

She began to play, a lonely, aching sort of music that rolled across the water to Mhairi and back over the land too, way beyond the dark line of the horizon and up, up into the night sky. The man stepped forward to look at Mhairi and she saw his face. He was slender and dark, with a long neck like a swan's and strong shoulders. His face was pale and kind, and his eyes … his eyes were a shock. They looked straight into hers as if he knew her. His eyes were dark brown and they were as deep and beautiful as a seal's.

If in that moment Mhairi had known what was to come, perhaps she never would have vowed to enter wishing night. But the music called her, and the land, and the man with the seal's eyes.

She slipped away from the bay when the woman stopped playing.

'It's cold, Jake,' said Ursula.

'Come on and I'll make you some coffee at my house,' he said. His voice was soft and light, with a different sound from the woman's. Mhairi could tell he didn't come from the island, maybe not even from Scotland. She had heard many people speaking there, none like him. He put out his hand to steady Ursula on the rocks. 'Thank you, Ursula. That was one of the loveliest things I've ever seen in my life.'

Round on the other side of the island was another bay with a long, silvery cockle strand. Mhairi powered her way round there with sure, strong strokes, feeling driven by some unfathomable emotion she had not felt before. She was quite alone as she reached the beach. Her body scraped along the first layer of not quite powdery shell as she came into shore, and as it did so she could feel it changing, becoming lighter, whiter. She spat water from her mouth and felt a warm cascade of hair shoot from her head like a shoal of fishes darting from a rock. Then there were two round breasts pushing out of her body and the heavy rudder of her tail fell away.

She felt her pelt float off into the tide as she climbed out of the water on two strong legs.

Her skin was spangled with a light film of salt and seemed impossibly soft to the touch. Everything was smooth, with the exception of the dark hair flaring between her legs. It looked ugly to her, like an outbreak of black coral sprouting from the glistening side of water-polished rock. The feet on the human body fascinated her most. She seemed to be able to move the bits separately. She stared at them for a long time, laughing as she wiggled the toes in the sand. It was powdery and felt cold against her warm feet. But it was soft, and caressed this light, white skin of hers.

There seemed to be so many joints and muscles in her new body. It didn't have the strength of her seal one but was far superior in its flexibility. She had to try it out. With the moon high above the beach and Ursula's music pounding in her veins, she sported herself in the pale light, lifting her arms, running, turning and twisting like seaweed in the water. The black land lay beyond her, the sea behind her, but here, on the beach between the two, she was happy.

Jake's Room

YOU COULD TELL this room was Jake's room. Everything in it was calm and peaceful: the light, sandy carpet; the careful arrangements of twisted bark and seashells; the muted lights throwing a dull orange warmth into the room. Ursula loved it because it was like him. It was completely unlike her own cottage, which was all dark reds and pinks and gold, cascading with velvet and roses and crystal and mirrors. People always looked at the glass figures of naked women and wondered if Ursula was gay, but she simply admired the beauty of these sleek female forms, their polished surfaces so unlike the lumpy malleability of her own skin.

Jake was grinding coffee beans, a nicety she never bothered with herself, though she loved the acrid smell it sent into the room. She amused herself with looking through Jake's record collection until he brought the coffee. Vivaldi, Mozart, Chopin and a large collection of Bob Dylan. When he came in with the two mugs, they were of some rough beige pottery, as she expected. She liked this, although her own mugs were china and decorated with either exotic flowers or cats. She thought their rough-hewn quality probably meant manliness.

Ursula and Jake both worked in the island school, she in the music and he in the art department. They were neither of them from there, which was why they had become friends. They slid away nervously from the islanders' suffocating combination of polite distance and insatiable nosiness. They were observed here, but not yet accepted. They therefore accepted each other, despite a ten-year gap in their ages. If occasionally Ursula's eyes were rather hungry as she looked at Jake, it was only the thought of what might have been had the age gap been reversed. And if Jake's eyes lingered rather longer than they might on the full curves of Ursula's bosom, it was only the thought of the comfort of previous female companionship. Other than that they were as circumspect with each other as two twelve-year-olds.

So they talked evenly about the seals, and Ursula refrained from saying that when she played to them she felt as if she were taking part in a strange and heightened form of communication that she had never experienced with a human being; and Jake refrained from saying that he had thought her very beautiful standing on the rock, playing her eerie violin music. They drank the strong coffee and some strong, peaty whisky and they pretended that the refined and sensible conversation they were having was satisfactory to them both. They didn't even look up when a white shadow flitted across the lighted window, simply thinking it a trick of the smoke from the fire.

Mhairi was finding it difficult to walk over the tussocky grass and almost impossible to see where she was going now that a cloud had gone over the moon. There was a wind coming up and she could feel little goosebumps prickling on her arms. She was astonished to discover how little protection this human skin gave her from the cold, but of course the humans she had seen all invariably wore clothes. Now she knew why.

The soles of her feet were the worst. She could feel every tiny pebble beneath them, every scrape and fissure of the rocks. She tried to keep to the grass but because she could not see, she kept stumbling over unexpected obstacles. She stepped into a squelchy pat of cow dung once, and found her nose involuntarily wrinkling at a smell she had considered a normal part of the atmosphere up till now. The dung stuck to her soles, cold and sticky. It seemed a most unpleasant substance encountered like this, in the dark and with no thick grey hide to protect her. She had to put her feet in the water of a burn to get rid of it.

But there was something mysteriously satisfying about the taste of salt on her tongue, the smell of the rough heather and bog myrtle. She even liked the feel of the cold wind whipping at this new white skin of hers. And when she came to the top of the hill and looked down on the silvery strip of beach and the waves fizzing white against it, she felt she was seeing these familiar things in a new way. She had a sense of the fineness of the forms they created, the wanton water teasing at the solid curve of the land.

Beyond them she could see the cottage she knew to be Ursula's. A pale grey square by day, by night it seemed to give off a soft glow. When she pushed the door open she felt flooded with light, not like the light from the sun, but brighter, pinkish. Like the colour the sun sometimes streaked across the sky at sunset.

Inside there was a bright orange light burning in the wall, such as she had often seen people making on the shore. When Mhairi went over to look, it gave off a fierce heat that made her start back in surprise. At least she was no longer cold, though she felt the need to wrap something round this extraordinary new body of hers, to protect it. She went upstairs, feet caressing the lush red grass growing on the ground.

To her surprise, when she reached the top she saw another naked woman looking at her. She was pretty, with generous features and dark eyes. Mhairi put out her hand to greet the woman, and the woman did the same, but all Mhairi could feel was a cold smoothness, like polished stone when the sea has worn away the top surface. She tried again with her other hand, but again encountered only the same feeling. Puzzled now, she walked round the woman to examine her, but lost sight of her and found only a flat piece of wood. The woman was still there when she turned back and it was then she realised that she was looking at herself, as you could sometimes do in rock pools when there was enough sun, though she had never looked like this before.

There was a sort of white mound in one of the rooms. Mhairi had never seen anything like it. She sat down and it was soft and comfortable. She rolled and stretched on it. It was like no rock or underwater coral she had encountered. She thought it would be a perfect place to sleep. But the urge to find some protection for her new skin was strong, and she felt so light and full of energy that she didn't want to sleep, not yet anyway.

She pulled at a knob jutting out from the box she had first seen herself in and it fell open to reveal an inner cave. There were so many colours and soft fabrics Mhairi could hardly choose one from among so many. She held them up against her body and looked at herself. One was a pale green colour like the sea off some of the island shores. Another was creamy, like the fleece of sheep. The one she choose was a rich crimson colour like the deep red peonies Ursula grew in her garden in the summer. Mhairi slipped it over her head, delighted with this further transformation. It seemed to her that the possibilities for change were endless in humans.

At the bottom of the cave she found many coverings for her feet. Some were difficult to walk in, though beguilingly pretty with their straps round the ankle and decoration on the front, but Mhairi nearly twisted her ankle just trying them on. Regretfully, she chose a flatter pair, which would help her walk on the rough tracks of the island and its rocky shore.

She started out from the little cottage, enchanted by the prospect of exploring the world beyond. She walked for a long time, straying off the path at times and at times feeling completely lost in a way she never did in the water. More than an hour after she started out, she realised she must have come full circle, because there, coming towards her, was the man with the seal's eyes.

He seemed astonished to see her.

'Hallo,' he said. Mhairi tried to say it back to him, but it came out muffled and husky.

'Are you lost?' he asked.

Mhairi shook her head and tried to tell him she was returning to the beach to find her skin. He didn't seem to understand her. This human language was harder than she had thought. She looked at him, her dark eyes communicating her anxiety.

Jake felt an electric charge go through him. The woman was very beautiful. He must help her.

'Where are you staying?' he asked, but she was shaking her head and the words came in an incomprehensible stream back at him. She must be cold, out in a silky dress at this time of night. He put out his hand to her. She would be afraid if he took her to his own cottage.

Ursula was still up when he got back to hers. He always walked her back, though there was no need in a quiet place like this. She came to the door in a Chinese patterned dressing gown, just the sort of thing he would expect her to wear. There was nothing minimalist about Ursula, he thought to himself, trying not to smile.

The girl stepped forward into the light. Ursula stopped. She felt as if she knew this girl from somewhere, though she was so exotic-looking she was sure she wouldn't have forgotten her if she did. The glossy black hair and eyes, the smoothness of her; everything about her was sleek.

'She seems to be lost,' said Jake. 'At least, I think she is. I can't make out a word she's saying. How on earth could she have got here without a car?'

'Could she be staying with someone in the village, do you think?'

'She doesn't seem to speak English. I don't see anyone local letting her just wander about on her own, do you?'

'Are you alone?' asked Ursula. The girl nodded. That puzzled Ursula and Jake. She did understand some English, then.

'Have you got somewhere to stay?' She looked doubtful and Ursula felt sorry for her. 'You don't think she could be one of those refugees, do you?'

Jake laughed. 'What refugees? I don't think they're exactly flocking here, are they?'

'I don't know. It was on the news tonight that they're coming in by boat, all along the west coast.' She whispered in his ear, 'That's my dress she's wearing.'

He turned to look at the girl. She didn't look like a thief. She must be desperate. 'I thought it was drugs that were coming in all the time.'

'Don't ask me,' said Ursula, amused. 'I mean, what else could she be? She doesn't look like a drugs runner.'

'And who knows what refugees look like?'

'I know, maybe she's the daughter of a very rich family and has been dropped here by Daddy's private plane.'

'I think she's dropped here from heaven,' said Jake.

The girl seemed agitated but Jake knew Ursula would be kind to her.

'I'll come back tomorrow morning,' Jake told Ursula. He headed back home, touched by the stranger. There was something curious, something questing in her. The sea was rising and he walked off the path and on to the beach, listening to the driving sound of the waves. The moon came out from the clouds, casting a phosphorescent light on the sand.

That was how he spotted the sealskin lying there, like a bundle of old clothes. He had never seen a complete skin like this, still with slits where the eye sockets would be, still with its tail. Whoever had killed the seal – and there were plenty of fishermen round here who wouldn't think twice about it – had scraped the skin completely so there was not a trace of blood or fat clinging to it. He couldn't imagine why anyone would do such a thing. Unless they were selling the skins and this one had simply dropped off the back of the load.

He stroked the soft pelt. It wasn't quite cold, and he wondered how long it had been lying there – he'd been out on the beach earlier in the evening and it hadn't been there. Neither he nor Ursula had heard anything, no sounds of gunshots or animal cries. Perhaps the Bob Dylan music they'd been playing had masked other sounds. *Me and Magdalena on the run*, he hummed as he walked back to the cottage, clutching the skin. He would take this into school on Monday. Already he was envisaging the project he'd build around it, the marvellously contoured shapes the kids would produce, the evocative images of the world under the sea.

Mhairi was tucked up in one of the sleeping mounds with a drift of duck feathers covering her. She was very tired and deliciously warm. She had till daybreak to retrieve her skin. She fell asleep, dreaming of glassy green waters lit by sunshine.

Ursula checked in the wardrobe. Sure enough, the new cerise dress she'd bought for the dance was no longer there. She sighed. The girl looked much more lovely in it than she could. She wondered where the girl's own clothes were and what the legalities of keeping a refugee were. She'd have to find something else to wear before next week.

Just before dawn Mhairi woke and slipped out of the house. She followed the path the man with seal eyes had taken. It seemed so simple in the grey half-light. She recognised the beach immediately, could see herself there, dancing with her new body, the sound of the waves pounding inside her head. But her skin was no longer there. She ran up and down the sand, calling, calling. The sky was lightening all the time. She heard the funny screeching noise of oystercatchers and saw a seal's head emerge from the water. It looked right at her, with an anguished expression on its face. Mhairi felt frantic. There was a pain in her head as if it would crack wide open.

The seal's body flipped as it turned to swim down below the surface of the water. It seemed to Mhairi as if something in her had gone with the animal. The sun was a pink bar on the horizon. As its light intensified and warmed the silvery beach, Mhairi longed to be twisting and gliding through cool underwater forests.

Rough Grief

THE FIRE WAS OUT, leaving Ursula cold in the grey light of morning. She wished she'd banked it up properly before going to bed, but she'd been so distracted by the arrival of the stranger. It was early for her to be up. She put the kettle on for coffee. For some reason it seemed to her that she was alone in the house. She ran upstairs, could hear no sound from the woman's room. Warily she pushed the door open. Nothing. No woman, but no attempt either to hide her absence. Ursula's dress and shoes were still there at the end of the bed.

For perhaps the only time in her life Ursula had a moment she took to be psychic vision. She knew with certainty that wherever the woman now was, she had left the house intending to leave forever. She also knew that the woman was in trouble somewhere. Trying to resist such thoughts she went back downstairs, only to find herself pulling on wellingtons and a warm coat. She took a blanket from the linen cupboard, just in case.

She set off towards the beach, with no real hope of being in the right direction, but as she approached she realised that the woman was there, half a mile away down the sand. She was running back and forth, naked, gesturing at the sea. Ursula thought she looked mad. She went towards her, trying not to frighten her. 'Please. Please don't,' she said, touching the silky skin of her arm.

It was as if the touch of another human being tore all convention away. The woman doubled up, sobbing, with a harsh, guttural sound that could have been a donkey braying or a rusty door being torn from its hinges. If it had been in another context, the sound would have been funny, but there was something inhuman in this rough grief, it seemed to Ursula, a wildness that went beyond unhappiness. This was the sound of the soul being ripped from the body, the sound of a pain that was as absolute as the rocks rearing up from the beach.

As the woman continued to honk and cry, Ursula put her arms round her and cradled her. The woman seemed astonished by being held. She rested her face against Ursula's, as if she had never touched another person's skin before. For one crazy moment Ursula wondered if she was from another world, an alien shipped in to enter the world of humans. There was something tentative, some lack of habituation in her acceptance of this very ordinary comfort.

'We'll go home now,' said Ursula, draping the blanket round her shoulders and taking her by the hand.

The stranger turned back often as they walked away, staring at the beach as though she had lost something there. Ursula supposed it must be her belongings. She made sweet tea when they got into the house, then sat down beside the woman. She seemed calmer when she was close to another person. She made a mumbling sound and Ursula realised that she was speaking a rather indistinct form of English. 'It's gone,' was what it sounded like.

'Do you have a name?' she asked. The woman nodded. As she said the name Ursula had the strangest feeling that she had met her before, though she knew she couldn't have.

'Marina?' That's pretty, and apt when you came to us from the sea.'

The woman let out a sigh, like the soughing of the waves. She rolled over in the blanket, burrowing herself into its warmth, her eyes staring emptily at the grey ashes in the fireplace.

Was she thinking of the land she had left behind, of her family and friends? Perhaps she was anxious about the future. Ursula would have to reassure her she was safe here, that no harm would come to her in this house.

But Mhairi was thinking of nothing. She was void, vacant. The sun was slowly warming the room, as the remains of her tea went cold in the cup. Something in her had died and she didn't know what.

Naming the Problem

JAKE LEANT FORWARD into the mirror, making sure he hadn't missed anywhere while shaving. The man looking back at him seemed tense, unsure of himself. Ridiculous to be this nervous for a village hop – and a woman he didn't really know, though Marina *was* more beautiful than any woman he'd seen before. He wanted to take care of her, wanted to take away that mysterious melancholy of hers, though he supposed it was mysterious only because they didn't know enough about her. If you were an asylum seeker, your life by definition must have been painful.

Neither he nor Ursula had found out where Marina came from. Her English had a curious intonation that they couldn't place and she didn't seem to know the name of her own country. One night there was a programme about Kosovan asylum seekers and they asked if she came from there. She nodded, but she nodded too when the second part of the programme showed Iranians. The woman from everywhere and nowhere, he thought, as he discarded the tie he'd been trying. The open-necked shirt made him look freer.

Ursula had handled everything magnificently, giving clothes to Marina, showing her where things belonged in the house, even teaching her how to cook some basic things. Marina didn't seem to have the first idea about modern kitchen equipment and they decided she'd probably come from some remote mountain village where life was lived as it had been hundreds of years ago. It was a miracle she could speak English at all. She certainly couldn't read it, had looked blankly at the newspaper when Ursula showed her a story about some refugees being attacked in Glasgow.

He felt this strange compulsion to be with her, a sense of connection that went beyond anything he had felt with a woman before. He didn't believe in that romantic nonsense about there being one person meant for you, but still ... maybe she was the one.

Ursula was staring into her own mirror with a sense of dismay. Having Marina to live with her was lovely, but it made her aware of all those subtle markers of age that she didn't notice when it was just her – the little ridge of fat above her eyelid, the fine hairs that appeared almost daily just below her lips. She sighed as she stared at her freckled skin. She looked just like a whiskery old seal she'd seen sunning itself on the rocks this week. She pulled off the dress she'd been going to wear. The comparison was too apt when you were wearing a swirly grey and beige dress that looked like the animal's dappled skin. She found a rich red blouse that brightened up her skin, but she felt beached, bereft. She knew Jake had fallen for Marina. Was this how it was going to be from now on? Was she forever going to be the older woman, the woman who was attractive but not quite attractive enough, good looking for her age but not slim enough or sweet enough to make people forget it? Marina tapped on her door. Ursula marvelled again at the firm white skin, the smooth contours of the younger woman's body. How sinuous, how flowing her curves were, perfect as glass.

'You look lovely in that,' said Ursula. Marina was wearing a turquoise and green patterned dress that reminded Ursula of a Hebridean sea. She looked anxious. Tonight's dance would be the first time she'd meet the people of the island. She had been for many walks along the beach with Jake, and once had gone with Ursula to a craft shop, where they'd chosen the dress and a couple of jumpers. Ursula had handed over some paper that seemed worthless to Mhairi compared to the vivid fabric.

'What is that?' she'd asked.

Ursula patiently explained. 'These ones are £20 notes. Look, this one's a five and this one's £10.'

She handed some pieces of metal over later when she bought them ice cream. Mhairi could not understand the shopkeeper accepting these coin things for such a delicious substance. It tasted like snow, only sweet, and sent the blood rushing round her veins.

The question of money was one that was puzzling Ursula. Marina had no papers, no identification, and without that she could not sign on for benefits. She'd looked blank when Ursula asked her about it. More worryingly, she seemed unable to read the simplest thing. It was hard to see how she was going to make a life for herself here. She had a desire to communicate that Ursula found touching, and it was fun to have her in the house, though it was distressing to hear her crying, night after night. The first time Ursula had gone in to comfort her, but there was something so primeval in this sorrow, something so beyond any comfort she could offer that she felt scared. After that she simply let Marina sob.

Now she studied the dark, worried eyes.

'Let's give you some perfume,' she said. 'And a bit of jewellery. Then you'll be perfect.'

Mhairi breathed in deeply as the aromatic spray drifted over her. She sat on Ursula's bed as the older woman brought out a box inlaid with mother-of-pearl. Inside were gold chains, bangles, strings of coloured beads, drop earrings glinting with precious stones. She liked a necklace made from what looked like pebbles from the beach, but Ursula said it was too heavy for her dress.

'And it's the wrong colour, anyway. Try this.' And she held up a fine pendant with a polished shell set in it. For some reason it made Mhairi feel happy.

They drove to the dance. She liked being in Ursula's car, liked the sensation of speeding along in this comfy little box with its smell of leather from the seats. From the window she could see waves whizzing past her, and the long beach. Somewhere in the back of her mind she knew they had some significance for her, but she had no idea what. Maybe she had come across the sea to this country, but she had no memory of the journey. Jake and Ursula used big words like 'amnesia' and 'post-traumatic stress', but naming her problem didn't make it any easier. It hurt her that she couldn't remember her own family or country. In not remembering, she had no idea who she was.

There were a number of whistles from men as the two women arrived, and many pairs of eyes following them. Mhairi saw the heads together, the whispering. The hall seemed dark to her, though there was tea being served in a brightly lit room just beyond it. The light fell on the long swan neck and fine cheekbones of a man – Jake, she saw with pleasure.

Music was coming from the stage, where a young man was selecting discs, but it wasn't music like Ursula's. It was louder, simpler, more exciting. People seemed to recognise the songs and shouted out the words with the singers. *She walked like a woman and talked like a man, oh my Lola* ... Sometimes the music got higher and faster. They'd snap the lights on and do very energetic and complicated dances that Mhairi couldn't follow, though sometimes she thought she recognised one of the sounds, a shimmering of taut strings that pierced the ear like the screeching of sea gulls.

As the night went on, men were holding women in the dark during the slow records. Many of them came to Mhairi and asked her to dance with them. Their hands felt hot and sticky, their sturdy bodies clammy and bulky. She could tell they were much stronger than she was. One beefy farmer called Hamish put his hands on her hips and thrust his body towards her. She thought she was going to suffocate, he was so overpowering. His breath was sour with alcohol, his eyes sour with his life. Scrabbling at his hands, she tried to break free from him.

'Stop it,' she shouted.

Others in the hall turned to look, tutting at her for making a scene.

'You stupid wee cow,' said Hamish. 'What's so special about you?'

Mhairi punched him in the face. His flesh squelched, as if she'd put her hand into a jellyfish on the shore. She was relieved when Jake came to her.

'Behave yourself, mate,' he said, propelling Mhairi away from the purple-faced farmer. Hamish backed off.

'Sorry, pal. Sorry. Didn't realise she was with you.'

Jake's hands were cool, his body slim. He drew her in but this was no invasion of her territory. It was as if he was seeking her permission. He placed a hand against her waist, the other arm round her shoulder.

Above them a silvery mirror ball started revolving in the darkness. Mhairi looked up, entranced by the glitter. It was like stars, only closer to the earth and more brightly coloured. The stars were flashing in her head and inside her and the silver of moonlight was shooting up and down her veins and through it all a sensation she had never felt before, a sort of burning deep down in her body. It was as if she wanted to urinate, yet she knew she wouldn't be able to. *Thump, thump* went her heart and she felt as if her belly was on fire. It was so pleasurable she didn't want it to stop. When Jake pulled her in closer to him, she felt she had to do something or implode. She kissed him on the lips, a wild kiss. There was darkness and surf pounding in her ears and she pulled at his shirt to feel the smooth, creamy skin of him. Around her people were looking shocked. Mhairi didn't understand why. Jake seemed breathless.

'Come on, we'd better go.' He glanced apologetically at Ursula, whose eyes met his, puzzled. Marina's lack of inhibitions did not seem normal, to them or anyone else.

'Let's go somewhere private,' he said.

She didn't mind, though she didn't see the need. 'Let's go to the shore,' she said.

Even when the coolness of the night air hit them, Mhairi did not feel calm. There was a turbulence and an ache inside that she had never experienced. She ran ahead of Jake. On the shore she pulled her dress over her head and began to dance, but it wasn't right. She wriggled out of her underclothes and tights. Whirling naked, on the shore, in the real darkness, with real stars spattering the sky, she was incandescent with pleasure.

Jake stood watching, wondering how many pieces his body would disintegrate into if he had to cope with any more sexual arousal. Marina was dancing towards him, long hair flying. In the cold of the night he was vaguely aware of the dark tangle emerging from luminescent thighs, of the curve of her hips, even of the soft blackness of her eyes, but all he seemed to be able to look at was her nipples, jutting out like twin raspberries from their dark areola. He wanted to drain their sweetness, crush the juice from them. He wanted the woman badly. Now she was tugging at his shirt again, pushing it back, tongue flickering over his chest, leaving little glow-worm slicks of her saliva.

'Please stop, Marina,' he said, pushing her away and then having to catch her as she fell backwards.

She seemed hot and half crazy, her milky skin radiating heat. 'Why? I like this,' she shouted.

He caught her by the wrist. 'You mustn't expose yourself like this,' he said.

'I'm warm enough, honestly.'

'But anyone could come along and see you.'

Her eyes were perplexed. 'You see me. That's all.'

He picked her dress up from the sand, unbuttoning it, though he felt clumsy. Her face reddened and she crossed her arms over her chest.

'I see. You don't like me.'

'There isn't a man alive who wouldn't like you,' he said. 'You're beautiful. A goddess. I feel as if you've dropped from the heavens.'

She took the dress from him, face immobile.

'Look, Marina. I'd like nothing better than to make love to you. But it would be completely irresponsible of me. You don't remember where you've come from, who you are. I would just be taking advantage of you.'

'I don't know what happened before,' she said angrily. 'I only know what happens now.'

'You could be married, for all we know. What would you feel then, if your husband turned up and you'd been with me?'

'What would he have to do with me and you?'

Jake sighed. He felt as if he was speaking in code, as if she simply did not understand the way ordinary people lived.

'I can't,' he sighed. 'You just don't know me well enough. I'd be exploiting you ...'

She walked away from him, back in the direction of Ursula's house, leaving her underthings scattered on the beach. Sticky liquid clogged her thighs. She wished she knew how they did things in her own country. This one was strange, confusing. She heard Jake gathering up her things, but strode on ahead. She knew him as well as she needed to. It was herself she didn't know.

The People of the Sea

THERE WERE STILL SOME INVITATION CARDS propped up on the mantelpiece, aquamarine with a gold deckle edge. Marina's choice, obviously. Jake smiled at the thought of his art school chums receiving such a card. He wondered how many of them would come. The island was an attractive draw in itself, despite its remoteness. A wedding, complete with its legendary whisky, would render it irresistible.

Things had happened very fast. He felt driven in a way he did not understand. He and his ex-wife had married immediately after art school, their wedding a final celebration of four years of bohemian living. Jackie had made her own dress, dark red velvet, ripped and slashed in the fashion of the times. The meal was a black buffet, with lumpfish eggs, squid in ink, chargrilled steak and black pudding. Even the salad was made from those dark bitter leaves that Jake found inedible. Jackie had decorated the cake, chocolate with black icing and red roses dripping blood, to go with her tattoo.

Jake now realised that this unconventional ceremony had been their formal entry into the world of grown-ups. His forthcoming marriage, with its traditional dress and cake and the ludicrously naff invitations, was actually far bolder. What did he know of Marina? He found her very beautiful, of course, but often he did not understand her. She behaved sometimes as if she was wholly without inhibitions, something Jake found strange in a woman he understood to come from eastern Europe, where societies were, he thought, more restrictive than our own.

But then he didn't really know where his future wife came from. He and Ursula simply assumed she had fled war and perhaps rape. She shivered sometimes with a sensitivity to his touch he would have thought came from fright had she not been the most directly sensual woman he had ever known. Jackie had been considered something of a raver in their circle, but there was an element of performance in her sexuality that spoke more of what she willed than what she wished.

One day Jake came home unexpectedly and found her alone in the flat, staring intently at herself in the mirror, one hand inside herself, the other caressing her nipple. The white of her breasts gleamed against her tight black velvet bodice; her black and purple panties were halfway down her thighs. Her hair was piled up on top of her head, with a couple of strands falling artfully across her cheek. It seemed to Jake that she looked happier in this exploration of the aesthetics of her sensuality than she ever did when he touched her. She called him over to join her that day, of course, but even as he licked her nipples and groaned at the smooth curve of her hips, he understood that she did not love him as he did her.

With Marina he felt desired as a man. Sometimes she was so frantic he could hardly resist her, but he refused to go to bed with her till they married, thinking that if nothing else between them worked, at least her residency in this country would be secured. He finished shaving and set out for school, feeling tired and edgy. Ursula was already there in the art room, looking dispiritingly fresh and examining the sealskin lying on his worktable. He had picked it up on the beach weeks ago, the night they met Marina, in fact. Jake's head throbbed as he studied it. It looked drab and ugly spread out there, and very dead. 'What possessed me to bring that in?' he sighed.

Ursula's eyes were amused. 'Headache?' she asked.

'Did I have an awful lot to drink on Saturday night?'

'You can't still have a hangover from then.'

He shrugged. 'More to the point, what on earth am I going to do with that?'

'There are all sorts of legends about seals, you know.'

'No, I don't know. I can just see our kids loving that. All those sensitive souls who thrill to songs about bitches and ho's. Yes, seal legends will be just the thing.'

'You really are crabby on Monday mornings, aren't you?' said Ursula, crossing to the kettle. 'Caffeine injection coming up.'

Jake stroked the skin. It was smooth but not soft, an unsettling combination. On the moon-flooded beach it had gleamed like a live trout, dark brown shading into taupe. Nice natural colours, he thought, though Ursula told him off when he said so. 'What an idea,' she said. 'You wouldn't call these colours natural if you lived in Andalucia, with bougainvillea and jacaranda outside your window.'

He bent to smell the skin, expecting it to be fishy, but it smelled tangy, like the sea. And there was some elusive sweetness there too, an indefinable scent memory that somehow resisted being pinpointed.

'How would a sealskin end up on the beach anyway?' he said. Ursula sighed. 'The fishermen hate them. I suppose one of them has killed the seal and skinned it.'

'I suppose so, but you know, there was no blood or fat inside it and it was still a little warm, though it was a cold night. Someone must have dumped it while we were having coffee, because it wasn't there earlier.'

'That's odd,' agreed Ursula. 'And what happened to the seal's body, then?'

Jake frowned. Thinking was making his head hurt.

'A sea cave,' he said. 'That's what we'll make. All green and gloomy.'

'I could compose some sea music, sort of mysterious, for the inside of the cave,' offered Ursula.

He felt suddenly awake. 'Green, gauzey material. Enamel. Chicken wire and papier mâché for the cave. Little lights like stars at various points in the rock. We'll make a kind of mermaid from the skin.'

'Don't mermaids have green fishy tails? And long blonde hair? The people of the sea aren't quite as colourful as that.'

Jake looked at the dappled surface of the skin. Ursula was right. The colour didn't lend itself to mermaid reproductions.

'The people of the sea?' he asked.

'There are all sorts of stories about seals,' said Ursula. 'The people of the isles thought they were humans who lived beneath the sea and had a King and Queen of their own. In some of the stories they're actually more moral than the humans are.'

'That wouldn't be hard.'

But Jake was abstracted, more interested in the practicalities than this romantic nonsense. He would have to find fabrics that were dark and mysterious, not too vivid. The lights would have to be soft and diffused, as if they were shining up from the depths of the sea. He didn't suppose there were any lights underwater, but you needed a bit of chiaroscuro with a subject like this.

'We could make it interactive, so that the lights and music come on when you touch jutting out bits of rock. Someone from the technical department could sort it out for us.'

'Maybe we could have the wind sighing in the background. Just to frighten them.'

'Yeah, and we'll make the little bastards pay to get in,' he said, and they both laughed, amused by the meanness of this notion, though Jake's face looked sweet to Ursula as he pensively stroked the stippled sealskin and placed it between sheets of tissue paper. It lay there almost like a living thing, its burnished browns and greys shimmering with the question of its very existence.

A Holiday to the World

'DID YOU SEE yon Brad Pitt on the telly last night? Is he no' gorgeous?'

The smell of fish spangled Mhairi's nostrils and made her feel cheery, but the shed was icy cold and she went back for her jumper before joining the other women on the line. The work seemed easy to her. You picked the fish up, slit it down the middle with your sharp-bladed knife, and tossed away the guts. Mhairi watched as gobs of blood and the soft coral of unborn fish babies slithered into the pail beneath her.

She had watched the film with Ursula and thought the star very handsome. He was Death, who had decided to come for a holiday to the world and find out what life was like. He knew everything about life but not what it felt or smelt or tasted like. Mhairi thought she was a bit like him, as if she was experiencing everything for the first time. When she first laid her head on Jake's shoulder she could have sworn that she'd never smelled human skin before. His scent was a particular mixture of the acrid and the animal. The top note was a citrony, sweet aftershave, then turpentine and beneath that the loamy smell of paint till finally, underneath it all, the smell of Jake himself, the smell of sweat and man. That was the one she liked the most.

'Did *you* see him, Marina? Whit do ye think o' him, then?'

'Very nice. He was quite like a fish, with those pale eyes and the soft lips,' she said, nodding enthusiastically.

'Whit's that, pet? She's an awfy indistinct speaker, is she no'?' said one of the women.

'Wonder where she's from?' said another.

'She's a quick worker, I'll gi'e her that. None of that cerry on about hoo disgusting the smell is. Just gets on wi' it. Pity she canna say much.'

Mhairi looked up and smiled. 'I can understand you,' she said.

'Did ye ever see a man like that in your own country?' one of the women asked, but Mhairi shook her head. She couldn't remember a single man from her own country. The actor was certainly much more attractive than any of the men around here, except for Jake, of course, Jake and his beautiful eyes. But there was something strange about the man in the film. Instead of trying to find out what the world was like through the life of an ordinary person, he'd chosen to inhabit the life of a hugely wealthy man, a man who owned lots of newspapers. In this country it seemed that money was very important and that the more you had, the more people respected you. You needed it for everything, even down to the very food you ate. Mhairi had watched Ursula and Jake going into the shop and buying fish when the sea outside was full of them. She thought she could have caught fish for them, though she couldn't remember how you did it. In her mind she saw herself swimming through the water and then standing up, holding the fish above her head in triumph, but she couldn't imagine the middle bit, the bit where she actually caught the fish.

No, it was clear you needed money to live here. That was why she was here now, in this cold shed that reeked of fish guts. She wanted to give Ursula some money back for the notes she was always taking out of her purse, whenever they needed something to eat. She couldn't wait for her first wage packet. Besides, she felt guilty about stealing Ursula's dress, though what else could she have done? It had been too cold to walk about in just this thin skin. She tried to give the dress back to Ursula, but she said no.

'You look much nicer in it than I ever could.'

Maybe she would buy another one for Ursula. There was a craft shop on the other side of the island where they sold dresses, flowing, richly coloured ones that came from India, a country on the other side of the world. Mhairi wasn't sure why the dresses came all that way from the East. The velvets and lace and chiffon seemed a strange choice for the rocky terrain and muted colours of the island, but Ursula said the craft shops were the same all the way up the west coast; they all stocked Indian garments.

Maybe she would buy Jake an Indian shirt, a nice orange one with gold embroidery. Or some paint. Or one of those books of paintings that he kept on the coffee table in his front room. The table was actually glass but she supposed they called them coffee tables because you put your mug of coffee down on them; there didn't seem to be such a thing as a tea table. Maybe she would buy herself one of those magazines that showed photos of film stars like Brad Pitt. Ursula was teaching her to read, a slow and difficult process, but in the meantime she liked looking at the women's beautiful dresses and the huge houses the people lived in. They had swimming pools and chandeliers and you could fit Ursula's house into theirs five times over. It was as if they lived in another, more exotic world.

She wondered how much money they would actually give her here. Ursula had shown her the amount in notes and coins at home, but she didn't know how many things it would buy. She hadn't got the hang of numbers yet. She decided she must have come from a very primitive place, as she could neither read nor count. She hadn't even known such activities existed.

'Maybe they bartered in your village?' hazarded Ursula, but Mhairi didn't know. She wondered what the village was like and why Ursula was so sure she had come from a village anyway.

But then Ursula seemed able to come to conclusions in a way Mhairi was not. She understood the world. Mhairi knew when there would be rain or when a storm would come and send waves spraying up against the harbour walls, but she didn't know how to tell the time and could never remember the Prime Minister's name. The way people behaved was constantly surprising to her. She picked a flower one day from a garden she passed in the town, so that she could show it to Ursula, but the woman who lived there started banging on the window at her.

Ursula laughed. 'No wonder,' she said. 'It's very rare to be able to grow those lilies up here.'

Still, Mhairi found it strange how much people wanted to possess things.

They finished early that day at the fish factory and she decided to walk home instead of taking the bus. She dawdled through the village, looking at everything. The gift shop seemed to have some new agate jewellery in its window. Maybe she would find something pretty there for Ursula. But she didn't step inside. There would be time enough for that when she actually had the money.

The road out of the village climbed up into the hills. Mhairi loved the quiet up here, the feeling that she was part of a vast world of living creatures. She bounced along on the heather at the side of the road, enjoying the cracking noise beneath her feet. She could hear a peewit's wheezing call somewhere close. High above her a kestrel trod the air currents, poised to swoop down and kill some small mammal. The peewit rose up suddenly in the grass ahead and set off on its limping run, wing dragging along the ground. *Poor little mother. Don't worry. I won't harm your baby.*

The heat of the sun seeped through her, warming her body, inch by inch. She followed the road up the hill towards the loch. She loved it there, the water so peaceful and dark. Sometimes the wind whipped little waves across its surface but the air was still today, gravid with the smells of the land. The loch surface would be serene. She longed for its coolness, for the cool green water. She wondered if she could swim.

As she rounded the corner she saw the loch spread out before her, but she hardly recognised it. It was gaudy in the high sunlight. Contained within its shores lay a whole hillside, running away from the bank, its purple heather splattered across the water like paint on glass. Mhairi wanted to walk on the underwater hills, crunch over its viscous bracken. She took off her shoes and started into the water to explore. It was cool on her toes, seeped up past her ankles. She wanted to walk up the steep incline of the hill ahead of her, but as she walked forward it started to ripple and break up and the more she pressed forward the more she knew she would never reach the top.

Her feet went from under her and she found herself suddenly trying to stay afloat. She flapped her arms but it felt awkward, unnatural. She should have another body for swimming, one in which she would be able to soar through the water with ease, feel it slip and slide around her. But her limbs felt heavy, weighted down, and she swallowed water, almost choking on its dank taste. She sensed there were other ways to move in the water, that perhaps she had experienced them before, but she was frightened at how clumsy she felt. She splashed around frantically till she felt the ground beneath her feet. Where had that other body gone? Would she ever be able to get back to it?

To Give Without
a Pounding Heart

MHAIRI STOOD ON THE BEACH beside Jake, gazing out to sea. Ursula was on a rock playing beautiful music, rather grand, not at all the sweet, rather mournful music that Mhairi was accustomed to hearing from her. Behind them the guests chattered and laughed, enchanted with the romantic setting, the exotic bride.

'Jake's gone native. He'll be cheering for the Scottish football team next,' said one to his wife.

'You're just jealous. He looks really handsome in his kilt.' 'The girl's a bit odd-looking, don't you think?'

'I think she looks charming, very natural.'

'What on earth is that she's got round her head?'

'It looks sort of seaweedy, doesn't it?'

'Hope it doesn't smell like that!'

'I think it's very pretty,' said the wife. 'It suits her, somehow. And the dress is perfect on her.'

The dress was silky smooth, a satin column skimming down Mhairi's body, with its long, slim waist and sleek curves; the skirt swirled out around her as she moved. Mhairi had been entranced with the dresses in the catalogue. Some had lace fizzing at the hem like waves on the shore. Others had pearls sewn inside them, such as she had seen inside shells. Still others winked and sparkled like stars in the night sky. She would have liked a colour other than white, perhaps sea green or that turquoise colour Jake had shown her in paintings of the sea by a Scottish artist, but it seemed to be some kind of tradition that only white was worn on your wedding day. Something to do with being pure.

She had finally chosen this simple style because she felt free in it, no sleeves to hold her back, the skirt flaring out from above the knee to offer her easy movement. Jake had made the headdress, entwining dark green crinkly material with shells and rockplants to form a coronet round her head. She herself had gathered wild flowers for her bouquet. They seemed more her somehow than the rich roses and peonies that grew in Ursula's garden.

As the minister intoned the words of the service and the guests sang hymns to Ursula's accompaniment, Mhairi's attention wandered. She could see some seals' heads bobbing out of the water, listening perhaps to Ursula's playing. They had such sad eyes, these creatures. Sometimes, when they came close to the shore to listen and Mhairi stared into their dark eyes, she felt as if they were trying to communicate with her, but she could never understand what they might be saying. Still, she was pleased that they were here today. They made the ceremony somehow seem complete.

Jake felt the muscles at the back of his neck tightening as he made his vows. He knew he was heading for a migraine. He remembered reading that one of the Lakota Sioux's most prized qualities was *to give without a pounding heart*, yet here he was, his heart pounding as if it would never stop. He wanted to give his life to this unknown woman beside him, he wanted to offer her his protection with a light heart, but he was afraid. Could he love her without knowing her?

Mhairi turned to her new husband and was perplexed by the pain in his face. The minister had told her she was to kiss him, but instead she reached up and stroked his temples. The simple gesture brought a film of tears to his eyes. He felt his body relaxing. This, the great adventure, would be all right. He took her hand and they turned away from their guests and walked across the rocks towards the sea. He could feel her body straining towards it. She seemed at her most excited, her most beautiful, when she could hear the waves booming against the shore, smell the stinging salt. He pulled her back towards him and she wound her warmth sinuously around him. Behind them, champagne fizzed like foam over a rock and their guests burst into applause.

'Not like Jake to be so impulsive. Must have been the *coup de foudre.*'

'Where is it she comes from, exactly?'

'Somewhere in Eastern Europe, I think. Probably softening Jake up for her Russian mafia pimp.'

'That's really not funny. She's obviously a refugee from some bloody awful regime.'

'And which one would that be, you bloody silly PC cow?'

Ursula found herself unexpectedly emotional as she watched Jake and Marina pick their way across the rocks, back to the path. No matter how much she told herself she was happy for them, there was a broken little part inside her which had thought that she and Jake might one day be a couple, once he'd come to terms with the pain of his first marriage break-up. What could she have been thinking of? Settle for a plump older woman? Men never do. They always find the younger woman.

'Another one bites the dust,' said Annie Spencer, another single member of staff.

'We'll have to start looking for toyboys,' said Ursula with a smile.

She walked briskly back to the village hall, where the wedding meal was laid out. Cold poached salmon, her famous potato salad, raspberries and cream, and of course bottles and bottles of champagne. She'd better watch Marina didn't have too much – she had that Eastern European tendency to go a little wild on alcohol.

'I can't thank you enough for this.' Jake was shyly touching her hand.

Impulsively she turned and gave him a hug. 'Oh Jake, what are friends for?'

'We will still stay good friends, won't we?' he asked.

'Of course we will,' she said, though she wasn't sure.

Mhairi watched her new husband with Ursula. She loved the woman as much as she loved him. Something in Ursula called to her. And the older woman was very kind to her. It wasn't she who had mentioned the stolen dress, Mhairi had had to bring it up herself. She still hadn't found the perfect one to replace it but she'd keep on looking. Her eyes scanned the wedding guests. How alien they seemed, with all their chatter about not very much. At least she knew that Jake and Ursula were interested in important things, Jake with his art, Ursula her music.

She was helping herself to some salmon from the buffet when Lucy, Jake's mother, came over to her.

'You must have some of the potato salad. It's divine,' she said.

Mhairi shook her head. 'I'll just stick with the fish, I think.' She tried to smile, but she sensed Lucy didn't like her. The woman's smile seemed as stiff as the silly hat perched on top of her head. Thank goodness she lived a long way away from here. Mhairi wondered how she had come to the island, by car and then ferry, or had she flown? For a second she had an image of powering her way through cool green water, light glancing off the dappled coat of seals in the ocean with her, the water sliding over her skin and then away again like a playful spirit. Salt stinging her face, gulping in the smell of ozone like food ...

'What a strange girl this is,' thought Lucy crossly. She seems capable of just standing there silently for minutes on end. What on earth was Jake thinking of? If only his father were still alive. Not that anyone had ever been able to change Jake's mind once he was set on anything. She had a bad feeling in her bones about this one. Probably a gold-digger, just out to get her green card, or whatever it was called. It would be a relief to get on that plane tomorrow morning and just fly away from this awful mess. After all, Jake was old enough to know what he was doing. You couldn't look after them forever. Could you?

As the night wore on, Ursula could feel her headache intensifying. These friends of Jake's seemed so unlike him, with their talk of house prices and how quickly their cars reached top speed and what foreign place they were going to on holiday and what it was going to cost them. No wonder he escaped here to the island, she thought, noting his own strained expression.

'Shouldn't you be whisking your child bride home?' she teased him.

His face momentarily lightened. 'Do you think it would be all right now? I don't like to leave Mother on her own.'

Ursula glanced over at Lucy, currently holding court on the subject of the marvellous consultant who had overseen her gall bladder operation. Mother will be all right, she thought, but said, 'Don't worry. I'll see she gets safely back to the hotel.'

Jake squeezed her arm. 'You're a true friend, Ursula,' he said. He and Marina tried to sneak out of the hall, but they were spotted and had to run the gauntlet of cheers and claps and picture-taking. Mhairi felt a little frightened as lights kept flashing in her face, but her spirits rose as they finally made their exit and began walking home. This was what she liked best, the feeling of sea salt on her face, the wind rustling through the silky fabric of her gown. 'Are you sure you want to walk?' Jake asked anxiously, but she flung her arms around him and said, 'Oh yes.'

The cottage was over two miles from the village hall and she set off briskly, launching herself into the night without looking back. Beyond the village there were no lights and they plunged forward into profound blackness. There were no stars and Jake felt as if the night was swirling around him like quicksand, as if with every step he was in danger of being sucked into oblivion. Marina appeared at ease in the pitch black night, holding her gown with one hand and almost dancing ahead, it seemed to him. She was in no danger of drowning in this blackness.

She reached the cottage before he did but waited for him to open the door. She always did, as if this was his territory and she must be invited in.

'You want me to carry you over the threshold?' he asked, but she looked blankly at him. 'Don't you understand me? It means the door, the entrance. It's our tradition here. A man carries his bride into her new life.'

She smiled sweetly. 'Okay,' she said.

He lifted her into his arms and pushed the door open. Before he left he had filled the room with dark red roses, specially ordered from the mainland. Now the sharp, heady smell engulfed them as they stepped as one into the room.

'For you,' he said, as she took great gulps of the scent.

'Oh...' Her body seemed to shiver in delight as he set her down and began to kiss her.

Mhairi thought she would remember this forever, the strangeness of it, the rich, overpowering scent. She knew it meant he loved her, but she liked the smell of the sea, or the smell of woodsmoke. The heaviness of the roses caught in her throat and made her feel sick. It was too much for her. She sat down on the sofa to steady herself and it seemed as if suddenly Jake was on top of her and she didn't know how he'd got there. She knew that men were stronger than she was, but his movements were so swift she hadn't realised he was making them.

She leaned back, feeling her back twist in the process. He felt heavy on top of her, and hot. Up until now she had thought he was a cool man, gentle and calm as the river that ran across the back of the farmer's field; she hadn't noticed before how much heat he had in him. His tongue drove into the back of her throat till she almost gagged, and then, unexpectedly, she began to feel warmth seeping into her skin, creeping throughout her body. He was sliding his clothes off and his skin felt warm, like an animal heated by the sun. There was a clump of seaweed hair and some pulpy bits on his body that squashed against her. His fingers slid between her legs, fumbling around in the space she had discovered inside herself, a secret place that opened up when you parted the lips that guarded it, like fronds of kelp at the entrance to an undersea cavern.

Up and down slid his hand, but his fingers, which seemed so gentle when he was painting or fashioning some sculpture out of driftwood, now felt rough; and the secret place, which opened and closed like a sea anemone if you stroked it, began to feel dry and sore. Mhairi thought she would explode as her body grew hotter and hotter and the pungent aroma of the roses caught in her throat and her bones felt crushed by the weight of this man who seemed like a stranger to her.

She looked at Jake's face but his eyes were closed and sweat was rolling down his cheeks like tears. As his bones ground against the bones in her hips, her back arched against the pain, which seemed to excite him. There was no escape here. Mhairi reached out for something to pull herself up with, but her hand came away with nothing more than one of the dark red roses; its thorn drove into her flesh and blood spattered her hands like petals. There was emptiness inside her and pain and, to her horror, blood began to lurch out from between her legs and all over her white dress. Small moans came sporadically from Jake and grunts of effort. In the dark horror of the blood and the roses Mhairi heard the sounds but could understand no words. Was this, she wondered, a man's way of telling her he loved her?

How Can I Live
Without my Blood?

CALLING THE SEALS was more important than ever to Ursula. She perched on the rock facing the sea as she opened her violin case and stroked the honeyed wood of the instrument. What crazed dramatic impulse, what aberrant desire for change had made her come here after splitting up with Michael? Was it not enough that she had lost her lover? Did she really have to lose her world too?

She could smell the spiky aroma of marram grass and sea pinks. This new world she had come to had its own beauties. She doubted whether she would ever again live in the city, though she'd grown up there. The water was choppy tonight, as if a storm was imminent. Her eyes searched the horizon but she couldn't see any of her friends, the seals. Her favourite had been gone for months now. Ursula hoped nothing had happened to her.

She drew the instrument up and tucked it under her chin, thinking about Jake as she tuned up. Now that he and Marina were married she was careful about going over there. Any young bride would want to keep her husband all to herself, not share him, especially with someone who could speak his language and laugh at the same jokes as he did.

The strings seemed as tightly wound as she herself felt tonight. Damn. One had snapped. As she searched in her violin case for a replacement, she caught a movement in the water and realised there were a couple of seals bobbing close to shore. They seemed agitated, not serene as they usually did. One of them was making a little whimpering noise, quite unlike anything Ursula had heard from them before. The seal poked its head out of the water, almost as if it were trying to communicate with something on land.

That was when Ursula saw Marina, crouched down on the rocks at the edge of the water. She was shivering, and as distressed as the seals. Tears dripped down her face and she clutched her stomach. Now that she was nearer, Ursula found it hard to tell whether the woman or the animal was whimpering.

'What on earth's the matter?' she asked.

The younger woman's eyes were swollen and scared. 'I think I'm going to die,' she said. 'It's the blood. It's so thick. Like sludge in a rock pool. Look at it.'

She seemed almost hysterical. At her feet was a wad of paper hankies, stained with thick gobbets of blood.

'Every time I think it's stopped it comes back again. Look. My new skirt is ruined. I bought that with my wages.'

The fresh blue cotton was spotted with blood. Ursula laid her violin carefully on the rock and strode to the water's edge, sending the two seals skittering back in panic. She dipped the pad that she rested her instrument on into the sea.

'Salt water draws the blood away,' she told Marina.

'But why is the blood coming? My stomach is aching with it. It's draining out of me and I'll never be whole again.'

Ursula was shocked. 'Didn't your mother tell you anything? You must have had periods before,' she said.

'My mother wouldn't tell me I was going to die,' Marina answered.

Ursula took her hand. It was very cold. 'You're not going to die,' she said. 'Put this round you.' She laid her own cardigan round Marina's shoulders. 'Don't you remember this happening to you before? It's your monthly period.'

'Monthly? How can I live without my blood?'

'Ssh. Don't panic. It's just part of being a woman.' Ursula sat beside her, knowing the heat of her body would calm Marina. The waves lapped against the rock they were sitting on. The sound seemed to bring Marina peace. As she slowly relaxed, leaning her head against Ursula's shoulder, the two seals drifted further out, their heads bobbing up out of the water occasionally, as if they were looking back.

Mhairi listened as Ursula quietly told her the strange story of her own body. She could not remember ever being so aware of what happened inside her. Was she stupid? Or had she once known but now forgotten these things? She watched the two creatures' slow progress through the waves and felt comforted by their presence.

'You didn't play for them, Ursula,' she said.

'Neither I did. Would you like me to play now?'

Mhairi nodded, sleepy. Being a woman seemed an exceptionally difficult thing to her. Why did everyone else seem to take it in their stride? It was terrifying, the blood clots, the sickness, the way she hurt so much inside.

Ursula looked at her weary face. She didn't want to disturb her by reaching for the violin. Instead she began to sing, an old Highland lullaby, about a woman whose baby is stolen by the faery people while the mother is gathering blaeberries. Strange to hush a child to sleep with the thought of being separated from what she loved, but the plaintive tune always worked with Ursula's little niece. *I found the wee brown otter's track, the otter's track, the otter's track. I found the wee brown otter's track, but never found my baby-o.*

Slowly the two seals in the water began to turn back towards the shore and the music. Mhairi watched them through heavy-lidded eyes. Her stomach ached. She could hardly bear the sadness of the song. She nestled against the warmth of Ursula's body. It made her feel safe where the music did not. The song, for all the beauty of its melody, was about despair and loss. She saw the frantic mother running up and down the hillside looking for her baby. Seeing a swan and a little yellow fawn. Flailing around in mountain mist. But never finding her baby. There was no happy ending with this lullaby. Mhairi thought the Scots must be a people of dark thoughts to comfort a child with such a story. She was sure her own country must have more peaceful lullabies, till she remembered she had fled a war there.

The seals were so close to the rock she sat on that Mhairi could see their eyes. *Hó-bhan, hó-bhan, Goiridh òg O, I never found my baby O!* Somewhere in the distance came the sound of a curlew calling, and a cold wind started to come up from the sea. The waves were choppy and rough and Mhairi thought they looked too dangerous to swim in, as if you would be tossed around in the swell, or sucked down by hidden whirlpools. Poor seals. She hoped they would be safe. She shivered and pressed closer to Ursula as the song went on and the two people of the sea turned their forlorn eyes towards her.

The Beginning of
Life as a Woman

'PLEASE CAN WE HAVE *meat* tonight?' Jake asked that morning. 'You only ever seem to think of fish.'

Mhairi was surprised; she hadn't noticed any lack of variety in their diet. Now she pressed her stomach against the sink, trying to ease the pain in her back. On the shore the wind sent a scurry of sand flying; foam plumed skyward as the waves sought the land. Mhairi thought longingly of swimming through water, her body elongated and fluid in the cool green, not bloated as it was now. Ursula had promised to be at the birth. She had told her about the options, the drugs to numb her body, the machines at the hospital, but once she'd mentioned birthing pools, that was it. For some reason Mhairi felt she would like to give birth in the water, see her baby swim up from between her legs like a little fish.

'She must come from some really primitive village,' Ursula told Jake later. 'She doesn't seem to know anything about the body.'

'She knows some bits of it,' said Jake with a grin. He had been astonished that Marina was a virgin on their wedding night, but she was completely uninhibited about the way in which she discovered her own body, and after the fiasco of the first night they very quickly found that, in making love, they understood each other in a way they failed to do during the day. Jake felt there was something occluded about Marina, a part of her he didn't recognise. He was sure it wasn't just the language and the mystery of her origins.

Mhairi peered into the shopping basket and picked up a carrot. Ursula had explained all about putting vegetables in with the meat to make it more tasty, though the lump of raw red beef sitting on the counter looked disgusting to Mhairi. The carrot had wrinkles all down it, like an old woman's thumb. Mhairi scraped at it with the knife, perplexed at her own clumsiness as the blade sliced through the carrot and into her thumb, dripping orange and red ooze on to the worktop.

Maybe the pains in her stomach were affecting her co-ordination, though she often felt awkward, ignorant, as though she had learned nothing in her life. Jake and Ursula were always asking her about her village, but she could remember nothing of what she had experienced before coming here. It made everything seem extraordinarily difficult to her – the way people spoke, what they did, even what they wore and ate. She supposed she must have suffered some brain damage, perhaps in the Balkan war. No matter how hard she tried, she still didn't speak like anyone else on the island.

As she glanced out the window she saw Ursula's cat sitting on top of the outhouse where Jake did his painting. She was a pretty little thing, licking her paws with the utter absorption that cats seemed to bring to everything. Mhairi loved the way Jake had taught her how to look, really look at things; she found the cat the most beautiful of the creatures around them, though she felt most affinity with the sad-eyed seals. Almost every night she ran over to the rocks where Ursula played to them. She wasn't sure which she liked better: staring into the animals' expressive eyes, or listening to the aching music that her friend conjured out of the violin.

A loud squawking broke out and Mhairi realised that a black crow had spotted the little cat and was croaking at her to leave the roof. Up the bird fluttered, screeching its vengeful message. *This roof belongs to me.* The cat stared back balefully, unwilling to be forced off a place she considered as much hers as anyone's. Only when a second crow joined the first and their harsh cawing filled the air, did the cat slide gracefully away into the bushes. Poor creature, thought Mhairi as the birds wheeled and dived, celebrating their territorial victory. Was she supposed to stay always earthbound, where she belonged?

As the pain in her stomach intensified she picked up the lump of meat from the counter. It smelled of blood. It wasn't unpleasant, though Mhairi wasn't sure she wanted to eat it. It wasn't so much the taste of cooked meat that put her off but the texture. It always seemed so hard to chew your way through it. Perhaps it was because she was pregnant and everything seemed to require so much effort.

Once she had the casserole in the oven, she eased herself on to the sofa and put the television on. This box in the corner seemed miraculous to her, the perfect way to find out about the world she now found herself in. At first she thought the people and animals she saw there had somehow shrunk so that they could live inside the set, but Jake explained that they weren't real, a concept she found hard to remember when her regular programmes came on, the ones about people in pubs or the police shows about American cities where people did terrible things to one another.

This afternoon there was a programme about an African tribe. She marvelled at how different the women were from her. They were black and very tall, around six feet, most of them, which Mhairi knew to be very tall for a woman, much taller than any of the women on the island. These black women were so slender that she wondered how they could survive. *They live mostly on milk*, the voice of the presenter told her, *and occasionally blood from their cows.*

He said the Dinka people worshipped their cows so much that only men were allowed to touch them. The tribes wandered wherever they could feed their animals, along the banks of the River Nile in the dry season and upcountry to the green plateaux of the north in the rainy season. *To exist, they must have space, land without boundaries, a wide, open horizon. Hemmed in, they sicken, turn into skeletons, wane, die.*

Mhairi thought of the great ocean surging beyond this little island. Land without boundaries, a wide, open horizon. The world she found herself in seemed a very sad place sometimes. Perhaps it was better that she knew nothing of her previous life. It would only make her distressed, the thought of the killings and the rapes she must have seen, the family she must have left behind. Jake and Ursula told her they thought she was probably a Kosovan but she didn't know what she was.

Her stomach continued to ache and she got up to try to ease the pain by walking. Up and down the living room she walked, for what seemed like hours; then she went into the bedroom, to look again at the pool in the corner. Jake had assembled it a few nights before.

'Won't be long now, darling,' he'd said, lifting the pieces out of the surprisingly small boxes it all fitted into. He put it together with his artist's precision.

Now she leaned over the padded edges, dreaming of the baby to come and pressing her stomach against the side to relieve the pain. There was a sharp pain in her back and she felt as if a sac of warm water had burst inside her and was running down her legs, quickly turning cold against her skin.

This was it. More than the monthly bleeding, more than lying with Jake, she felt this was the beginning of her life as a woman. Now she would understand why she was here and what her life was about. She phoned Ursula and the midwife and went back to lie on the sofa, but the pains were filling up the whole of her mind till she could think of nothing else. She cupped her hands underneath her belly, cuddling the baby hidden inside. She liked the weight of it, the feeling that she was bound somehow to the earth, to the land, in a way she hadn't been before. Another mother at the antenatal clinic had said *she* felt like a great big whale. Mhairi wasn't sure why that was supposed to be a bad thing. Whales seemed perfectly attractive animals to her. Even the killer ones had their own predatory beauty; and anyway, most whales only ate plankton.

There was a knock on the door and Ursula rushed in.

'I came straight,' she said, setting down her violin case. 'I was at the church going through some music for the end of term service. Where's Jake?'

Mhairi flinched. She had been so happy thinking about her baby she had forgotten to phone her husband.

'Can you phone him?' she asked.

Then the midwife came bustling in the door. 'How are you, dear?' she said, scurrying into the bedroom to look at the birthing pool without waiting for a reply. 'Oh my. Isn't this exciting now? I've never done one of these. Don't you worry, though. We're going to be just fine.'

The thought of anything else had simply not crossed Mhairi's mind. Birth surely was something that came naturally? Now for the first time she began to feel fear. With each surge of pain that went through her body came a question: what if her ignorance about the world left her incapable of giving birth? What if, in her stupidity about life, she produced a damaged baby? As the pain intensified and she needed all her energy to cope with it, she felt relief that it drove such troubling thoughts from her mind. Not for the first time she thought that physical problems were much easier to deal with than mental ones.

'Your blood pressure's very high, dearie,' said the midwife. 'Try and relax now.'

By the time Jake arrived the midwife was filling the pool with warm water, run through a hose from the bathroom.

'You should have waited for me, Morag. I'd have done that,' said Jake, arms sliding round Mhairi's stomach. 'All right, my love?'

She nodded, but she felt nothing about this was all right, not the pain, not the fear, not even the kindly little woman so excitedly testing the temperature of the water.

Ursula went through to the kitchen to make tea. 'Something smells nice in here, Marina,' she called.

Mhairi had such a tight feeling in her chest she could hardly bring herself to grunt in reply. She watched as Ursula poured tea and handed round biscuits, but it was like seeing something through murky water at the bottom of the ocean floor; the others seemed very far away from her, distorted. All she could hear was the slow trickle of water into the pool and the thumping of her own heart. All she could feel was the terrible throbbing that had colonised her insides and was taking on a relentless energy of its own, like the pistons she'd seen on television driving an old-fashioned paddle steamer. In and out the pain moved, on and on, taking her into uncharted waters, into a place where she felt as if all the thoughts in her brain had been sucked out and replaced with the sensation of red light pounding behind her eyes.

It was probably an hour later when she heard Morag's voice. 'That's it, dearie. You can get in now.'

Mhairi pulled her sea-green maternity dress over her head, startling Ursula, who was about to take the dishes out to give her privacy. The older woman was not surprised to see that she was naked under the dress; there was something almost wild about Marina. She looked natural without her clothes, completely unself-conscious in a way few women were. No doubt this freedom was one of the things Jake loved about her. Ursula caught sight of her own plump figure in the wardrobe mirror and sighed – she had put on a stone in the year since Jake and Marina married.

Mhairi climbed up the little stepladder and slid into the bath. Once in the water her face and whole body relaxed. The pain was still there, but much less than it had been before. Now when the contractions came, she twisted and turned in the water, letting the pain slide away from her. Time ceased to have any meaning as she drifted, suspended in her liquid safety net.

'That's remarkable, you know,' said Morag. 'Her blood pressure's gone right down. I'm going to speak to the consultant about this. I think it would help lots of my women.'

Jake sat on the steps beside the tub, occasionally wiping his wife's brow with a damp facecloth. She looked so ecstatic lying there in the dark water that he felt excluded somehow. Ursula slipped into the living room and brought back her violin. She played a slow, melancholy Gaelic song that she often played to the seals. Mhairi's eyes went dark with recognition, then she closed them, a small smile on her lips. Behind her lids she could see surging currents of water and fish sliding by; she could see strange clumps of seaweed fluttering in the green gloaming; she could sense the rush of the water her body displaced when she swam; she felt completely and utterly at peace.

It was dark now in the room, but no one moved to turn on the lights. Jake lit a scented candle Ursula had given them and the smell of lavender spiked with rosemary permeated the room. Mhairi's body seemed to ripple with a particularly strong contraction and the midwife stared into the pool.

'The baby's coming now, I think.'

Mhairi's hand went down between her legs and she felt the little boney head and soft hairs, wispy as algae, mingling with the rougher hairs on her own body.

Then there was a sharp pain that made her face contort.

'Don't stop playing, Ursula,' she said, but Ursula's bowing limped on, slow and tentative.

Morag slid her hand into the water. 'I can feel its little fist balled up beside its head,' she said, laughing. 'This wee thing doesna want to come out. He's punching you.'

Mhairi smiled. 'I don't blame him,' she said. 'It's lovely in here.'

She felt her body convulse again and she was pushing. She desperately wanted to see her child but she had a huge sense of compassion for him. Who would want to leave this fluid, beautiful world where you were safe, for the strange and dangerous world of the earth, for the world of humans?

But there was no denying the child. His little head started to appear and the cave inside her that had held him all these months was widening, opening, releasing him. He swam out between her legs and floated, arms spread wide as if giving himself up to the world. His body was white as mother-of-pearl, glowing against the dark water of the pool.

'I've never seen so much vernix on a newborn,' said Morag. 'This wee fella was in it for the long term. He really, *really* didn't want to come out.'

Mhairi felt the tissue of her womb giving way inside her and the placenta appeared in the water, a huge red sea anenome tinging the water pink with its dye. She looked at her son, bound to her still by the umbilical cord, spiralling out from him like a curly white telephone wire. She never wanted to be separated from him.

Ursula had stopped playing, tears in her eyes. Jake was silent, in awe. The midwife cut the cord but Mhairi knew that now she would never be alone. This child would understand her. He could not do other as he was of her blood, of her flesh, born of the water. She scooped him out of the blackness, and let him rest, nacreous white against the matt white skin and dark areola of her breast. He began to breathe, quite gently, his little body waxy and warm against her skin. Mhairi closed her eyes. Her baby seemed happy to be here, but she longed to return with him to the underwater world, where it was green and pain-free and exquisite; she longed to twist and turn with the changing currents; she longed to swim free, her baby surging through the water by her side.

Made Anew

'YOU NEED TO FASTEN THE SEATBELT, love,' said Jake, leaning over her to click it into place. Mhairi felt a flicker of disappointment. She was so looking forward to flying. She wanted to wheel and whirl in the air like the gulls that flocked over the water looking for fish, or the eagles she saw in the glen on the other side of the island.

There was a loud droning and the plane started to roll along the runway. Then Mhairi felt only exhilaration as she looked out her window and saw the ground tilt away from her. Up the machine lifted, leaving behind the sheep-scattered hills with their rocky outcrops, the little cottages punctuating the landscape. There was Ursula's, with its dark red peonies reduced to an exclamation mark, though the garden was laden with them; there was their own cottage, and inside the two children, safe with Ursula.

The night before, Mhairi had sat on the bed, filled with dread at the thought of leaving Sam and Mary.

'They'll be fine,' Ursula said. 'My job involves a modicum of understanding children, you know.'

Mhairi nodded, thinking what a curious word 'modicum' was. Ursula saw her quizzical look and laughed.

'A little bit, Marina, that's all it means. They'll be quite safe with me, you know. And I can't wait to have them to myself for a night or two.'

Mhairi was relieved. One part of her was afraid to let the children out of her sight, but the other part longed to be away, to see more than this little island. In the four years she had been here she had never been off it. Now she would see the big city and its streets and cars and shops. She would see magnificent buildings and crowds of people of every different shape and colour. Her spirits had lifted, as today they lifted with the take-off of the plane. She was avid to see what lay on the mainland.

Jake glanced at his wife, rejoicing in the radiant enquiry of her look. Sometimes he was afraid he couldn't make her happy, not because she was ever lacking in affection for him, but because she seemed sometimes to be restless, to want more than he could offer her on this little island. He felt absurdly happy, and continued to be so throughout the short plane journey and the taxi ride to the hotel, throughout the raiding of the mini-bar and the ceremonial bouncing on the bed. Loving his wife so passionately was not anything he had expected in life. Neither the tepid marriage of his parents, nor the soggy ending of his own first marriage, their 'drifting apart' as Jackie had put it, had prepared him for this sense of being with the person he was meant for. Nuzzling into Marina's neck, opening his eyes as her unsettling call signalled her climax, he knew he could never be happier than here.

The following day they went shopping. 'Stop worrying about the money,' he said. 'My aunt left us far more than we'll ever use.'

'Depends how much I spend today,' she teased. Her tastes, though, were simple. She wanted *National Geographic* magazine, whose front cover showed an undersea probe in the Pacific Ocean, and he insisted on buying her a mother-of-pearl necklace she admired. She refused the high-heeled shoes he offered her.

'Where am I going to wear them at home?' she asked.

'In the bedroom, perhaps?'

'Ah, a present for *you*,' she teased.

The department store had a magnificent central hall with wooden galleries and large chandeliers. Jake stood there studying a leather file case he could use to protect his drawings when he went to the beach. Was it worth spending so much on something this beautiful when he had a plastic one at home that probably did the job better? He ran his hand over the fine grain, savouring the scent of the leather. It smelt of tradition and satisfaction and being a man. Then he realised Marina was no longer with him. For a moment he panicked. What if she was lost somewhere and he never found her again? What if someone from her country had seen her and abducted her for political reasons? He ran up and down the same six-foot track of floor several times, seeing nothing, before calming himself. How stupid he must look. She had simply wandered away somewhere and was looking at handbags or something.

'She's lovely, isn't she?' he heard from one of the make-up counters.

'Do you think she's foreign? There's something different about her.'

Marina was sitting in a chair with a little circle of women around her, as a make-up artist smudged pearly colour round her dark eyes, painted new contours on to her face. Jake watched in fascination as an entirely new Marina emerged. This woman was more sophisticated than his wife, less simple; she was more seductive but less sensual, more overt but less open.

Mhairi was enchanted by the process of being made anew. Was this what it had been like when she first came to this country? This feeling of transformation? This sloughing off the old self and becoming someone different? For a fleeting moment she wondered who her old self had been and if she would ever remember where she had come from, but this moment was too exciting for her to linger in the past. She looked up and saw her husband.

'Would you still recognise me?' she called out, laughing.

'Told you she was foreign.'

'I think she's just Highland, maybe a Gaelic speaker.'

Jake smiled at his wife. 'You look beautiful to me whatever,' he said, though he silently preferred the old Marina, the real one, as he preferred to think of it.

She seemed to pick up his ambivalence, almost as if she had an internal radar attuned to him. Her eyes flicked once to the mirror and then she shrugged, her sense of excitement seemingly gone. She was serene for the rest of the afternoon, but he couldn't help regretting whatever signals he'd given off. It was as if something in her had been subdued.

In the Indian restaurant that night, though, her exuberance returned. She was intrigued by everything, the puffy naan breads, the spicy prawns, the sickly sweets made of condensed milk. It was as though in exploring this new cuisine her sense of adventure had been returned to her. 'The colours are fantastic, aren't they?' she said, staring at the red and gold renditions of Indian legends adorning the walls. 'They're so bright they hurt your eyes.'

'You're so bright you make me feast my eyes.'

She giggled, taking another slug of her bottled beer. Her cheeks were pink – she rarely drank at home. 'Do you think we'll ever go to India?' she asked.

'Why not?' he said, excited at the thought, though he couldn't tell whether the old or the new Marina was suggesting it. 'We can afford to do these things now. The world is our oyster.'

'I love oysters,' she said, though Jake couldn't remember her ever having eaten them. Maybe her memory was coming back.

'You like anything from the sea,' he said.

They left the restaurant and began wandering through the streets back to their hotel. It should have been simple, but somehow they lost their way and ended up by the river. It was dimly lit and deserted, except for a couple staggering along together by the waterside. They seemed mismatched, the girl thin and pale, the man red-faced and burly, so different they could have been two separate species. Mhairi caught the scent of the water in her nostrils, the eddying of a myriad little insects, a myriad motes of mud. The smell surged and ebbed in her mind, but only the smallest shard of memory came to the surface, something to do with a small boy. And a woman?

'I think I might have been here before,' she said.

'Could you possibly have come into the country here in Glasgow?' asked Jake, puzzled. 'Why would you have ended up on the island?'

He was afraid suddenly. If Marina were to remember where she came from, perhaps she would no longer be the woman he knew. Perhaps she would no longer want to be with him. He looked across at her sleek dark hair, her brown eyes. He longed to touch her skin, to feel the heat of her body against his. Then he would be safe. *They* would be safe.

She caught his anxiety. 'It's too dark round here. Dodgy,' she said. 'Let's get a taxi. You've got that number they gave you at the hotel.'

Her heart was thudding as they pulled away from the river. She wasn't sure what this place meant to her, only that she had been here. The how and the why eluded her. The taxi scudded through the dark streets, past pale wraith-like women standing on street corners, groups of drunken men, eventually some elegant couples strolling past busy pubs. Mhairi was looking out but she saw none of it properly. She was seeing a bridge over the river and a woman with the eyes of a cat. Some memory was floundering in the depths of her mind, but she could not pull it to the surface. It was important, but it was floating away from her. She knew what it was like to have water rushing against her skin, and dank river smell in her nostrils, but she didn't know what that meant. She felt as if she was drowning.

Jake caught her by the hand and walked into the lift with her. 'You look lost. What's the matter.'

She smiled at him and leaned her head against his shoulder. 'I don't know.'

In the room he pulled her on to the bed. They lay there, arms around each other, neither moving, though he could sense a fine tremor running through her body like a reverberating nerve.

'Darling. Did terrible things happen to you?'

'I can't remember ...'

'You're safe now. You're with me.'

'I know,' she said, but she felt as if nothing about life was safe. If her memory, her very sense of who she was could fluctuate with the waters of the River Clyde, what else could disappear in her life? Her home? Jake? Her very children? She sat up abruptly.

'We have to phone home, Jake. I need to speak to the kids.'

'No problem, love.' He picked up the phone and dialled. For the first time in a long time, Mhairi was seized by the strangeness of the act; in this piece of plastic the voices of her children would be heard, like the whisper of the sea in a seashell, as insubstantial and incomplete compared to hearing them speak as the seashell's whisper is to the crash and boom of the sea. Suddenly the whole room seemed strange to her: the clear piece of water in which she could see her face, the chunks of wood supporting where they slept, the pale fire that burned from holes in the ceiling.

'Marina, you look ghastly. Hold on, Ursula,' Jake said into the phone, putting his arm round his wife's shoulders. He was frightened by the pallor of her skin, the bewildered look in her eyes.

'Marina, are you all right?'

Even Ursula's voice had sounded strange, dissonant, as if something was not quite right. Panic consumed Mhairi utterly. What if Sam had fallen and broken his collarbone? What if the baby had swallowed something poisonous? Would either of them be alive when she went home? She could see the walk up to the cottage, hear the crunch of gravel under her feet, smell sea and grass. And then the opening of the door and the body of Sam sprawled on the floor as he sometimes sprawled in sleep, his fists bunched, his mouth open. And the baby, the baby, the baby ... dead, dead, trussed up in her sleeping suit like a battery chicken in its polythene wrapper.

'Why are you crying, Marina? Please don't cry,' said Ursula. Jake pulled the phone back. 'She's worried about the kids, Ursula. They're fine, aren't they?'

'Of course they are.' Ursula thought of the mothers she'd seen on the television news, weeping at war graves. Poor Marina. In a strange place, away from the island that had given her safety, no wonder she was disoriented and anxious about the children. Perhaps she had lost children before? Ursula looked across at Sam, his sleek dark hair and brown eyes so like his mother's. He was holding wee Mary in his arms, feeding her from the bottle. Such beautiful children. She wished they were hers.

'Tell Marina I'm going over to give them both a great big kiss from her.'

'Yeuch, you are not, Auntie Ursula. Get away from me,' said Sam.

'Ursula's giving them a great big kiss on your behalf,' Jake told his wife. She turned her face into the pillow. Great honking sobs broke from her and Jake marvelled as always at her lack of inhibition. She sounded like sea lions he'd heard barking at the circus when he was a kid.

'Thanks, Ursula. I'll talk to you tomorrow.'

Jake put the phone down and slid down against his wife. 'Marina, Marina. Don't cry. They're fine, love. There's no need for you to worry about them at all.'

She turned into her husband's body. 'I can't bear it. It's too hard having children. I'm scared when I'm not with them.'

'Look, we'll go back tomorrow. Just don't worry. There's nothing wrong with them.'

He kissed the tears from her eyelids, ran his hand down her side. She seemed to have exhausted herself. Her eyes were open but she lay quietly, as still as if she were asleep. He wondered what horrors were lurking below the surface of her mind, waiting to pull her into their depths. She should have had some kind of counselling. He should have brought her to Glasgow way back when he first met her. Why had he not insisted? Why had he not made her face her truth, whatever it was. It would have protected her now, when she found herself in a situation she did not know. *Stupid, stupid bastard, congratulating yourself on looking after her, when all the time you were just keeping her for yourself.* He sat up and rifled through the phone book. He'd go into one of the refugee organisations and ask them what help was available.

He turned to put the directory back and felt her catching his jumper. 'Where are you going? Don't leave me.'

'Relax, love. I'm not going anywhere.'

She pulled him back to her. Fierce, hungry, she sought his mouth, bruised his lips with hers. She seemed frantic, pulling at his belt buckle, popping the buttons on his shirt. What was she so in need of? He wasn't sure it was him.

In the street below, traffic rolled past the hotel in successive waves, the sound like the rumbling of lava from a volcano that Mhairi had seen in a film. She surged against Jake, craving his heat, his electric skin. Let liquid fire wash over them, let the red hot heat of their bodies purge her of this fear. She dug her fingers into his buttocks, clawing at him, pulling him inside her. Let him come into her world; let his soul be seared with her terrible sense of dread. She gripped him with her thighs, clung desperately to him as together they plunged again and again into the cauterising terror of the volcano.

Blood, Bone, Breath

'OH MUM, NOT CHICKEN AGAIN. Can I have some of your herring?'

'Hey you, you're a kid,' said Mhairi. 'You're not supposed to like fish.'

Her son shrugged. 'Well, I do.' He flung his wet bathing suit down on the kitchen floor. 'Will you come to the competition tomorrow, Mum?'

'Not if you leave that there.'

'But *will* you? Mum, *please*.' Mhairi looked at her son's eager face. Didn't he know she was teasing? She swooped down to cuddle him, held him against her, tight. Children probably needed time to learn about humour, just as they needed time to learn to speak. Sam leaned back against her for a moment, then squirmed from under her arms.

'Yuk, yuk, yuk,' he said, but he was half-smiling.

'Something smells good.' Jake and Ursula struggled through the door holding cardboard boxes, full up with fabrics and paint.

'Hurray,' said Sam. 'Auntie Ursula!' He caught one of her boxes just before it toppled over.

'You *are* quick, Sam,' she said. He followed her through to the living room, intent on investigating the boxes.

'Sam,' called Mhairi. 'Make sure you've washed your hands. I'm going to serve up in a minute.'

She turned to the fridge and took out two herring fillets. She could hear Sam's clear voice as he came back from the bathroom.

'Are you going to play to the seals tonight, Auntie Ursula? Can I come?'

Ursula looked enquiringly at Jake. 'Will we have time?'

He looked up from the floor, where he was separating out some of the fabrics from the boxes. 'You don't have to help me with this anyway, Urs,' he said.

'Course I do. But we'll sneak out and play for a wee bit, will we, Sam?'

'And Mummy, too,' he said.

'Of course. Mummy always has to come.'

'Mu-mmy. Herring. Yum yum.'

Mhairi walked past him to the fridge. She stopped herself from ruffling his hair and satisfied herself with smiling at him instead. 'Let's have some wine, Ursula, will we?'

'That would be lovely. I feel in need of a tonic.'

'And a gin too, Auntie Ursula?' piped up Sam.

Ursula grinned at him. 'What do monkeys sing at Christmas?'

'Don't know,' said Sam, eyes searching hers for a clue.

'Jungle bells, jungle bells,' chanted Ursula as Sam made retching noises.

Mhairi poured the wine. 'You look a bit peaky, Ursula.'

'Just "the change",' she said. 'One minute you're so exhausted you can hardly stand and the next you're sweating like a pig. People think you're deranged.'

'Och, you're too young for that.'

Ursula made a face. 'I wish I was. I didn't intend to start quite this early, I must say.'

Jake came back into the kitchen, lugging a large box. Sam followed with a smaller one. 'I'm helping Dad,' he proclaimed.

Ursula jumped to her feet. 'Sorry, Jake, I got sidetracked.'

'No, no. Don't you stir yourself. You girls just get stuck into the wine while us chaps wear ourselves to a frazzle, eh Sam? Let's take these into the living room.'

'Is that all of them, Dad? I'm not tired you know. I could carry lots of boxes.'

'Right, let's leave the ladies to their girl talk and we'll get the rest in, son.'

Mhairi plonked the roast chicken on top of the cooker and poked a skewer through the plump breast. The juices ran clear. 'So? Have you been to the doctor, then?'

'Yes, it's all perfectly normal, nothing to worry about, which is depressing in itself. But it's not as if all these female hormones are exactly useful.'

'Certainly not – homicidal urges every month and a never-ending desire for chocolate.'

Ursula was surprised. 'I don't think I've seen you eat chocolate.'

Mhairi blushed. 'I keep a little stash of it, actually,' she said, remembering the first time she'd eaten it. It was the first time Jake had given her money for housekeeping and she took a bus into the local Co-op. She had no idea what to buy and chose the prettiest wrappers. Jake picked her up after school and they unpacked the shopping together. He laughed when he realised there wasn't the makings of a single meal.

'I suppose we could have bread and mayonnaise with some tomato puree on the side,' he said, but had stopped laughing when he saw her stricken face. 'You didn't know what half of it was, did you love?'

She shook her head.

'We'll go round again tomorrow and I'll show you what we need,' he said. 'Don't look so upset. Here, this'll cheer you up.'

He popped a square of dark chocolate into her mouth. It was as if the bittersweet taste slid into her brain and she slowly became calm.

'The Spanish thought it was a miracle substance when they saw the Aztec armies using it to keep going,' said Jake, seeing her rapt expression. She made a mental note of the name *Aztec*, another thing for Ursula to show her in the big encyclopaedia. After that she always made sure she had some of the miracle substance in the house.

Now she opened the end cupboard to show Ursula. 'See? That

box is for after dinner, seventy per cent pure cocoa solids.'

'You spoil me, Marina. My life would be very dull without you and Jake.'

It was Mhairi's turn to be surprised. She felt, even now, after seven years on the island, that it was always Ursula who gave to her. Ursula had taught her to read and write, had lent her books and records, shown her money and fashion and even how her body worked. What on earth had she offered Ursula?

Five-year-old Mary tugged at Ursula's dress. She held out a drawing of a woman with a bright pink face and orange hair.

'That's you, Auntie Ursula,' she said.

'It's lovely, Mary. Can I take it home and put it up on my wall?'

The little girl nodded solemnly. 'I've did one of Mummy, too. Would you like to see it?'

She took a second picture from her notebook. This one showed a face outlined by sleek black hair. The dark brown eyes were enormous and somehow, despite the crudeness of the child's drawing, full of pain.

'Is Mummy sad in this?'

Mary cocked her head to one side, considering. 'No, she's always like that,' she said. 'I think maybe she just *looks* a bit sad sometimes.'

Throughout the meal Ursula found the thought of the little girl's picture nagging away at her. Could a five-year-old, innocent of analytical intent, and unskilled in representing reality, really see in a way adults could not? Was Marina really that unhappy? After seven years of living here and loving Jake and having his children, was she still not where she wanted to be?

When the meal was over Jake took a roll of black bin bags from the cupboard.

'Right, team,' he said. 'Let's get all this sorted.'

They trooped into the living room, the women opening a second bottle of wine, the children tripping each other up in their excitement at the prospect of helping.

Jake drew a pair of scissors through the tape that held one of the boxes closed. He ripped back the lid and started drawing out what appeared to be theatrical costumes.

'Remember these, Urs?'

She didn't at first, till he plonked a trilby on Sam's head. 'Oh yes, *Guys and Dolls*.'

'*Luck, be a lady tonight*,' sang Jake.

'What a pity it was the kids who did the show, with such magnificent voices around,' she teased.

'My Daddy's a *good* singer,' said Mary.

'I'm just kidding, pet.' Ursula cuddled the fierce little girl.

'That's naughty, Auntie Ursula,' came the reply, loaded with that absolute level of reproof that only the very young or the very religious can muster.

'I think I surpassed myself with these,' said Jake, delving into a second box and producing a series of sequinned turbans adorned with pineapples and bananas and cherries.

'Are they from the pantomime?' asked Mhairi.

'Yes, remember Nancy MacLeod doing her Carmen Miranda?'

'Let's save the artificial fruit – we can use that again. The rest we'll just get rid of.' He thrust a pile of scuffed Arabian slippers into the bin bag. The sequins on the end winked like luridly coloured stars.

'Are you sure ...?' Ursula started but met with a raised eyebrow from Jake. 'I suppose you're right.'

'We don't want to take a load of old rubbish into the new school, do we?'

'No, start fresh. You're absolutely right.'

Outside the cottage it had started to pour, a sudden summer deluge that looked as if it would never stop. The sky turned unnaturally grey, as if night had come early.

'I think we're in for a night of this,' said Jake.

'We'll have to play for the seals tomorrow night, kids,' said Ursula. 'Fingers crossed it'll be dry by then.'

'Oh no,' said Sam. Mary solemnly crossed her fingers.

Mhairi was looking curiously at the dappled skin that Jake now drew from the box. She felt uneasy but didn't know why.

'Remember this? We had that fantastic display on the people of the sea, with Ursula's music playing in the background.' He turned to his wife. 'I found this the very night I met you.'

Some distant memory was prickling away in Mhairi's mind. She ran her hand over the dry skin. It should be wet, moist, she thought. It should have a living creature inside it: blood, bone, breath. It should smell of salt water and sand, not this tacky glue; should be searing through green waters, eyes wide open in the dim waters of the Atlantic. This was as dry and sad as the transparent little crab shells that littered the beach. It was not as it should be.

Ursula, watching her, had a sudden feeling of dread. Some former premonition, of she knew not what, flickered into her mind and hovered there, impossible to dismiss. Yet there was nothing amiss here. She looked at Jake, at the gentle smile he gave his children. Their heads by now were lower than their bottoms in their eagerness to reach the treasures in the box. Only Marina sat apart, body and face rigid as her fingers explored the sealskin, flicking off the sequins that had been glued there for the school display.

As the rain battered the window and turned the sky ever darker, Jake turned on the lights. The room became cosy, warm, a little cove of safety against the storm outside. At last Mhairi looked at them all, those she loved most in the world – at sweet Jake, her lover and protector; at Ursula, with her passion and her humour. Most of all she looked at the faces of her children as if, for all the times she had carelessly or casually accepted their presence, she must now imprint every feature in her memory, every curved cheek, every eyelash. In this familiar room, with the people who should have made her feel safe, she suddenly felt cold and very, very afraid.

A Long Line of Swimmers

THE ROOM FELT HOT and stuffy. Mhairi slipped out of bed and slid the window open. The rain had stopped but there were still clouds scudding across the moon. She could smell the salt of the sea, hear big waves crashing on the shore. In the surging and the soughing of the water, it seemed as if there was a kind of music, too strange and deep for humans to hear. She knew that if she had once heard this music, had her ear been attuned to these resonances and not the sounds of everyday life, she would not have been able to live. She strained now to capture its elusive notes. As the moon grew full and drew the waves towards their own crashing dissolution, it seemed to her as if the sea was calling her, as if its savage harmonics, and not Ursula's finely wrought music, were more truly her own.

Jake stirred but failed to wake as she felt under the bed for the sealskin. He had put it on top of the black bags, ready for the bin, but she couldn't let it go. She took it to the open window and stood, watching the sea. The skin felt purer now, with the tangy air rushing through it. She laid it against her cheek. It was rough, but that somehow felt right. Jake's hands were rough when he touched her, the fingers scarred with glue and parched with paint. Down below the water, rocks were rough with barnacles when you brushed against them; coral reef was sharp and scratchy, belying its delicate appearance.

In her mind she tried to slip under the waves, tried to penetrate the underwater forests that surely lay there, but everything was black and cold and wet and she could see nothing. She pulled a chair over to the window and spread the sealskin over herself like a blanket. The salt wind stung her face, but she felt warm underneath the skin, as if her own blood was pumping through it, electrifying it. Jake turned in the bed, restless without her, but she needed to be by the window, with the pounding of the wind and the water and the yell of a lone oystercatcher, lost on the shore without its mate.

That morning it was Jake who woke first.

'Marina?' he said, as grey as a ghost in the early light. He was puzzled, hesitant. 'What on earth are you doing there, love?'

He lifted her out from underneath the sealskin to carry her to the bed. The skin fell off her but Mhairi grasped on to the end of it and held it tight. She didn't want to be without it.

She held on to it, all the time that Jake was kissing her, all the time that he was nuzzling her neck, all the time that he rubbed his body the length of hers. It was in her left hand as she caressed him with her right, as she ruffled his hair with her right hand, ran her right hand down his thighs and in between his legs. She slipped out from under him then and lay on top of him, drawing the sealskin over her back. With it on top of her she felt strong, as if all the heat from the animal that once lived inside it had transferred itself to her. He marvelled at the dark hair sticking to her head, the sleek lines of her shoulders emerging from the skin.

'Jake,' she said. 'I will always love you.'

He had no time to say anything in return. Mary came pounding into the room, flinging the door wide. 'Mummy, are you playing a game? Are you a seal what comes out of the water when Ursula plays it a song?'

'It's not a game, darling.' Mhairi pulled her daughter on to the bed and cuddled her under the sealskin.

'It's dark in here, Mummy. It smells funny, like a fish.'

Jake slid his dressing gown on and headed for the kitchen.

'Mummy, you've got no clothes on. Aren't you cold?'

Mhairi held her little girl against her, remembering her as a baby, remembering the feeling of her little minnow mouth nudging the breast for milk, remembering how tiny she was, and how replete she felt with her child clamped to her, a mollusc clinging to its rock.

'Maybe we're all supposed to go about with no clothes on,' she whispered, but Mary shrieked. 'Mummy, you're very, very bad.'

'Am I, my wee darling?'

'No, you're the best Mummy in the whole world.'

The children were fractious at breakfast time, Ursula subdued, Jake uneasy – and yet Mhairi did not want the meal to end. Afterwards she moved slowly as she stacked the dishes and wrapped Sam's swimming trunks in a clean towel. She went into the bedroom before they left, looked at the salt-spattered window, the plain wooden furniture, much of it made by Jake. She did not want to leave.

'Why have you got that damn skin with you, Marina?' said Jake. She shook her head, slid into the seat beside him. She rested her hand on his thigh all the way to the swimming baths. It was hot and steamy inside, as she imagined entering a jungle would be, though everything here was light and bright, not dark and mysterious. Despite the heat, she kept the sealskin with her, ignoring the curious glances of other parents. She could not be without it now.

Sam was paler than normal and she pulled him to her. 'I feel sick, Mum,' he said.

'You'll be fine. You come from a long line of swimmers.'

Jake and Ursula exchanged a puzzled look.

'Do I, Mum?'

'Yes. Here, touch this for luck.'

He stroked the skin and smiled at her, nerves gone. He went to move off from her, but she held him to her, just for a moment longer, then let him run off to join his little friends. Mary snuggled down beside her.

'Sam's going to win, isn't he, Mummy?'

'Let's hope so, sweetie.'

As the races began she wondered how the children swam so confidently in such noise. The lights were retina-burning bright and the children's shouts and splashes were amplified in the crucible of the water. Clutching the sealskin to her, she knew that swimming was for cool green water, quiet water where sounds were submerged and came to you from long distances away.

Sam put on his goggles and began shaking his arms and legs as he'd seen swimmers do on the television. He was first to respond to the gun and plunge into the water. Compared to the other children he looked totally relaxed in the pool, propelling himself through the artificially turquoise water as if it were his natural element. The muscles on the other children's shoulders tensed and strained, but Sam torpedoed through with the grace of someone who has not had to work for their gift.

'Gosh, he swims like a fish,' said Ursula.

'He swims like a seal,' said Mhairi.

'You're in a funny mood today, love,' said Jake, squeezing her hand. She leant her head on his shoulder. She felt wearier than she had ever done in her life. Down in the pool, Sam was winning every race in his age group while she sat there, knowing how soon he would come to curse her and this talent, the only thing she was leaving him with. Mary was even younger. How soon would she forget her mother? How long would it take her to be happy again?

Ursula looked at Marina's eyes, darker than ever in her pale face. How much she had changed since she first came here as a gauche, even wild, young girl. Life here must have been strange to her, yet she had dealt with marriage and motherhood and keeping a house when it seemed she knew nothing of any of it. Ursula's eyes went from Sam, waving up from the pool, to the sleepy face of Mary, cuddled into her mother, to the lively eyes of Jake. It was only when she looked finally at her friend and the bereft expression on her face that she knew, with that sharp sense of premonition she had felt before, that Marina was leaving.

At the end of the races Sam came running up to them, hair up in a spiky tuft on his head.

'Yeah ... Sup-er swimm-er!' he said, flexing his muscles.

Jake ruffled his hair. 'Well done, son.'

Mhairi hugged him. 'I'm proud of you,' she said and kissed him.

'Mu-um,' he protested.

The lady sitting next to them leaned over and patted his arm. 'What a super wee swimmer you are, Sam.' She turned to Jake and Mhairi. 'You'll have all the other parents after you now. I hope he's not as good at football as he is at swimming. It'll be war.'

Jake rolled his eyes. 'He seems ready for war already.'

The lady beamed at Sam. 'Och, boys never change.'

'Mum.' Sam was tugging at Mhairi's skirt. 'Jamie McDonald is crying because I beat him.'

'Oh no. It shouldn't be like that. You can't help being a good swimmer.'

'Well, he says I did it on purpose. He's crying, Mum.'

'It's not your fault he's hurting, my lamb.'

'Mum, am I your lamb, too?' demanded Mary.

'You are, my darling. I love you both so much it hurts.'

'Why does it hurt if you love us, Mum?' asked Sam.

'I don't know,' she said. 'But it does.'

Jake was jubilant as they all got back into the car. 'Where to now, people?'

'To the shore,' said Mhairi. As the car moved off Ursula suddenly felt as though she was going to heave. She had always been a good traveller, but today everything felt disoriented; everything was somehow wrong. Why was Jake not as frightened as she was? Were men really a different species, as so many of her women friends supposed?

Mhairi was trembling by the time they reached the harbour where the fishing boats came in. A long white beach led away from it; there were already several families taking their Saturday afternoon stroll along it.

'Not here,' she said. 'Our own beach.'

It was as if Jake noticed for the first time that something was wrong. 'Are you all right, Marina?' he asked.

'No,' she said. 'I can't bear this.'

Jake looked at his high-strung wife in astonishment.

'What is it?' he said, but Ursula told him, 'Shh.' She remembered the fine eyes of her favourite seal, the one who no longer came to hear the music; she remembered the two seals bobbing anxiously in the water as Marina went through menstruation. What exile was this? How could they have been so wrong about everything? She felt sick to her stomach.

They reached the long white stretch of beach where Mhairi had danced seven years ago, where she had shed her pelt and entered a world which was not hers. Jake took her hand as they walked along, puzzled by her apparent distress but also remembering nights of making love here, when the children were asleep, gliding in and out of his wife as the waves lapped on the shore and the salt air stung their bodies. He turned to look at her, wondering if she too was thinking of those most beautiful nights of their marriage, but she was holding her side, hardly able to breathe.

Now, finally, he really was alarmed. 'Marina. What on earth's wrong?'

'I don't want to go,' she said. 'But I can't stay.'

'Go where?' The wind was whipping the waves up, pelting the sand with a cappuccino froth. There was going to be a storm. The children had started to shiver. He needed to get them into the house. Out on the horizon he saw two black spots bobbing on the water. Were they fishing floats? buoys? Ursula recognised them at once.

'My sisters. They've come to get me,' she said.

'Who's your sisters, Mum?' Sam was dancing from rock to rock, sure-footed.

'He doesn't get that from me,' said Mhairi. 'It's quite sore moving over stones. Our skins are tough but we have to kind of rock from one to another.' She turned to Ursula. 'I did love dancing,' she said.

Mary embarked on a lop-sided Highland fling. She was generally regarded as being good for her age, though both Mhairi and Ursula cracked up laughing when they saw her, hopping from one foot to the other, nearly toppling over.

'I can dance, Mum.'

'I know you can, my darling. Jake, you'll have to explain to them.'

'Explain what? Don't be ridiculous,' he blustered.

Ursula squeezed his hand. 'There's nothing you can do to prevent this,' she said.

In the water the two seals raised their heads and uttered a strange, mournful cry.

'I'm coming,' said Mhairi. She knelt beside the children. 'Sam, you'll have to look after Mary when I'm gone.'

Mary's eyes were solemn. 'Mummy, you're not to go.'

Sam looked puzzled. 'Where are you going, Mum?'

'Not far,' she said. She felt as though her heart, that heart which had powered her for thousands of miles underwater, was going to explode.

'Don't forget me,' she said to Jake, and kissed his lips.

He snatched at the sealskin. 'Are you mad? You can't leave us.'

'I must,' she said. 'Ursula, please look after them all for me.'

Ursula pulled her in against her. 'Is there no other way?' she said.

'I wish there was, but I have been breathing someone else's air. I need sea and salt. I need the dark waters beneath the surface, I need to be free.'

'Come back,' said Ursula. 'You know I'll play for you ... always.'

'I know.' She nuzzled Ursula's cheek. 'It's not so bad. You never need to buy fish again. I'll bring you some ... always.'

Ursula tried to laugh, but she knew it came out like a wheeze. 'There's a limit to how much herring I can eat,' she said.

'Never.' Mhairi hugged Sam and then Mary, squeezing them so tight they gasped for air. 'I love you.'

'What have I done wrong?' said Jake, pulling at her dress. 'Where are you going, Marina? Don't go.'

She hugged him, rubbing her sleek hair against his face. 'I am Mhairi,' she said. 'I love you, Jake. I will be your wife for ever.'

The wind was howling now and a grey rain slashed their faces. Gently Mhairi took her skin from Jake. Her children were crying, frightened. Jake and Ursula gripped hands, willing the tide to turn back, the seas to still. Later they all said the sky lightened at that moment, rendering the sand, which had looked grey in the storm, a light, brilliant white. None of them saw the moment when Mhairi put the skin on. It was as if one minute she was a woman, much loved, and suddenly she became a seal, clumsily flopping across the last few yards of sand until she reached the sea.

For Mhairi it was as if she suddenly became whole. She plunged into the dark water, hardly feeling the cold. Down she dived, disturbing cloudy swarms of plankton. It took her a moment to remember how to propel herself forward with her front flippers, but once she felt the water parting beneath them, she surged through the waves with the freedom of a bird soaring and wheeling through the blue sky.

It took only a few minutes for her to reach her sisters. They lunged against her, bounding out of the water in delight that she had returned to them. With thunder crashing about her and lightning searing her eyes, Mhairi leapt and turned, in an ecstasy of movement so intense that her sisters thought she had returned to them as a dolphin.

Together the three circled the bay again and again. On their second circuit they were joined by some younger seals. The sisters peered at them and said they were their children. It seemed to Mhairi as if there was no pain in this conjunction, and no fear. They were not frightened that their children would die in the night or cease to breathe without them. They were simply there.

The seals finally turned to go. On the shore the people of the land were huddled together, the children sobbing, Jake and Ursula leached of all feeling. They were sodden with the rain, their hair slick against their heads as flat as any seal's.

Only Mhairi turned back as they left the bay. Her head surfaced from the water, the brown eyes taking in the people she loved on the shore, the scrubby slope behind them scored with harsh rain. There was no music, only the ugly gasps of the humans crying. She raised up her face towards the storm, welcoming the hard pellets of moisture that lashed her skin. And as she spun and glided in this element that was her own, the sounds of the thunder and the sobbing and the whoosh of the water as she powered through it dissolved into a myriad notes of the most bittersweet music that she had ever heard.

A FAERIE
CHILD

Nine Rosebushes

THE BLOOD JUST WON'T STOP. Mara prods her gums but they seem firm. She *knows* it's coming from the back of her throat, can feel the liquid massing, a viscous bubble somewhere in her gullet. It will rise and rise till it emerges in a thick red globe, like the adder beads her grandmother told her about when she was young. Mara's blood ran cold at the thought of Midsummer Night, and seven great snakes hissing and hissing, while one little white one wound in and out between them, shaping their glutinous saliva into the iridescent bead.

'Pray you find one, Mara,' said her grandmother. 'They protect pregnant women. I lost three bairns before I had your mither and she lost five before she had you.'

'Ugh,' Mara said. She hated snakes. But now she'd give anything for an adder bead. The blood forming in her mouth is only a portent, she knows. Nine babies she has lost. She can't lose another one.

> *Nine beanrows will I have there, a hive for the honey-bee;*
> *And live alone in the bee-loud glade.*

Nine rosebushes are what she has, every one of them with blossoms dark and red as blood.

'Mara, please don't be so mawkish,' Stephen pleaded with her as she dug into the dry earth, only days after losing the first one. She might as well live alone. Does he care that their children have gone, seeping away with her blood, over and over again? She thought *she* was dying that first time, as the blood came away inside her, more than she believed possible. She didn't realise it was her child dying.

The first bush flowered as if by magic. The garden had resisted her until then. Everything she planted withered and died, even the night-scented stocks, which a kid could grow. But the rose, her Crimson Glory rose, flourished as if she had nurtured it with her blood. How long had she been carrying her child dead inside her? How did she not know?

The next time she did know, because of the pain, a knife scraping and scraping at the walls of her abdomen. She would have endured anything to keep her baby. It was summer and the first rosebush was in flower, emitting a heavy fragrance that she couldn't get enough of; her lungs were hungry for the lushness of the scent. On hot days it almost overwhelmed her, the rich perfume, the sound of bees buzzing round the garden, bearing the message, *This was my child, this was my child.*

Did she jinx the second baby by thinking so much of the poor, lost, first one? Her mother bought her the next rosebush, just before she died. It was a different variety, Munstead Wood, plum-ripe, almost purple, the sort of bloom that looked as though it should flower in mud or thrive in the forest, clinging parasitically to the roots of an ancient tree. Its dank, fruity fragrance came from the swamp. There was a comforting sense of decay in this one, as if its inherent corruption matched the reality of the world.

The number of rosebushes in the garden grew, though Mara stopped telling Stephen about the events they signified. If he realised, he didn't say so. Perhaps he was afraid. Or perhaps he simply thought his wife, like many women, had a passion for the flower whose ruffled petals, curling round a secret, hidden core, so much resembled the inner crevices of their own bodies.

Mara spits into the sink, recoiling from the gobbet of clotted blood that lands on the pristine white porcelain. She tries clearing her throat, but more saliva bubbles up, streaking the sink with pink. Again and again she tries to expel it from her body till at last she grows afraid that she will expel the baby, too. This time she hopes for a girl. Only a girl will understand what she has had to go through in the name of love. Stephen certainly doesn't.

Mara wipes her face with a damp cloth, thinking, not for the first time, of her husband and the mysterious country he's in. It's hard to imagine what Azerbaijan is like. All she knows is that it has mud volcanoes and that Stephen is there as much as he's here. She has no idea what he really does there. Marine engineering? Something to do with oil rigs, she supposes. He started with marine drawing, which conjured up images in her head of underwater forests, of coral reefs and strange, serpentine creatures gliding in and out of bone palaces. Then he went back to university to study some more and emerged as a marine engineer, though how could you engineer the tides of the sea, the waves that crashed to the shore like smashing china?

Abruptly she sits down on the toilet seat. If she sits very still and waits, perhaps the baby will stay with her. There is no pain, only a sensation of nausea and sudden, terrible emptiness. She doesn't need to see the doctor or go for a scan. She knows the baby is no longer alive.

A World Elsewhere

MARA TAKES THE LAST BATCH of cherry scones out of the oven, splitting them in two and buttering them lavishly – her mother-in-law always boasts you can sink your teeth into any scones *she's* buttered. The thought of it makes Mara sick to her stomach, but she takes a bite to try, wrinkling her nose at the impression her teeth leave behind, as if some voracious squirrel has passed by and taken a chunk out of the scone. The slick yellow fat coats her tongue and the inside of her mouth in the most disgusting way, but it tastes unexpectedly comforting and she ends up cramming the whole lot in her mouth. The perfect way to put on weight, after all. She can hear Betty chattering away in the living room and ventures another, swiftly rubbing the grease off her mouth before lifting the tray to take the rest in.

'Och now, Mara, you mustn't be doing so much in your condition,' says Betty, bustling forward to take the tray off her.

Alex raises her eyebrow in that comical way she has. Dumb insolence, the teachers called it at school. It always made Mara crack up.

'Infanticipating again?' she says drily, making Mara bite her lip with laughter. Alex has chosen the term deliberately, she knows. Betty's always using those stupid old-fashioned phrases.

'Now you know what trouble poor Mara's had,' says Betty, handing out plates and napkins before wielding the silver teapot. You'd think it was *her* house, not Mara's. Probably thinks it is. Just because she gave them the deposit ... 'We mustn't jinx it by talking about it.'

Mara sinks back on to the sofa, grimacing at her friend over Betty's immaculately coifed head.

'You're looking a bit peaky, dear.' Betty pats her hand as she hands her a cup of tea. 'I've put some extra sugar in to buck you up.'

Alex splutters into her cup. 'Oops, bit of scone went down the wrong way. Delicious, by the way. All those hours in home economics paid off in your case.'

Mara smirks. She and Alex spent their time in home economics bouncing on the beds they were supposed to be providing with hospital corners, and spraying furniture polish in the air to make it smell like they'd done the dusting.

'I don't know what they taught you girls in school,' sighs Betty. 'Mara couldn't boil an egg when she married Stephen. I had to take her in hand myself, didn't I, dear?'

'You should have taken Stephen in hand,' says Alex. 'Mara and I weren't cut out for domestic service.'

Betty tuts in shock. 'A girl needs to be able to look after her man,' she says. 'Poor Mara's done very well. She keeps an immaculate house now.'

She looks round with approval at the polished wood table, the lace doilies and the frou-froued Royal Doulton figurines she's given Mara every Christmas without fail since she and Stephen married. In darker moments Mara dreams of auctioning the lot on ebay and absconding with the profits. The frozen frills of an earlier age, the ladylike daintiness of their portrayal of femininity are so far from the chaotic mess of her own experience of being female that they feel like a constant rebuke.

'If only she could carry these poor bairns to term. But then poor dear Peggy was the same. It's probably some genetic failure in the family,' pronounces Betty, with the satisfaction of one who knows her own genome to be perfect.

Mara almost laughs out loud at her friend's shocked expression, though Betty's continual insistence on knowing her mother better than she did herself grates on her nerves. So what if they were schoolfriends? You can bet she wasn't there when Peggy was sliding down the bathroom wall, in despair as her blood and her baby soaked out on to the floor. Betty's the sort of person who probably doesn't even like sex, too funky for her. Mara reckons she only let her husband do it to her the once, when Stephen was conceived. No wonder he turned out the way he did, a simulacrum of a man with seawater in his veins, not red blood pumping round his body.

She sighs. You can't fault his sperm, at least. Nine times he's got her pregnant. Betty's right, nothing wrong with *her* side of the family.

'Maybe this time you should consider bedrest?' says Alex.

'I'll ask the doctor,' says Mara. 'It doesn't seem to make much difference what I do. We've tried bedrest and we've tried keeping active. Neither worked.' She looks out at the nine rosebushes in the garden. In the light breeze that lifts other flowers and sends the leaves rippling, they are steadfast, firm. There's her dark Shakespeare rose, with its complex formation of petals, its powerful scent. Would her boy have been a writer? Beside it is the Wild Edric, a lighter red than the others, but with a heady fragrance so pungent it could drive you mad. Such a romantic rose, named after a Saxon lord who married a fairy queen. They fought one day and she rode off, never to return. They say his ghost haunts the hills still, searching for his lost love.

'The restless dead', her mother called it, a phrase that had been handed down from her own mother. As a young child Mara found it a terrifying idea, that the dead still wandered the world, unable to find peace. This wasn't the usual ghosties and ghoulies, the daft Disney films with their anodynely comic characters. This was real. It could be her own grandmother, her mother, trapped in spirit form, haunted by their own unfinished business.

Now she *wishes for* the restless dead, longs for her babies to come back to her, to thread their way through her dreams, brushing her cheek with the lightest of touches, demanding her attention. But no matter how much she desires it, her babies never come to her.

'You need to be sensible,' says Betty, not unkindly. 'I don't think some gentle work hurts, but you can't do that heavy lifting and stuff you've been doing at the hospital. Ask them for a nice wee desk job, dear.' She lowers her voice dramatically. 'And when Stephen comes home next month, you mustn't let him ... you know.'

This time Alex snorts outright, to Betty's surprise.

'Oh no, dear. You know what men are like. Even though he is my son ... We have to protect this wee thing now,' she says, leaning forward.

Mara recoils against the back of the sofa – surely her mother-in-law wasn't going to pat her stomach?

Betty's eyes look moist. 'I've waited so long for a grandchild,' she says. 'We don't want anything to go wrong now.'

'Nothing will go wrong this time,' says Mara. 'We're not allowed to do lifting any more. The poor patients have to struggle up themselves.' For the first time she notices that Betty's little feet barely touch the ground. She's so used to thinking of her mother-in-law as all-powerful that she seems not to have noticed that she's also tiny. If only she didn't expect to be called *Mum*. Mara had a mum and it wasn't Betty. Occasionally she relents and calls her *Ma,* which isn't something she ever called her own mother, but for the most part she doesn't name her at all.

Betty stands to go, smoothing her tight dress down over her convex, but curiously un-lumpy stomach. She has the look of a plump pouter pigeon, probably has on one of those pink corsets women used to wear in the old days. She pats Mara's hand.

'Now mind what I say, pet. Go and see them about an easier job.'

Alex giggles as soon as Betty goes out the door.

'Lord, she's a hoot.'

'She's all right, she means well. Hey, want some wine instead of that tea?'

'When the cat's away, eh? But you can't have any if you're pregnant.'

'I'm not,' sighs Mara. 'I lost the baby again, but I can't bear to tell her yet.'

'Oh, love. I'm so sorry.'

'Don't tell anyone, Alex. I'm not ready.'

'Course I won't. I wouldn't.'

Mara touches her hand as she goes to the kitchen. 'Sauvignon or Chardonnay?'

'It's way too early in the afternoon to be drinking something heavy like Chardonnay – let's have that.'

Mara slips her shoes off and swings her legs up on the sofa. 'Might as well play the part,' she says.

Alex laughs and lounges back in her armchair. 'How decadent is this?'

'This is the sort of thing I imagine you do all the time, in that bachelor girl flat of yours.'

'Stop it. You're beginning to sound like her.'

'Any minute now I'll be telling you I'm tipsy, or half seas over.'

'Are you all right, though, Mara? Seriously.'

'Not really. She's hell bent on being a grandmother. I feel there's no time to breathe. As soon as I've lost one she's asking me about the next.'

'Look, I know you don't want to think this, but there are worse things in the world than being childless.'

Mara gazes at her friend. Maybe in London, when you have a fancy job and glamorous friends who're all actors and writers, that would be okay, but not here, not in the middle of nowhere, where every dumb beast in the field can reproduce.

'What else is there?'

Alex leans forward in her chair. 'Remember our mantra, Mara? There is a world elsewhere.'

Mara tries not to look out at the garden. *My babies are here.* The words ripple round her brain. *My babies are here.*

'Where did we get that anyway? Was it Shakespeare?'

'You know it was.'

'I don't remember being that smart. Come on, what could I do elsewhere? I'm not clever like you, Alex.'

'I'm not clever. I'm just lucky I found something I was good at. Remember we were going to share a flat in Paris? I was going to be a writer and you were going to be an artist?'

'Well, you nearly got there. You're in publishing.' Mara tops up their glasses. 'And I nearly got there – Stephen used to be in marine drawing.'

Alex doesn't laugh. 'Do you love him, Mara. Really?'

My babies are here. Outside, the roses look black against the bright sunlight. Mara leans back against her cushion. Tipsy's quite a good word really. 'I'm with Prince Charles on that one,' she says. 'Whatever love means ...'

'Oh God, Mara, are you really settling for that?'

'What else is there? I'm not young any more. I don't expect to be starry-eyed at my age.'

'You're not old.'

'I'm thirty-four. In one year my fertility halves.'

'There's more to life than fertility.'

'I want a baby.'

She's shouting. Is she shouting?

Alex puts her glass down in capitulation. 'Well, maybe Stephen'll do the business.'

'He has up till now. Super-Spunk! It's me that can't follow through.'

Her friend's face twists. 'I'm so sorry, honey. It's not fair.'

'It's not anything. It just is.' Mara slides off the sofa. 'We need to raise our alcohol levels. That's all there is to it.'

Alex stands to go for more wine, elegant in her neat little cardigan, the skinny jeans. Thin, even. When did that happen?

'It's okay, I'll get it. I'm not pregnant any more, remember?'

'Sorry.'

Mara stands at the kitchen window, wishing wine still came in bottles you had to open with a corkscrew – she can't go back in there yet. From here she can see right up the glen, where the hills curl round the river like a fox protecting its cubs. She always thought she'd be safe here, that nothing bad could happen to her in a place called the Fairy Glen. She must have been mad, thinking of cosy little flower fairies instead of remembering all the stories her mother and grandmother told her – of snatched babies swapped for fairy changelings, or cowrie-clad shellycoats leading wanderers astray. Of Tam Lin riding in procession behind the Queen of Elfland and his true love throwing her green mantle over him while the fairies turned him into an adder and a red-hot brand of iron and finally a naked man.

Nothing more dangerous than the last. Look at the heartbreak it's brought her. She smiles at last. More wine, definitely. She takes the ice bucket from the cupboard and smashes the bag of ice cubes against the fridge door to free them. The next bottle of Chardonnay will be really cold. Time to listen to tales of bohemian life in the city, of sex in penthouse flats and designer handbags and lovers who eat sushi from your naked body. There is a world elsewhere.

A' Women Want a Wean

MARA IS WAITING in the corridor when Jen's boss comes out.

'You can go on in,' he says, jerking his head in the direction of the operating theatre.

Gingerly Mara opens the door and pokes her head round. She hates the theatre, with its pools of blood on the floor after operations. Sure enough, there's a dark red slick underneath the operating table.

'Oops,' says Jen. 'I'll get rid of it. I know you hate that.'

She drags her mop over the gooey liquid, smearing pink all over the vinyl, before finally erasing all trace of its presence.

'Nearly done. I'm starving, are you?'

Mara nods. 'I'm always starving these days.'

'Eating for two, doll. That's it.'

They're early. The canteen is only half full when they get there, and the hot food is just being put into big chafing dishes.

'Oh goodie,' says Jen. 'We get first choice.' She drums plump fingers on the counter, humming as she decides what to have. 'Cheeseburger and chips. And coleslaw on the side.'

'Trying to pretend you're healthy?' teases Mara, pointing to the macaroni cheese, glistening with comforting fat.

'Want chips wi' that, hen?' asks the assistant.

Mara shrugs. 'Why not? And a bit of salad on the side, please,' she says, ignoring Jen's sniggers.

'So when's Stephen home?' asks Jen.

'Tonight. He gets into Edinburgh Airport this afternoon and he'll be home by seven.'

'Big night the night, eh?'

Mara smiles, wondering what it'll be like to have him back this time. There's always that moment of adjustment, when the whole house has to be re-calibrated, no longer her personal refuge but a home where two people live, where there will be a man's underpants in the laundry basket, newspapers piling up on the coffee table, the smell of aftershave and of him.

'So did you see Alex, then? Heard she was back at the weekend.'

'Aye. It was nice.'

'I think she's got a bit snobby now, a bit up her ain arse.'

Jen chomps into her burger, muffin top visible under her tunic top. She never seems to worry about her weight. Her husband and three children are as chubby as she is; can't be healthy, really.

'It was good fun. She doesn't change. Not really. She thinks I should stop trying for a baby.'

Mid-mouthful, Jen's jaw drops open. 'Oops,' she says, scooping up a wodge of undigested bun and stuffing it back in her mouth. 'I think she's lost the plot there.'

'Maybe she's right. Maybe I should stop putting myself through this time and time again.'

'A' women want a wean,' says Jen, with a note of finality.

What else is there? Later, as she lights the candles for her romantic dinner table, Mara tries to imagine what her future could have been if she *had* moved away, but it's like the surface of a crystal ball, misty and impenetrable. Maybe she would have gone to art school. Or maybe she wouldn't have got married at all. She could have shared a flat with Alex. She could have worn designer clothes, had lots of lovers.

She is not going to buy another rosebush.

When Stephen's key turns in the lock, she shoots a last scoosh of perfume on her throat. He's almost tentative as he enters the cottage, till she hugs him. Then his body relaxes against hers.

'You look bonny,' he says, taking her hand. 'Maybe this time we'll be lucky.'

He's brought her chocolates from the airport and a fine lavender pashmina, whose soft fabric she rubs against her cheek. He wraps it round her shoulders.

'You look really pretty in that colour.'

They eat the lamb casserole she made the day before, leaving it so that all the flavours would intensify. He refuses a second helping but makes no comment when she takes one. As she eats, he takes out his camera phone.

'This is where I went on my day off this time. It's called Yanar Dagh, and it's a mountain that burns all year round.'

The image is tiny, and strange, a picture of a hillside aflame with fire.

'The fire never goes out. There's natural gas inside the mountain and it's always alight. There are streams running off it that look quite calm and normal, but you can light the surface of the water if you have a match. It's amazing.'

Mara pores over the images, fascinated by the hill blazing in the darkness, the sky behind it midnight blue.

'That one was taken in one of the teashops you can go to around dusk. That's the best time to see it,' says Stephen.

'It's beautiful.'

He stands and kisses the back of her neck. 'So are you.'

They leave the dishes and go straight to bed. Mara wraps the lavender shawl round her naked shoulders. In the light of the bedside lamp her skin is creamy, glowing. Stephen puts his hand on her stomach but she raises it to her lips and kisses his fingers, pulling his dark head on to her breasts. He moans with pleasure.

'I've missed you, love.'

'I have a good feeling this time, Stephen. This time it'll be all right.'

He flinches at her certainty, but it doesn't matter. This time it *will* be all right.

The Clootie Well

THE HOUSE SEEMS EMPTY without Stephen. She knows by the end of the month she'll fret about his return, anxious that he'll irritate her or somehow curtail her freedom, but for now she feels alone. In the silence the ticking of the clock seems loud, threatening almost, and she can't be bothered watching the telly.

The cat sits on the hearthrug, daintily licking her chops after devouring a whole sachet of some lamb slop.

'I know where I'll go, puss.'

Slowly she gets to her feet. The weight of all the creamy sauces and chocolate she's stuffed herself with is beginning to slow her down. Where is her sewing basket? Rummaging around in its depths she fishes out a length of emerald satin ribbon and some strips of brightly coloured cotton, red and purple. The ribbon is beautiful. If anything should work, it will.

As she heads for the door she realises the cat is following her, padding along behind her as if they're going for an evening stroll.

'Come on then, Sukie. Let's go.'

She turns the outside light on and picks up her big storm lantern. It'll be dark by the time they get back. The leaves rattle in the trees like dried beans in a jar. She pulls her jacket closed, wishing she'd brought a scarf. Sukie trots behind her for quarter of a mile and then abruptly stops and starts squawking at her. The sudden sound lasers through the stillness of the glen.

'Really, puss. What a racket. Was there ever a louder wee cat than you? That's enough to waken the dead.'

The little cat cries out as though she's being tortured.

'Come on, then,' says Mara, but the animal stays where she is, as though faced with an invisible boundary she must not cross. It puzzles Mara, but she needs to go on now. As she turns to resume walking, the cat yells at her again.

'Go back, then. I'll see you in a bit.'

She walks on, trying to ignore the animal's calls yet feeling she has somehow betrayed her. Dusk is smudging out the last of the evening sunset and the pink tinge on the hills dissolves to grey. She climbs the stile at the end of the rough track and starts to move towards the river when she realises she's turned too early. Switching the lantern on, she searches for her own markers, the spray paint on the rock that looks like a crow, the ribbon round one of the tree trunks.

At last she finds the right path, picking her way meticulously across the uneven grass. The river is hissing like a nest of snakes and above her the hills loom like a hawk ready to strike. She started out too late, should have left it till the morning. A loose stone tumbles away underneath her feet but she manages to keep her balance. Finally she's there, in her secret glade, under the whitethorn tree with the sound of the skirling water in her ears.

Is it just because it's getting dark that it looks different? She walks round it, switching the lantern on so she can see properly. Yes, there's the strip of white velvet she started it off with, and next to it, a piece of the black lace mantilla that used to be her mother's. It was painful cutting it up, but if you're making offerings to the gods they should be valuable. A scrap of her wedding veil is round the other side. She finds it, caught in the prickly spines of the tree, but beside it is a wispy silk scarf and beyond that, someone's regimental tie. Other people must have found her shrine and added their own wishes to hers. Blue shimmery chiffon, long strands of strawberry-patterned fabric, a yellow gingham ribbon. So many sad people in the world, so many wishes.

Carefully she tiesher purple material next to the white velvet. The red should go beside her mother's black lace. But she needs somewhere special for the emerald satin, somewhere hidden, where it will glow like the sparkly lametta boas she puts at the foot of their Christmas tree. Stooping, she drapes it along one of the lower branches, winding it in and out to secure it. Damn, she's caught her finger on a thorn. She should have been more careful.

Scudding black clouds start to darken the sky and the wind turns snell. Standing beneath her tree, its votive ribbons flying like the prayer flags on a Tibetan stupa, Mara closes her eyes and wishes. Let the spirits of the earth and the running water give her what every woman should have; let the gods and goddesses gather under the shelter of this tree and conjure up the cells, only the cells, she will do the rest; let the heavens rage and storm, let the lightning split the sky, so long as it brings forth the tiniest living child. Let God ... Oh God, let there be a God ... If He or She is out there in the vast emptiness of the sky, please listen.

If only there would be a sign. Mara clasps her hands the way they were taught in Sunday school, remembering the highly polished patent shoes the girl in front of her wore, the naff posters of Jesus with children in an assortment of skin tones. But belief seems as hard here underneath the whitethorn tree, as the river rushes downhill with the speed of a fairy raid, as it did in that stuffy classroom. Does the answer to a prayer depend on the belief of the person praying? She wishes she could believe but her head's a jumble of nonsense, of Christ and saints, of elf-children and brownies and changelings, of selkies and shape-shifting horses with seaweed in their hair. *Please*, she whispers, but there is no reply, just the soughing of the trees and the first patter of rain.

The road home seems interminable. She puts the lantern on full beam, terrified she'll fall as she tries to get back to the path. Somehow when you're staring at the ground as you walk, the distance seems longer. Her jacket is too thin and no longer meets in the middle, making her shiver. When the dusk turns to darkness she nearly falls, missing her footing on the uneven surface. Instinctively she hugs herself with her arms to protect her belly, till she remembers. It doesn't matter if she falls. There is nothing there.

She is bleak and cold by the time she gets home. Sukie is already installed by the heater, licking her fur in the most contented manner, though when she realises Mara is back, she slides to her feet and starts yowling for food.

'You little hypocrite,' says Mara, cheered by the cat's insistence on being attended to. She slices up a chicken thigh for her and puts it on the kitchen floor, chewing at the last one in the pack. It's gone before she's even had a chance to savour it, so she searches for something else to eat. Ready-made macaroni cheese; good, she can heat it in the microwave. It would be nice to have a glass of wine with it but she daren't keep any in the house in case people see her buying it or disposing of the bottles.

The hot cheese is comforting, a good coating for her stomach. Normally she'd have a salad with it but she has a feeling that it would cut the fat and reduce her calorie intake, and she *needs* to be this big. There's a whole apple pie in the fridge so she puts that in to heat while she has some crisps and a cup of milky coffee. Cream, there must be cream somewhere, she knows it, but despite rummaging in all the cupboards, the best she can come up with is canned custard. When that dings in the microwave she puts it in a jug and brings it and the pie through on a tray.

Slowly relishing every mouthful of hot fruit, every slippery spoonful of creamy custard, she eats her way through the pie. Mindful eating, that's what Alex does, rolling even a tiny raisin round her mouth many times to take the full flavour from it. It's supposed to help you lose weight, but all it does for Mara is make her want more. There are sausages in the fridge, eggs she could fry, cans of beans in their slurry of tomato sauce. She wants to eat and eat till her stomach swells up like a Buddha, till she becomes a giantess bestriding the world, all-powerful, all-fertile. She never wants to feel empty again. Scraping the last spoonful of yellow custard from the plate, she gets to her feet and heads towards the kitchen. Will she never feel full?

The Baby Shower

'ARE YE STAYIN' ON for Ellie's baby shower?' asks Jen, stuffing one of her chips in her mouth before she's even got to the checkout.

'A baby shower? I thought that was an American thing.'

'A' the young lassies are havin' them these days.'

Mara looks doubtful. 'Nobody told me about it.'

'Might be worried you'll be upset to see the baby, like.'

'Oh no. I'd love to see the baby.'

They walk over to a window table and put their trays down. Outside the sky is dreich, filled with impending rain. Mara slathers brown sauce on her chips, trying to eat slowly.

'I don't have anything with me. You need to bring something, don't you?'

'Och, you'll get a wee teddy or something in the hospital gift shop. Get a pink one. It's a wee girl.'

Five girls, Mara's had five girls. Five clots of tissue draining out of her body, except that the second was more than that, almost ten weeks old, an ectopic pregnancy that nearly killed Mara and did kill her daughter. She and Stephen were so excited, thinking this time, after three losses, this time she would finally bring their baby to term ... The pain started in the middle of the night, a stabbing in the midriff, jolting her awake. As soon as she sat up, clutching her side, Stephen was awake.

'Mara, are you all right?'

She could sense the blood seeping on to her nightie, rolling down her legs. When Stephen switched the bedside lamp on, the sheet on her side was stained pinky red. Mara felt she was going to be sick, but she didn't want to vomit, didn't want anything leaving her body. She must hold it in, she must. From a long way away she could hear Stephen calling an ambulance, babbling in panic, then everything went black.

When she woke up she was in a room with blue sheets and plastic leather chairs. Wrong colour sheets, she thought. We had a girl. She could hear her husband's voice in her ear.

'You're pale as a ghost. Please come back to me, Mara. Please.'

'I haven't gone anywhere,' her voice said. It seemed very far away from her, as if it was in a tunnel with fog swirling all around. Could your voice just go walkabout? Did it have an existence of its own? Did your brain? Stephen started crooning to her, begging her over and over again to stay awake.

'We'll try again,' he said. 'I promise you. We'll just keep going till we have our baby. Don't leave me.'

She wanted to leave him, wanted to follow her baby, who was haloed in light at the end of a long tunnel. Mara's mother was holding her so she knew the baby was safe. She wanted to go with them but her damn body refused to give up. Slowly she came back to herself, felt the blood flowing again, movement returning to her limbs. Stephen looked shell-shocked. Maybe he did love her. She attempted what she hoped was a smile at him, though she suspected it was a botched job, a lop-sided rictus more scary than reassuring.

'Thank God,' he said. It came out almost as a sob. 'We'll try again, Mara. I promise you.'

Now Mara wonders whether she can go and celebrate the arrival of someone else's baby. But maybe she'll get a chance to hold it, feel the warm body snuggling against her breast.

'Okay,' she says to Jen.

'They're holding it in the committee room on the first floor,' says Jen. 'I'll meet you at the end of my shift.'

In the hospital gift shop Mara ponders over a pink teddy with a squashed face and a plush pink cat with a chiffon skirt, surreally inaccurate representations of the original animals. The cat, then. She buys the largest bunch of flowers in the bucket, fifteen quid – pink roses and stargazer lilies whose smell instantly makes her feel ill. It doesn't matter. She needs to be there whatever the cost.

At four o'clock she heads down to the maternity unit.

'Jen's in the birthing pool,' says one of the other cleaners.

'Literally?' says Mara, to a grin from the other woman.

Jen's sluicing out the pool when she arrives, so Mara plonks herself down on one of the wooden chairs.

'Always a pleasure to watch others working.'

'Cheeky mare,' says Jen. 'Gorgeous wee boy's just been born in here. You should ha' seen him. Thick black hair and blue eyes, a wee sweetie.'

Mara eyes the turquoise egg at the bottom of the bed. 'Do you think they really help?'

'Why no'? Whatever it takes.'

'I fancy the birthing pool.'

'I had one with Jamie, ma last one. Helps you take the pressure off your lower back.'

'You ever done that floating pool thing, where you're in the pool in the dark?'

'I've never worked out what it's supposed to be for.'

'Stress. I suppose.'

'Och, that's what alcohol's for.'

Before they even get to the party they can hear the noise, a bee-hum of talk and laughter that thrums through the empty corridor. Inside, the committee room is decked with pink and silver helium balloons. Ellie looks surprised to see Mara but kisses her cheek.

'How are you doing? You must be past the morning sickness stage by now.'

'Oh yes,' says Mara. 'That's long gone.' She keeps her head turned away from the lilies. Funereal flowers anyway, even though they're so pretty. She thrusts them into Ellie's hands and places the cat among the piles of pink teddies, pink rabbits, pink bootees, pink ponies. 'The baby'll probably end up wearing nothing but black after being bombarded with all this pink.'

'Aye, she'll be a Goth like our Rachel.'

Ellie's teenage sister Rachel is busy pouring champagne, her dyed black hair sticking up in tiny spikes all over her head.

'You could have one wee glass, no?' she says to Mara.

'I'll stick with lemonade, I think,' says Mara.

'Your turn next, Rachel,' says Jen, slugging down half the contents of her glass in one easy motion.

'Have to find the chap first,' says Rachel.

'You'll need to get rid of the Goth make-up, then. It scares men half to death, that.'

'Poor wee things.'

'I'm serious. They're easily intimidated.'

'Och, who needs men anyway? I'm not sure I want a life of nappies and rubbing cream on people's bums.'

'Don't knock that part,' says Jen.

Rachel rolls her eyes at Mara. 'Your pal's sex mad.'

'Hey, you cannae beat a regular sex life,' says Jen.

'She's right. You don't want to end up like John Betjeman and find you haven't had enough sex in your life,' says Mara.

'Believe me, I get enough.'

Mara looks at the tartan mini-kilt, the raccoon eyes, and doesn't doubt it.

'Wouldn't you like to have a baby?' she asks.

Rachel picks up a glass of champagne in her free lace-gloved hand. 'It's not on my agenda at the moment.'

'Don't hang about, girl,' says Jen. 'You know what my mammy used to say. You turn down the walkers and the riders go by.'

'What if I'm the rider?'

Jen looks across at Ellie, who's picked the baby up from her pram and is jiggling it in her arms. 'You cannae do it without a man.'

Rachel looks irritated. 'There's more to life, you know.'

'Actually, there isn't. You can mess about if you want to, but there's nothing more important than children.'

'Speak for yourself,' snaps Rachel, walking away.

Mara buries her head in her lemonade glass. 'Why are you getting so aerated?' she asks.

'Stupid wee lassie,' says Jen.

Mara gazes across the polished mahogany table at the throng of women now clustered round Ellie, all cooing over the baby. 'How old is she, sixteen? You were still mourning Kurt Cobain at that age, swearing you'd never love another man the way you loved him. She'll learn.'

'He *was* beautiful, wasn't he?'

'Is that a cake over there? I'm starving.'

Jen bursts out laughing. 'You won't want to eat that yin. It's made of nappies.'

'Really?' Mara goes over to inspect it. Sure enough, it's built up from layers of rolled nappies, tied with pink satin ribbon. There are sausage rolls on a plate beside it, and little cupcakes with pink icing. She automatically shoves a hot pastry into her mouth, but the crowd round Ellie and the baby is thinning now so she walks over there instead of tackling the cupcakes. Where was it Ellie worked? Was she someone's PA? The gynaecology man, maybe?

'What are you going to call her?' she asks, staring hungrily at the child.

'We thought Blue Ivy, like Beyoncé's baby.'

'That's a pretty name,' says Mara.

'I like your name. It's unusual.'

'Just plain old Mary, really. But you know what my mum was like – she'd never have plain if fancy would do.'

'She was quite a character. I was in her class at school. She was my favourite teacher, such a laugh.'

Mara sighs. 'I know. I miss her a lot.' She glances down at her thickening belly. 'Especially just now.'

The other woman looks stricken. 'What a shame.' Impulsively she thrusts her baby at Mara. 'Would you like to have a wee go of her?'

Gratefully Mara cradles the baby, marvelling at her mammalian absorption in sleep. With her eyes glued shut, her pink button nose and tiny fingers, she's like the picture of a baby otter Mara saw on the internet, its mother staring defiantly at the camera as she holds her child tight. It's at the moment the baby snuffles in satisfaction that Mara feels something crack inside her, like a dam bursting; no, not a dam, a wild torrent of storm water, ripping trees and rocks and earth from the banks of the river as it hurtles on its vertiginous path down the mountain side. She is swept up in the current, tossed into the churning water. A high keening noise bursts from her lips as she clutches the little pink cocoon to her.

'Mara!' Jen is at her side in an instant. All around people are murmuring, poised in the inertia of wanting to help and being afraid to make things worse. The mother stands frozen in terror. Mara stares at her, not seeing her. All she knows is the warmth of the baby in her arms, the way she tucks neatly into the crook of her arm. How can she ever let her go?

'Don't cry, Mara.' Jen's hands are gentle but insistent as she slides them under the baby and slowly prises her away from her friend. 'It won't be long till you have your own baby. Don't cry.'

Mara struggles to make sense of it but she must. She must pull herself together, divert their attention away from her. The baby's eyes open for an instant, then she snuggles back into sleep. Jen puts her carefully into her mother's arms but Ellie flinches as Mara speaks to her.

'Sorry, Ellie. Your baby's really beautiful. I'm a bit tired, I think.'

Jen holds her arm firmly as she marshals her to the door. 'Go on with the party, folks. Nothing to worry about.'

Once they're in the corridor a babble of noise breaks out behind them. Jen turns to look back but Mara keeps on walking. There is nothing in that room for her.

A Faerie Child

WATERY LIGHT FILTERING THROUGH the lace curtains, a view up the glen towards the hills, this room is beautiful. Mara surveys the pale lilac walls, the ivory cot. Her baby will be happy here, so why does she feel so low? Hormones. Must be. She has cramps in her stomach, pain in her lower back, and she feels miserable. Her period must be starting, again.

She trails to the bathroom, clutching her handbag. Yes, the blood has started. Tucked in a secret pocket of the bag is her mooncup, tied up in a little bag with pink ribbon. What a boon that's proved to be – no incriminating tampons or bulky pads, just a little cup to collect the blood. Ha, the way fairies are supposed to collect dew. She scrunches up the silicone and slides it inside her body. There's a relief in dealing with practical matters.

Things are beginning to fall into place. The universe is finally conspiring to help her. The local paper had an article about a new private maternity hospital opening up, so when she went for her check-up to Dr Johnstone, she told him that was where she was giving birth. It was in a stern-looking Victorian building that used to be an asylum and didn't look as though the facilities were any better than in their hospital. In fact it didn't look as cheery. It was all a bit elegant and sterile, with none of the brightly coloured curtains and photos of exotic places they have on the walls of their baby unit, though at least you'd have a room of your own there.

When she told him the doctor looked alarmed. 'My dear Mrs

Niven. There's no necessity for you to go there. Borders General has marvellous facilities and staff. Besides, these places are ferociously expensive.'

'That's not a problem,' said Mara. 'My husband probably earns as much as you do.'

'Really? I thought he was an oil worker.'

'He's in management, actually,' said Mara. 'He makes at least £600 for every day he works, often £700.'

'Hmmm.' Dr Johnstone was ponderous both physically and mentally, adjusting his waistcoat before he spoke. 'Well ... be that as it may, the National Health Service really is the safest place for any mother.'

Mara liked him but this was the time to be ruthless. 'Hasn't exactly worked out well for me.'

He cleared his throat and sighed. 'No, no, I suppose it hasn't. You'll at least come here for check-ups until the birth? I *would* like to keep an eye on you.'

'Actually, no,' said Mara. 'I've worked out my treatment plan at the hospital. It's all taken care of, Dr Johnstone. No need to worry.'

Back in the nursery she sets the mobile spinning, a flock of little white ducks bobbing up and down on the air. Stephen will be home soon. What will it be like to be close to another human being again? Will she be able to hold things together? She hears the car scrunching up the track and delves into her handbag again, dousing herself with *Secret Obsession*. Betty's picking him up today, and the old witch is uncanny. That'll put her off the scent, literally.

By the time they come into the house she's reached the bottom of the stairs. A brief flicker of shock on Stephen's face.

'I knew I should have been keeping an eye on you,' says Betty, bustling forward. 'You look awfully peaky, dear.'

'I don't want any fuss,' says Mara, entwining herself round her husband. He breathes in deeply. 'Ah, the scent of a woman,' he says. 'Hoo-ah!'

'The kettle's been boiled,' says Mara. 'Who wants what? Or would you like something stronger?'

'Gracious, what an idea,' says Betty. 'A nice cup of tea will be fine. I'll make it myself, in fact.'

'No.' Mara uses her weight to block her mother-in-law's path. 'You sit down, Ma. I'm perfectly capable of making the tea. I've made some sandwiches too. The scones are bought, I'm afraid.'

'Good grief, I wouldn't expect you to be making scones at this stage.' Betty looks quite affronted at the suggestion.

'I would normally,' says Mara, determinedly serene. 'But I was making new curtains for the nursery. They're so pretty – lace. Why don't you go on up and see them while I serve up?'

She winks at Stephen, who smiles and follows his mother up the stair.

'Mara,' he calls down, leaning over the banisters. 'You didn't paint this yourself, did you?'

She walks into the hall holding the teapot. 'It's a really pretty colour, don't you think?'

'Oh, Mar, you shouldn't have done that. It's dangerous in your condition.'

'I feel great,' says Mara. 'I've got rid of all the fuss and I'm feeling really good. Don't you worry about a thing.'

'What do you mean, you've got rid of all the fuss?' Betty's voice is steely underneath the anxious tone.

'I mean, I've taken control of the whole process. And do you know what, Betty, I'm happier and healthier than I've ever been at this point in a pregnancy. It's going to turn out all right this time, I know it.'

She hands round the tea and the best china side plates. Tuna mayo sandwiches and Stephen's favourite: ham and mustard on white bread.

'Oh,' he moans, as easily distracted as she knew he would be. 'I've been dreaming about these sandwiches.'

Betty takes a delicate bite of tuna. 'I don't like it, Mara. What do you mean, you've taken control? It's not safe. You should leave these things to the doctor.'

'You know what, Betty? Nothing in this world is safe. I'm sick of living like there's an insurance policy for everything. I've followed doctor's orders every time and look where it's got me. This time I'm in charge.'

She feels so good she only has one small sandwich. It will be all right. She's going to make sure it is.

Stephen finishes his third sandwich in as many minutes. Goodness knows how he's not fat.

'Mara, I've got a present for you.'

'A present? You know we agreed you weren't to do that. It's just a waste of all this big money you're earning if you fritter it on me.'

'It's not like that. This woman came to Baku last month from England and it turns out she makes these.' He thrusts a small box into Mara's hands. 'It's to help you during the actual birth.'

Mara slides off the giftwrap, hands trembling, while Betty peers over her shoulder. Stephen is not usually a romantic man. Inside the box is a creamy porcelain egg with a tiny baby nestling in it. Its skin is waxy, its face lifelike, a faerie child deposited in Mara's hand.

'Turn it over,' says Stephen, laughing. 'Its bum's coming out the other side.'

Sure enough, a small pink rump is poking out of the back of the egg.

'It was for the women to hold on to during labour. Very tactile, see? You hold it in your hand and it helps take away the pain.'

Betty looks in astonishment at her son. 'I've never heard of such a thing,' she says.

'I'm telling you, Mum. This woman Nancy knows all about it, all about the history. She was showing it to the boss' secretary and I heard her.'

'You've got hidden depths, son,' says his mother.

Mara simply holds on to the little figurine, her fingers tracing its miniature nose, the curve of its puckered lips, its little bum. It's a boy, for sure. Gently she hooks her finger on to the tiny feet protruding from the shell. Is this little manikin a sign to tell her what sex her child will be? The cool surface of the egg is somehow comforting. This time it will be all right. It has to be all right.

The Other Wee Ones

WHAT WILL HER BABY BE LIKE? How do you look forward when you don't know whether it'll be a boy or a girl? In Argos yesterday, Jen tried to tell her it was bad luck to buy things too early. They'd gone for lunch in Gala and stopped off to look at baby clothes on the way back. Mara really wanted a red Emma Bunton frock with pink cats on, but what if it was a boy? She settled for a Little Bear giftset and a wee white Winnie the Pooh hoodie. Only £4.99 in the sale.

'Whit for are you buying that giftset?' demanded Jen. 'It's twelve pieces, Mara. What if something goes wrong?'

'Nothing's going wrong this time,' said Mara. 'I'll make sure of that.'

'You must have enough clothes at home.'

Mara looked blankly at her friend. 'The new baby can't have those. They belong to the other wee ones.'

Jen's mouth gawped open like a fish, but she said nothing.

Now Mara lays the new clothes in the top drawer of the chest in the baby's room. Layers of tissue paper enrobe the things she bought before, the tiny pink nylon party dress with one of those daft flower headbands, the blue stripey bodysuit and matching hat, the lemon cardigan with a duck appliqued to it. This one was Emma's, this Rob's, this Poppy's. Carefully she puts them in the bottom drawer, right at the back. Stephen won't be poking about in here but no point in taking the chance of him finding them.

'Give them to the charity shop,' he'd urged. 'You can buy new ones if you ever decide to try again. We mustn't dwell on the past.'

She wonders if he ever does. He's never referred to the babies they lost. Maybe it was too painful for him, too. She wishes she knew. What is it they call it, the elephant in the room? Only this is a whole troupe of baby elephants. Nobody ever looks up at their entrance or talks about them. It's as if they never existed at all. A void, that's what they are, a great, gaping void at the heart of their marriage – and they both a-void talking about them.

'Mara, Jen's here.'

'Just coming,' she shouts.

She can hear the noise of Jen's kids as soon she leaves the nursery. Nadia and Lily are singing a song at the top of their voices and Tom's banging on the toy drum he carries round everywhere with him. The low murmur of the adults' voices forms a counterpoint to the din of the children.

'Okay,' says Mara as she enters the room, 'who's going to help me make my scarecrow?'

'Me,' shouts Nadia.

'Me,' shouts Tom.

Mara smiles at Lily. 'She's going to be a witch this year.'

'Will she have a big horrible wart on the end of her nose?'

'Do you think she should?'

Lily nods.

'Our scarecrow's the Queen of Elfland,' says Nadia.

'She must be pretty. That's not going to scare any crows away, is it?'

Lily looks doubtful. 'Well, anyway, I like crows.'

'She's got green high heels with sparkles in them,' volunteers Nadia.

Tom gives a tremendous flourish with his drumsticks. 'I think a witch is much better. The Queen of Elfland's just a stupid *girl*.'

Nadia tosses her head. 'She could put a spell on you, stupid.'

'I'd fight her off with my drumsticks,' says Tom, brandishing them like cudgels.

'Well, none of you'll be safe from my scary witch,' says Mara, raising her voice to a cackle. Lily shrinks back but Nadia and Tom start to giggle.

'I'll make the tea, will I?' asks Stephen.

Mara nods, already absorbed in sorting out the materials for the witch.

'There's sandwiches in the fridge.'

'Nutella ones, Auntie Mar?' asks Nadia.

'Why don't you go and peek in the fridge?' says Mara. 'You could help Uncle Stephen bring them in. No sneaking one off the top, mind.'

Nadia grins. 'I deserve one for helping, don't I?'

'Hmmm, maybe you have a point, little girl,' says Mara in her witch's voice, to much hilarity from the children. She leans forward and stares into Tom's eyes. 'Guess what else there is?'

He purses his lips, a snaky grin creeping over his face. 'Is it frogspawn?'

'Maybe.'

'No, it's worm cake, isn't it, Auntie Mar?'

'Oh yes, a delicious big worm cake for you, my dear. And a great big chocolate cake for the girls.'

Lily lets out a loud squeal, whether from horror at the idea of worm cake or delight at chocolate cake is uncertain.

'Yum yum,' says Tom, rubbing his stomach. 'I love worm cake.'

Stephen brings in a tray of food, accompanied by Nadia bearing the plate of Nutella sandwiches.

'I'm watching you, Miss Nadia,' says Mara.

Nadia swipes a sandwich off the plate. 'My earnings,' she says.

'Cheeky wee git,' says Jen. 'Here Stephen, will I be ... will I pour?'

'Thanks. I'll just go and get the rest,' he says.

Lily lodges herself in at Mara's side. 'She should have stripey stockings, Auntie Mara.'

'Have a look through that bag, pet. There should be quite a few pairs in there. Remember we bought them off a street stall when we went to Glasgow that time, Jen?'

'Yeah, a quid, weren't they? I never wore mine. Too funky for me.'

'Fit for witches, though, eh Lily?'

The little girl laughs and draws out a black and red pair.

'Perfect,' says Mara.

She can see Jen is working up to saying something. She's eating her sandwich slowly, which is not like her, and she keeps glancing sidelong at Stephen. When he gets up to refill the teapot, she leans forward in her chair.

'Mara? Have you heard about the clootie tree up the glen?'

'Yes.'

'Was it you that started it?'

'What if it was?'

'I didnae take you for one of thae pagans.'

'I'm not.'

'What's this?' Stephen's voice is as quiet as his tread.

Jen looks down at her feet.

'What's a pagan?' asks Tom.

'Someone that dances round in the scuddy and sings funny songs,' sniggers Nadia.

'No one's a pagan,' says Jen, shooting her daughter a sharp look.

'It's just something very traditional,' says Mara. 'A religious thing. To the Virgin Mary, mostly. I've seen one up north.' She turns to Stephen. 'Remember we went on that holiday to the Black Isle?'

He nods, bemused.

'That's all it is.' She shakes the dummy out of the plastic bag. 'Here, Tom. You get the dust out of her, will you?'

'Yay!' Gleefully he attacks the doll with his drumsticks. 'Take that, you nasty old witch.'

'Don't get carried away, son,' says Jen. 'It's no' that dusty. It's only been in the garage, no' the coal cellar.'

'Auntie Mar hasn't got a coal cellar.'

'Smart Alec.'

Mara pulls a long black dress from the pile of clothes she's gathered and tugs it over the doll's head. 'Here, you do the socks, Lily, will you?'

The little girl tugs and heaves till her younger brother shoves her out of the way and finishes the job for her. Nadia delves into Mara's costume bag, emerging with a plastic witch's mask covering her face.

'*Fee, fi, fo, fum. Something wicked this way comes,*' she intones.

Lily looks doubtful. 'You say that for a giant, not a witch.'

'It looks good, that,' says Jen in conciliatory tones.

'Got it in a wee newsagent in Melrose,' says Mara. 'Only cost me a few quid. There's a big pointy hat in there as well.'

Lily pulls out the hat and plonks it on her own head.

'You don't look scary at all,' says Tom dismissively.

'What's a scarecrow festival for anyway, Mum?' asks Nadia.

'Tourists, I suppose,' shrugs Jen.

'Not at all,' says Stephen. 'It's to scare the crows away from people's gardens and houses. You don't want your eyes pecked out by a crow, do you?'

Nadia squeals in delight. 'You're silly, Uncle Stephen.'

'No, he's not,' shouts Tom at the top of his voice. 'A crow could come and peck your eyes out any time.'

Lily looks alarmed, till Mara picks her up and cuddles her. 'Ignore them, pet. They're just messing. We need a broomstick for this old witch, don't we?'

'You haven't made one, have you?' asks Jen.

'Course not. Got it off the internet.'

Stephen wanders to the window. 'Hardly anyone will see our scarecrow up here, will they?'

'Loads of people come walking, especially at the weekends,' says Mara.

You just have to look at that clootie tree,' says Jen.

Later, when they've all gone, when the sandwiches and cake have been scoffed and the witch set flying from the guttering, Stephen turns to Mara. 'I'd like to see it. The clootie tree.'

'It's nothing, Stephen. Just a whim, really.'

His voice is firm. 'Still, I'd like to see it.'

They walk up the glen, the tips of their noses tingling in the crisp autumn sunshine. Once they leave the track, Mara leads the way, Stephen following anxiously behind her.

'Are you sure you're all right? The grass is pretty uneven here.'

'I'm fine. Don't worry.'

As they approach the secret glade, a young couple emerge, the girl looking tearful.

'You see, it's not just us,' says Stephen.

'No ...' But Mara can't imagine anyone else could be walking round with the same nuclear ache in their head as she has. She glances at her husband, striding along with a worried look on his face. What does Stephen really feel? Does he lie in bed at night, crying for the children he has never met? Does he give them names and imaginary talents, inventing worlds through which they move? Does he blame her?

They round the bend into the secret glade, to find even more scraps of cloth have been left on the whitethorn – some streamers of lilac lace and a pretty pink satin ribbon that Mara's sure the crying girl has left. They are alone. The fluttering ribbons glint in the October sunshine, a myriad faerie banners streaming forward into the future. Will *they* ever reach the future they long for or will the treacherous imps of fate thwart their desires?

Stephen stands silently, gazing at these vivid embodiments of other people's yearnings, of their own. He takes Mara's hand in his. Although he says nothing, it feels like a moment of communion, as if, without a word being spoken, he is telling her he is with her. Mara's eyes prickle with tears. Over the sound of the breeze in the trees around them she can hear the rustling of the river, like the whispering of little voices all around. Over and over again they call to her, the wee ones she has lost. Can Stephen hear them too?

They Know what to Do

WHY SHOULD SHE START thinking about her mother now? It's not her birthday or the anniversary of her death; there's been no specific trigger to remind her of the past, yet the sense of her not being there is as sharp as it was on the day she died. They'd been going on a few days' shopping trip to Glasgow to buy Mara's wedding dress and what her mother jokingly called her *trousseau*. Mara had only seen the word in books and wasn't entirely sure what it meant.

'It means something pretty to go away in and some sexy fripperies that your husband can take off on your wedding night,' teased her mother.

'Mum!'

Her mother just laughed. 'I wish I still had my wedding night lingerie. It was water green silk cut on the bias, the most beautiful nightie I've ever had. Your father told me I looked like a mermaid in it.'

'Was he romantic then, Mum?'

'Oh, sometimes.'

'I don't think Stephen is really.'

'He's a dark horse, pet. He may surprise you yet. You know what they say, still waters run deep.'

They'd been in a teashop upstairs in Buchanan Street, done in the designs of Charles Rennie Mackintosh. Her mother had ordered plain toast with some butter on the side.

'Won't you have a cream cake, Mum? They've got your favourite, those pastries with the sugar shell.'

'I feel a wee bit queasy, to tell you the truth. I'm just going to the ladies. I'll be right back.'

But she wasn't, and when Mara went to investigate she found her mother prone on the floor, her face pale and waxy. A massive heart attack, the doctors said later, though she'd shown no sign of heart trouble before. She was always a smoker, though. They said that could cause it. It didn't seem right, to get married so soon after her death, but Stephen was going out to the job in Azerbaijan and didn't want to wait.

Losing the first baby without her there was very hard.

The blinds are drawn so the room is pitch black, but there's no peace in the darkness. Mara's head is pounding and the big bed feels empty without Stephen. Maybe her mother was right. Maybe he's more romantic than he appears. He made her feel loved, that day at the clootie well. When it was time for him to go away again towards the end of the month, he really didn't want to go, with the baby coming, but she told him not to be daft, it wasn't due till some time in November. She'd just whisper in its little ear not to come out yet, till daddy came home.

What is she going to do? No more miscarriages. She can't take another loss. She's been every day to the clootie tree, even cut a strip off her wedding veil to give to the spirit of the glade, whatever that is. If only she could feel there was something there. She clutches the little birthing egg, feeling its weight, running her thumb over its smooth surface and funny little bumps. She's tired but there's no rest anywhere.

Maybe, instead of lying down, she'd be better for some fresh air. It's too lonely lying in this empty bed. Slowly she labours to get up. It's as if she's moving through water. Her new body is too heavy, like inhabiting the body of some massive sea creature, a seal or a fat walrus. If only she could swim away to somewhere where there's no pain.

Downstairs she pulls on her warm coat and sets off walking away from the glen, towards the main road. Away from the clootie tree.

She must try not to obsess. It's only a mile to the main road, and she's warm by the time she reaches it. It feels mild today, though the horses in the field opposite are already wearing dark blue winter blankets. She stops a little further on, near the farmer's barn. A flock of house martins are swooping in and out of the eaves, constantly moving flashes of glossy blue-black and white. Shouldn't they have gone south by now? They fly round the yard together, then split and dive in opposite directions, as if trying different flight paths. In and out they weave, sometimes together, in families perhaps; sometimes flying solo, each taking their own path. How beautiful their brilliant spiderwebs of flight are, but functional too, as if they're practising moves for the long journey to the warm. They'll be gone soon.

She mustn't walk too far, she still has to go back. Turning, she heads for home, just as the birds, as if at some pre-ordained signal, all wheel round together and swarm into the afternoon air. She watches as the flock, ragged at first, forges itself into a single entity. They know what to do. She'll know too, when the time comes. The baby will come, in his or her own way.

Waiting for the Eighth Wave

NO-O-O-O-O-O-O-O! Mara can hardly breathe. Bang, bang, bang. The phone smashes into pieces. She drums her fists on the floor. How could Alex do this to her? All that rubbish about how there are other things in life and now she goes and gets pregnant. It's not fair. Not fair. She'll have her baby with no problem, when Mara loses hers as easily as a hen laying eggs.

The cat examines her solemnly, her eyes flaring yellow in the half-light. Such an unblinking stare, no wonder people thought they were evil spirits. Mara slowly gets to her feet. She must look a right sight – tears, snot, dishevelled hair.

'Oh Sukie, what am I going to do?' she says, crushing the little creature against her chest and causing her to squirm away, protesting loudly. 'Bugger off then, you horror.'

Alex sounded so happy, babbling away as if only she knew the meaning of life. How diplomatic she'd been, asking how Mara was and how Stephen had taken the news.

'What news?' Mara had asked.

'You know, that you've lost the baby.' Alex's voice was almost a whisper.

'Alex, it was a mistake. I meant to tell you but I didn't want to jinx it. It was just some blood loss.'

'No! Oh Mara, I'm so happy for you.' That was when the floodgates opened and she started going on about her famous writer boyfriend and how she couldn't believe it when she got broody and how she thought he'd walk away but he was as keen to have children as she is and she didn't want to upset Mara by telling her the news, but now she knows everything is okay would Mara be her bridesmaid because they're getting married, in the village, at Christmas.

'I never thought I would,' she said. 'Me married, isn't it amazing?'

Mara held it together till Alex was off the phone but now she feels as if she's locked into one of those mediaeval racks she saw on a trip to a castle dungeon once, relentlessly boring deep into her body, burning her to the core and stretching her insides to breaking point. The pain is so intense she almost faints. She gasps for breath, emitting high-pitched moans of anguish, until at last she leans back against the wall, spent. What is she to do now? Stephen will be back in a fortnight and she needs to find her baby. She can't go through a miscarriage again.

Slowly she rises from the floor. It's down to her. No one can help her now. She walks to the bathroom and splashes hot water over her face and neck, then sprays perfume over her chest and wrists. She'll go to the private hospital and see what she can find.

In the car she has to lean forward to see, the light is so poor. Once out on the main road the mist surges round the car, enveloping it in a moving shroud that drifts and curls but remains impenetrable, forcing her to slow to a crawl. She puts her headlights up but they reflect light back at her so she dips them again. It's so hard to see. Where is her baby in all this?

She inches her way along the road to the hospital. On her last visit she thought there wasn't much security at all, really. There was no proper reception desk, you just wandered straight down the corridor towards the patients' rooms or upstairs to the café. She's memorised the whole of the glossy brochure she picked up in that posh baby shop in Melrose, so she knows where the incubators are. In Borders General there's a proper buzzer system for the special care unit, but at the asylum, as she thinks of it, the staff all have electronic security tags. She'll just have to keep her wits about her.

She drives into a woodland car park about half a mile from the hospital. No one else is around anyway, but her car is easily hidden at the far end of the space, miles away from the road. Her handbag is a big loose shoulder bag, which easily hides the petrol she brought with her. No one can tell what it is as she decanted it into a malt whisky presentation bottle ages ago, a beautiful one with a picture of misty islands and water. If only she could escape to her own island. They'd be safe there, her and the baby. And Stephen, if he wanted to come.

As she walks towards the old Victorian building she imagines what will happen when she sets it alight, sees glassy conflagrations mirrored in all the windows, tongues of flame leaping out of doors and licking round pointy turrets. Hell-hot fire slowly taking hold till the whole building is ablaze, incandescent with heat, gold and purple and green and turquoise radiance dancing through it. The noise of flames and creaking timber and masonry roars in her ears and her heart is pumping like a ticking bomb, ready to detonate. The whole place will explode, an elemental firestorm of heat that will raze it to the ground.

No one's to get hurt, though. Their systems better be working. It wouldn't be a good start for the baby if someone lost their life. Bad karma. She must focus on the positive. That way everything will turn out all right. She'll lay the trail of petrol upstairs, set the fire and then run downstairs. With the alarm going off there'll be chaos. She'll be able to take the baby and find her way out the warren of corridors at the back of the building. One of the mums is bound to be sleeping or maybe the nurse will be in the bathroom. Mara will pick up the baby and usher the mum out ahead of her, then slide off in the opposite direction in the pandemonium. Her baby will be waiting for her. She knows it.

Inside, the place seems deserted. Maybe the roads are too bad for anyone but her to make it through. It's a sign. She splashes the petrol all over the corridor. Her hand is trembling as she lights the match and it takes several attempts before she gets it to light. A blue light inches along the trail of the petrol and suddenly leaps upward. Hardly able to breathe, she heads downstairs, keeping her face down. There's bound to be security cameras all over the place. But she hasn't even reached the bottom when there's a monstrous hooting sound and the fire alarm goes off. Mara keeps walking, pulling her scarf up round her neck and mouth. A nurse runs past her, taking the stairs two at a time. Then there's the sound of loud hissing, as if a thousand snakes have been let loose. Is the fire taking hold more firmly? Mara lets out a breath in relief. She must stay calm now and do her job.

The nurse is shouting something and another one comes out of one of the mothers' rooms, holding a baby in a blue sleepsuit.

'It's okay. Panic over. The sprinkler system has kicked in.' She walks slowly back down the stair, ignoring Mara and talking to the other nurse. 'That was amazing. There was quite a wee fire blazing up there and all this water suddenly started gushing out of the ceiling. I tell you what, it makes you feel quite safe, that does.'

The other nurse looks suspiciously at Mara. 'Can I help you?'

Mara just wants to snatch the child and run but she'd get nowhere.

'I'm looking for the café. I was upstairs seeing my friend and she said it was one floor down.'

'No, one floor up,' says the nurse abruptly, as the baby starts to cry loudly. She turns away from Mara towards the room she came out of. 'There, there. We'll go and see Mummy. She'll give you some yummy milk.'

'One floor up,' repeats the first nurse, looking suspiciously at Mara. 'What did you say your friend's name was?'

'I didn't,' says Mara crossly and stomps up the stairs, sensing the nurse is watching her ascent. There's no point in staying here. It's ruined now. She'll have to go to her own hospital. But there are no newborns, unless one's been brought in today. Briskly she starts walking back to the car, which seems much further off on the way back. If only the baby would come and she could lose this weight.

The mist has lifted slightly now so she keeps off the road and walks through the woodland to the car park. Deep breaths. She *will* have her baby today. She must. Moss, damp leaves, the smell of bark steam in her nostrils in a bosky bouillabaisse that she draws deep into her lungs. It speaks of times long gone, times when people lived on the land, honouring the seasons, knowing when every berry or blossom was due. Sometimes she feels like a throwback to those times, when birth was an arduous process, dangerous for mother and child and not the high-tech, fast-track conveyor belt it is today. Not everyone was privileged to give birth then so why is it expected to be a matter of course now?

In the car she sits for a long time considering her options. Berwick's the nearest, but she's not sure if the baby unit has started up there and anyway, it'd be too small. She'd stand out like a sore thumb. Alnwick's maternity unit is on its own, right in the middle of the hospital, so people would be able to see her coming and going. Newcastle, then. That's a big hospital. No one notices one person in a crowd. It's not even twelve yet, she could be there before two.

She heads south towards Jedburgh. It's ages since she's been there. It would be nice just to stop and see the town, maybe visit Mary, Queen of Scots' house. She was always fascinated by the death mask, its stillness and serenity. How could you be so composed if you were going to have your head chopped off? The queen must have been a very dignified person to be able to transcend the horror of the death she was given.

There's no dignity in any of this, Mara knows, but she can't help that. She can't help any of it. If she doesn't find her baby soon, she'll never be a mother and then she might as well not be a woman. What's the point of all the bleeding and discomfort and mood swings if you don't have a child?

At Jedburgh, she nearly swerves into the pavement from looking at the tall, narrow house with the tiny windows that a queen looked out of. After that, she puts her foot down. She feels as if she's driven, not driving, as if she's being urged onward by elfin creatures, disporting themselves in the currents created by her car, forcing her ever faster. There is neither will nor choice involved in the journey. It's as if there is nothing in the world beyond her desire.

She crosses the border into England, with low-lying hills rolling towards a horizon of infinite possibility. It's beautiful and bleak, but there's no time to stop and admire the landscape. She must press on. As the road turns towards the east, the countryside becomes more normal, the sort of land you can pass through without needing to look. Her speed picks up now and she feels as if she's riding the wind, as if there's nothing can stop her now.

It's when she reaches the big roundabout leading into Newcastle that she has her brainwave. She won't go to a hospital at all. She'll go to Gateshead, to the big shopping centre. Where better to fade into the background than a place filled with people looking at shiny objects of desire rather than at each other?

As she follows the line of traffic across the Tyne Bridge, her spirits soar. Finally, this is going to work. The bridge's elegant arch and dark green struts roll forward in an iron cavalcade, bearing her closer and closer to what she wants. Soon ... soon she will have her baby.

She chooses the basement car park, where there are fewer people, so she can strap her baby carrier across her chest without anyone seeing. Good, no one's around. 'Sorry, but this is the last time I'll need you, Jemma,' she whispers to the soft-bodied baby doll as she straps her into the sling, her little pink hat just poking out at the top.

This is the moment when she thought she'd be sick, scared, but she feels light, as if she could float upstairs like thistledown, a will o' the wisp. The lights are almost blinding when she reaches the third floor. No particular reason to choose it, just it seems luckier than the ground or the second. She's never been able to understand the Chinese selecting eight as their lucky number. Odd numbers seem much more attractive to her. *Waiting for the eighth wave*, she remembers Alex saying, describing a beach she was on in Dalian, where all the skinny Chinese counted the waves before plunging in at what they judged the most propitious moment. This is her propitious moment and she is determined to ride the wave as soon as she spots it.

The malls are crowded, with harassed mothers and lounging teenagers. Funny she's never thought about her baby growing up, just about her being a baby. Her? Where did that come from? She will take whatever is sent to her. She plods past the glittering storefronts, the mannequins dressed in absurd outfits that only the stupidly wealthy – or perhaps more accurately, the wealthily stupid – would contemplate. Occasionally she bends her head to comfort Jemma. 'Not long now, sweetheart. Not long now.'

She walks for hours, first through the bigger stores, then past the food court. She'd love to stop and have a coffee, but someone's bound to talk to her about her baby. At last she sees, right in the middle of the mall, a cluster of stalls, as draped with endless necklaces and earrings as her clootie tree is with people's wishes. The jewellery looks hand-knitted, home-made in amongst the polished artefacts in the famous department stores, the obscenely priced jars of face cream in the shop windows. There are lots of young girls clustered around it, examining the trinkets with as ferocious a level of concentration as if they were collectors of high-end antiques.

'Aw, look at this one, Lola,' says a girl with bare legs and a minute skirt, picking up a pair of skull earrings with red stones glowing in their eyes. Most of the girls seem to be half dressed here, which surprises Mara given that the weather's so dreich. The girl called Lola moves over to the stall and it is then that Mara sees her baby. Her baby. She's a girl, with a funny little pink pixie hat like two rabbit ears.

'Man, they're great,' says Lola, piling her blonde hair up on top of her head and trying the earrings up against her ears. 'Where's the mirror? I need to see these.'

Mara's little girl is fast asleep. She doesn't hesitate. It's the matter of a moment to slip her out of her buggy and tuck her in beside Jemma. No point risking putting Jemma in her place, but she does whip the rabbit ears hat off the baby and stick it on top of the pram.

'Ye knaw, I can just see mesel' in these, Sat'day night down the club,' the girl Lola is saying.

'Will yer mam babysit, then? I thought she wasn't gan to,' her companion replies.

Mara doesn't hear the answer. Her bulk, the baby sling, her navy coat mean no one even sees her. She's almost at the bottom when the first signs of commotion come floating down the lift shaft, but she doesn't wait to hear the girl's panicked screams or the sound of shoppers running this way and that, searching for a lost baby. This is the way it's meant to be and she feels a huge sense of peace.

The baby stirs as Mara slides behind the steering wheel, but then gives a little snuffle and rubs her face against Jemma's soft chest. Not a hitch as Mara drives straight out of the car park without fastening her seatbelt and heads back to the bridge. She turns the radio on. There's no news bulletin yet, but she keeps the volume on low as the soft music seems to soothe the baby.

It's after four now and the teatime traffic is just beginning to build up. Luckily her road home is less congested than the A1. No need to panic. Smoothly she changes gears, brakes and stops as if in a dream. There's a big supermarket off the main road just out of town. She'll stock up with what she needs for the journey, the carrycot, the baby feed, the disposable nappies. She's got everything else at home. Then she'll feed and change the baby. Her baby. Maybe she'll even get a cup of coffee and a sandwich. She's tired now, despite her elation. No, not elation. What she feels is relief.

By the time she's put the baby into her carrycot and started back on the road again, it'll be quite late. Late enough to be dark by the time she gets home. She will drive up through the silent glen, her headlights the only light in the darkness. When she pulls up at her door, she'll carry her baby in her arms into the house. There will be no one to see her, no one to know.

She's not a heartless person. She'll call the baby Lola, after her mother.

Sister, Little Sister,
my Love, my Sister

'I'M COMING HOME. I'm not waiting till the end of the four weeks,' says Stephen. 'I can't wait to see her. Are you all right? Why didn't you call my mum?'

'There was no time,' says Mara. 'And anyway, I was upstairs, sorting out stuff in the loft. There was no way I could get down to the phone.'

'But you're both okay? There's no harm done?'

'No, I'm fine. And she's gorgeous. Stephen? I'd like to call her Lola.'

'I hoped we'd maybe give her my mum's name. And your mum's too, of course.'

Is he joking? Elizabeth, like the Queen? He must be mad. 'She's her own wee person. I just want her to be herself.'

'Whatever you want. Anything.' She can hear from his voice that he's close to tears. 'I didn't really believe this day would ever come.'

'I know. Are you sure you should come home? You might lose your job. This wouldn't be the time ...'

'The boss is pretty good. I'll ask him.'

She has about forty-eight hours at the most before he gets here. Damn, she should call his mum but she can't handle old Betty yet. Will he call her? That's a risk she'll have to take. She'll need to get rid of all the stuff that might incriminate her, the clothes she was wearing and Lola's, the carrycot she bought in Newcastle, the dark blue Wallaby sling thing – the poppy red one is much nicer. She puts her coat on and straps it on. She loves the way it keeps the baby cuddled close to you.

'Come on, Lola. Let's go and have a bonfire.' The baby squirms a little, then reluctantly settles. There's only one place to go, the clootie tree. She puts the carrycot into the back of the car for the moment and they walk up the path, Mara humming quietly, trailing the stuff in a shopping trolley. Nearly dark, so there's no one around, thank goodness. She breaks off branches from nearby bushes and piles them up around the clothes, scrunching up the newspapers she's brought and tucking them strategically into the pile. A couple of firelighters so that the blaze gets going quickly. Then whoosh, it all suddenly takes and the flames spurt into the evening sky, a geyser of heat and shards of light that bounce off her coat.

The crackling of the fire wakes the baby up and she starts crying, a panicky wail that alarms Mara.

'Don't be frightened. It's only a bonfire, sweetheart.' She takes a step back from the fire but the baby carries on, the sound becoming louder and louder. Mara tries to rock her, but ends up jiggling her awkwardly and causing her to start screaming in earnest.'

'Oh God. Right, we'll go home in a minute. Stop that now.'

Lola continues to wriggle against Mara's chest, still clearly uneasy, so she starts to croon softly, a Scottish lullaby her mother used to sing to her, about a little girl lured into a fairy hill and trapped there.

Sister, little sister, my love, my sister,
Can you not pity my grief tonight?

I am in a little bothy, low and narrow,
Completely open, with not a scrap of thatch on it,

Only the water of the hills running down like a stream,
And the mighty hill of the white-maned horses.

The strange, otherworldly tune, meandering and sad, seems to stun Lola into silence. Mara feels the little body relax against hers. This is the happiest night of her life. There's a primitive satisfaction in watching scintillae of fire float into the darkness, in hearing the river drumming out its counterpoint to the rustling flames.

Once the fire is out, she will gather up the ends of metal from buckles, any last scraps of material left and she'll get in the car and dump it somewhere off the road. The motion should soothe the baby and stop her from crying. There's time enough tomorrow to face that old witch, Betty, and to hone her story of what happened at the 'birth'. For now, she draws the sweet smell of the woodsmoke deep into her lungs and cuddles her baby. In the presence of the unseen hills, of the deer settling down for the night, the crows curving their wings in sleep in her fairy glen, she silently sends her thanks to the goddess of the tree, to whoever out there in the dark night has granted her wish.

A Changeling

THREE CARS CRAWL SLOWLY towards the house, their blue lights flashing, suspensions bouncing on the rutted track. The noise of the sirens is deafening, a strident wail that pierces the peace of the empty glen and reverberates inside Mara's head. They're coming to get her. *Nee naw, nee naw, nee naw* ... No! No, please no ... She thrashes about, trying to get up and escape from them, but Stephen is holding her down.

'Mara, what on earth's the matter? You're having a bad dream, love.'

Mara sits up in bed. A trickle of sweat is running down her spine and she wants to tear her nightie off, she's so hot.

'Is it just a dream? There's no one outside?'

'Course not.'

'Check, Stephen. Please.'

He goes to the window and draws back the curtains. 'Nothing, like I told you. Who did you think was there?'

'I don't know ... Oh no, is that the baby crying?'

'Yes, I was just in with her, trying to get her settled. Will I bring her to you?'

Thank goodness. That must be what made her think of police sirens. Lola really does have a powerful set of lungs.

Mara swings her legs down from the bed. 'Yes, that'll be lovely.'

But she feels limp, exhausted. When Stephen reverentially places the baby in her arms, she stares at the little thing in incomprehension. Why is her face all red and crumpled like that? Doesn't she want to be here? Maybe she's just hungry.

'Would you go and do her bottle, love?' she asks Stephen.

'Course.' He beetles off, grateful to be doing something for her.

Mara leans over to get a tissue to pat herself dry and Lola squawks even more loudly, *alarmingly* loudly. Mara stares at her, perplexed. What's wrong with her? Maybe she's missing her real mother. She cuddles the baby even closer to her, but her little fists clench and she almost chokes, she's so cross.

'Now, now. Don't cry, pet. Please don't cry.' She slips her finger into the tiny hand, marvelling as everyone does, at the miniature perfection of the nails, though amused at how old the wrinkled little fingers look. So tired ... Mara leans back on the pillows, still clutching Lola. She feels as exhausted as if she really had given birth to her. Partly Betty's fault, of course. *Ooh, the baby doesn't look as if she's just a couple of days old.* How did she manage with the cord? The placenta? Getting downstairs from the loft with the baby? Why didn't she call immediately? Why Lola? That one was easy. *The wee lassie on EastEnders.* Betty was totally outraged by that. *For heaven's sake, after somebody on a SOAP.* Blah, blah, blah. Mara's had enough of it. She's going to throw all her bloody doilies out and get new furniture in. This place is like a museum, a care home for distressed gentlefolk. That old witch better watch out or she won't get to see her granddaughter.

Still, she asked so many questions that she gave Mara a head-ache. Later, when her mother-in-law was gone, Mara looked up some answers on the computer. Luckily Stephen cut his mother off at the time. *What is this, an interrogation?* he'd said. *Mara's tired, Mum. Give her some peace.* Mara can't tell whether he's really as unsuspicious as he seems. Or perhaps he doesn't want to look too closely. He clearly adores the baby, with a simple whole-hearted-ness that now eludes Mara. Lola's little fists flail as if she wants to thump her, though thankfully she seems to have exhausted her lung capacity and emits nothing more than crabby little bleats. Such a cross face, though, as if she were a changeling, a disgruntled faerie child crying to return to Elfland.

'Here we are.' Stephen breezes in with her bottle. 'You look done in, love. Will I do it?'

She nods, pleased at his enthusiasm. Lola calms down with the bottle in her mouth, her frown gradually relaxing as she sucks the tepid milk. Mara tries not to think of the first Lola, of how bereft she'll be without her child. An irresponsible teenage mum, a wee tart that's only interested in going out clubbing. Shouldn't have had the baby in the first place, she'll never be able to look after her properly. It's strange there's been so little about it on the news, but then Mara's deliberately kept the telly to a minimum and Stephen is too engrossed with his first child to bother with it.

He looks happier than she's ever seen him, even during the occasional times during their marriage that they've had sex with the lights on. What will it be like if he does leave his job and try to get work back here? Will they still like each other? Will she be happy with him round the place all the time? Maybe it won't happen. He'll never be able to earn the money in the UK that he makes in Azerbaijan. And she wants Lola to have nothing but the best. Dreamily she thinks of the heavily embroidered pink dress she saw on one of the shopping channels, the beautiful little red shoes in the posh baby shop in Melrose. If her baby's a changeling, she's going to look like the bloody Queen of Elfland.

'Hey, would you like a cup of tea now?' When she nods, Stephen hands Lola back to her. 'Back in two ticks.'

Once he's gone, Mara stands and walks to the window, cradling the baby. In the grey light of almost dawn, the rosebushes in the garden look black, waxy. Overhead, a skein of geese flies past in strange, forked formation, streaming forward into the sky. Their melancholy honking floats back to her when they are long past, the sound of ghostly geese no longer there. Suddenly Lola's body feels immensely heavy, a dead weight in her arms. Mara steadies herself on the windowsill, looking down in dismay at the restless child, whose nose and mouth seem to dissolve, distort, turn her into a goblin child. It's as if she's never seen this little face before, doesn't know who this baby is. She stares into Lola's eyes. Where are *her* babies? Why are *they* not restless, struggling to free themselves from the spirit world and get back to their mother? Why do they not come to her? Where are her babies?

THE
DIVA

Black Holes

THE DIVA WAS NOT A SCIENTIFIC WOMAN but it came to her at a particular moment in the middle of passionate sex with her lover that she understood the theory of black holes.

This was a scientific theory about the pull of gravity causing matter to collapse in on itself. As far as she knew you couldn't actually see or reach black holes but that, she knew, proved nothing. The physical presence of a phenomenon was no gauge of its existence. It seemed many accepted theories could be proved irrefutably through mathematics, the language scientists use when they don't want other people to know what they're saying.

A delicious warmth was beginning to seep into the diva's left foot. This was always a sign that she was on the verge of orgasm. But it was a very tricky moment. She had to keep all the tinglings and tremors in her body under control, at the exact level they were at when the left foot came into play. The paradox was, it required an inordinate amount of effort to reach the warm, misty state in her mind which was the prelude to the uncontrollable and perhaps unbearable experience that she sensed lay just beyond her.

This time she felt an ache in her stomach, as if she suddenly missed someone she loved. Then it was as if her whole insides were imploding, sucking in her lover's member, drawing him in and in till he disappeared and her own body disappeared and she was left alone in a dry, arid wasteland where only the ache existed. Later she thought it must have been that night that she conceived her child.

The diva was a Scot, the first of her race to reach international eminence since the divine Mary Garden, who was Debussy's first Mélisande. From the first she knew she was an exotic. She had to be. Her name was Mercedes McMorine. It was a lot to live up to in a city like Glasgow, where pretensions of any kind were firmly discouraged. 'Don't be so affected,' her teachers would say when she told them the latest fey instalment of the family saga she created from the raw material of her eleven brothers and sisters. Sometimes it was even, 'Don't tell lies.'

'Miss, my brother Kevin's on Sir Edmund Hillary's expedition to the South Pole.'

Sigh. 'Don't tell lies.'

'Miss, do you think I'll suit purple velvet when I grow up?'

Sigh. 'Don't be affected.'

Mercedes loved her name. She knew it marked out her otherness from the people around her. She couldn't imagine where her mother had found it.

'It's the name of a car,' her father said, rolling his eyes heavenward. He thought it was affected, too. His other children had rational names like Betty and Tom and Nancy and Johnny.

'It's after Mary, Our Lady of the Mercies. In Spanish,' said her mother, crossing herself.

The McMorines lived in a block of what, in those days, were thought of as high flats. 'The tallest in Europe,' Mercedes' brother Billy, the next one up from her, told her proudly, though she thought that somewhere on the Continent there must be a building higher than ten storeys.

The flats were teeming with children, running, fighting, jumping in and out of the lifts, dropping flaming paper twists down the rubbish chutes, but only the McMorines had eleven. The McMorine Millions they were called, and there was much curiosity about the sex life of Mr and Mrs McMorine. Peggy Phillips, the old spinster lady who lived down the stair, used to blush whenever she passed Mercedes' mother. She pretended not to see Mr McMorine, though she always asked Mercedes how he was, with (Mercedes thought) indecent interest.

The McMorines lived in hysterical squalor. There was always some drama, some trauma going on in the midst of chaos. For many years Mrs McMorine was certifiably batty, as she struggled with eleven children, fish on Fridays, washing, ironing, chickenpox and neighbours who thought the sounds of eleven children walking up and down the hall were socially unacceptable. Her life was made immeasurably harder by the fact that she hated housework. She much preferred dealing with any drama or trauma to clearing away the dirty breakfast dishes or the mince that got ground into the carpet on Mondays.

Mr McMorine was a shy man who suffered deep embarrassment about the chaotic state of the household. It was not, however, deep enough for him ever to consider putting away his piles of books and papers on ancient Roman customs, the origins of matter and the West Highland Way. 'For heaven's sake, Alison,' he would say when Mrs McMorine suggested that her sister and family come to tea. 'This house isn't tidy enough to have strangers in.'

He was not without a sense of humour, though. One Saturday night the McMorines had settled down to their customary treat of thirteen assorted fish, pie and black pudding suppers eaten out of the paper. The pickled onion jar was making its rounds of the sitting room when there was a knock on the door. Mr McMorine went to answer it.

'Come in, Father,' he said, causing a frenzied bout of paper rustling as the twelve remaining family members tried to stuff their chips under cushions and down behind the television set. Mrs McMorine came close to a clinical seizure at the thought of the parish priest seeing them in such working class squalor. It wasn't him of course, only the paper boy.

Mercedes was third of the children, not young enough to be the pet, nor, in a family of mixed boys and girls, singular enough in gender to be valued. Nobody much noticed her really, though her mother always had a soft spot for her most romantically named offspring. In the midst of all those people Mercedes sometimes felt very lonely. She read a story in the newspaper once about a girl who was going to have a hole-in-the-heart operation and it struck her that that was what she had, a hole in the heart, an empty place that nothing could fill up.

It upset her to think about it, though she couldn't help it sometimes. Once her father came in and she was crying because she knew she couldn't have an operation, that she would never be rid of the hole in *her* heart.

'What's the matter, love?' he asked gently.

'I'm depressed,' she said.

'That's a very big word for such a little girl,' he said, and as she cuddled into him she felt a perverse pride that she had reached beyond her own littleness.

When she was thirteen her father brought back the family's first record player. It was when she heard Maria Callas singing that she first began to sense she would find a way to a world beyond this one. Their flat was at the top of the building, on the tenth floor. In the day you could stand in their living room and look at all the little dolls' houses of the city and beyond them to hills. Mercedes thought the Highlands were beyond that. She had only a hazy idea of what they were like but she knew if she saw them they would match her longing for grandeur in the world around her.

At night when you looked from the window the city was a glittering jewelscape of light. Mercedes' mother had bought lamps with pink satin shades. 'Very tasteful, dear. *Woman's Weekly* does have some very good ideas,' said her father dryly when he saw them, but Mercedes thought they made the room all rosy and magical. As Callas' voice throbbed out of the machine Mercedes felt gripped by some inchoate yearning, and anger too, but she was consoled that the primitive fury she held inside her was felt by another person.

Her favourite was a song sung by a lady called Norma. Her father frowned as he read the record sleeve.

'This sounds a lot of old hogswash.' He said Norma was a Druid priestess who betrayed her vows and fell in love with her Roman oppressor. Then the Roman went and fell in love with a younger priestess, even though Norma had two children by him. Mercedes thought the ending, when she gives up her two children to her father and then is burnt to death with her lover, was the saddest, most noble thing she had ever heard.

Her favourite bit was when Norma called on the goddess of the moon. The song started very slowly and sweetly, but it was sad from the beginning, too. Mercedes burned with satisfaction that this appeal to the awesomeness of the beyond was being made to a female deity. The record cover showed a woman with strange, cruel eyes and fierce strength. On her arms, burnished copper and gold bracelets glinted like weapons. For years Mercedes was never sure whether Callas was the priestess or the goddess herself.

Her voice was rich and barbaric. It seemed to flow up to the top notes like liquid, with a sound so painful and so beautiful that Mercedes found her eyes blurred and made the lights of the city go all hazy on her as she listened. From out of the calm sound of the chorus, the voice lifted and soared. Mercedes thought of a bird rising in the sky but as the voice began to roll and trill she could think only of the poor bird falling, dying, its wings fluttering finally along the ground.

In later years, when she sang *Casta Diva* in front of international audiences, she sometimes felt as if the primeval power of Callas entered her body. She would feel the pit of her stomach lunge as she prepared herself for the top notes. Her arms and legs would tingle with the sensation of her own power. By then she knew that in this prayer for peace the priestess understood her wish would not be granted. She knew then that the beauty of the beginning contained all the pain and horror of the ending.

Sometimes, when she reached the final section and was begging the goddess to spread on earth the peace that she made in heaven, she would be enveloped by pain so intense that the only release was to draw deep down into her diaphragm and forget everything. Nothing existed but the certainty of pain, the knowledge of loss. Only then would she find the power to reach the top notes, to lose herself in the thrilling sequence of trills that brings the aria to a close.

It seemed to her always that the aria was no prayer. There was no hope in it. It was a threnody, a lamentation for death to come, and in her mind it resembled nothing so much as a terrible and terrifying descent into prolonged sobbing.

What Makes You Think You Can Do That?

THE FIRST REQUIREMENT for being a diva was a voice. Mercedes at least knew that. As she progressed through various local and school choirs, though, she worried that when the time came she wouldn't have a voice at all. Sometimes her music teacher would look across sharply at her as she strove to push her throat into the thrilling realms of the singers she heard on records. 'It's far harder to correct someone who sings sharp than someone who sings flat, you know,' she would say, looking down her pinched nose.

At concerts there was always fervent applause when Mercedes finished her piping, young girl's rendition of the solos people expected, *The Road and the Miles to Dundee*, or *By Yon Bonnie Banks*. But Mercedes understood that this was simply child's stuff, that it was far more arduous and bruising a task to seek applause as an adult. She worried that her thin soprano would not make the transition to the wild and compelling instrument she longed for it to be. She worried that it would disappear altogether, swallowed up in the swirling mass of hormones that she knew would soon begin to circulate around and inside her.

She knew all about sex. Her mother had told her when she'd first asked, which was at a ridiculously early age. Then she'd forgotten all about it again till her older sister Nancy got pregnant and Mrs McMorine pressed a pamphlet into her hands. *My Dear Daughter*, it was called, and it told you all about being modest when you were with boys because they carried a little seed bag around with them. This sounded most inconvenient to Mercedes, though she would have liked to be able to pee up walls. She and her friend tried it once, just to see if they could do it, but Mrs Henderson on the ground floor knocked on the window at them and told them to go away, dirty wee besoms.

They called sex 'the facts of life' then, which rather put Mercedes off. The facts of life always seemed to her the least interesting part of it. When she was still at primary school one of her classmates began to menstruate and some of the other girls worked themselves into a frenzy of secrecy and female pride. Sophie Pringle, whose enjoyment of life was and always would be directly proportionate to the amount of melodrama it entailed (in later years she had countless offspring by different fathers, dropped out and became a hippy, dropped back in again and married a financier who turned out to be crooked, then ran off with a drug dealer she met while visiting the financier in Saughton prison) sidled up to Mercedes.

'Anne McCluskey's got blood in her pants,' she whispered.

'Oh,' said Mercedes.

'You know what that means, don't you?' demanded Sophie. Mercedes shrugged.

'It begins with a P,' thrilled Sophie, rolling her eyes warningly in the direction of the boys in the class.

The only thing Mercedes could think of was *period*, but she couldn't imagine that was interesting enough to merit such drama. 'Period,' pronounced Sophie triumphantly. For ever after she thought of Mercedes as totally unworldly.

People tended to, anyway. She read too many books and was always too wrapped up in her own thoughts to take any part in baiting the teachers or pulling Anne McCluskey's temptingly red plaits. Even her father thought she was odd. He came into the room one day when she was listening to her current favourite, Callas singing the

Mad Scene from *Lucia di Lammermoor*. Mercedes didn't think the music sounded very mad, so she was at the window looking down on her favourite audience, the city, and trying to think what kind of madness came out in that polished way. She tried a tentative warble along with the record. Her father gave a dry cough behind her.

'I'm going to be a singer when I grow up, Dad,' said Mercedes. 'What makes you think you can do that?' frowned Mr McMorine.

Later she heard him telling her mother what a strange girl she was.

'You should do something about her, Alison. She's not in the real world,' he said, returning to his study of the 1932 Fort William to Mallaig railway timetable.

Mercedes didn't worry too much because she knew that the world was stranger than she could ever be. One night they had a concert at her school. She was standing on the stairs behind the stage, waiting to go on with the junior choir. It was a bit crushed because there was also a group who were going to do a routine with Indian clubs. Clara Kirschbaum, the German teacher, was singing a solo on stage. She was a fat, not altogether ugly woman who seemed even more exotic and other to Mercedes than she felt herself to be.

Clara was cosmopolitan, colourful. There was something completely un-Scottish about her. She had no inhibitions about eating huge amounts of fattening foods in public, nor of saying extravagantly bitchy things about the other teachers. She wore short skirts that showed off her plump knees. Once on a school trip she had even been seen to drink a glass of red wine when the teachers nicked off for lunch in a hotel. Sophie Pringle heard Sister Mary Joseph talking about it. She said Miss Kirschbaum wasn't fit to be in charge of young girls.

Now the teacher was singing some extract from an opera. Mercedes didn't know what it was. Her father was currently in the middle of a passion for the music of French barrel organs, so her operatic education had temporarily been arrested.

Clara had a slightly shrill voice and Mercedes could tell she would never be of the first rank, but she had an authoritative delivery and deliciously surreal panache. She made her stocky figure and crinkly hair actually seem romantic. But the Indian club team giggled when she hit the high notes.

'What's that?' said the gym teacher. 'The tune the old cow died of?'

Mercedes said nothing, though afterwards she felt as if she had failed in some way by her silence. She ought to have braved their ridicule and stood up for Miss Kirschbaum.

It would only have been like standing up for herself.

Who Dares Wins

THE DRESSING ROOM SMELT LIKE all dressing rooms. It was a strange smell, sweet smell, smell of sweat, smell of face powder and clothes worn the night before, smell of fear.

In Mercedes' room were the types of thing you find in all dressing rooms. Her lucky champagne cork, a red feather fan with a postcard of a flamenco dancer pinned to the corner, huge long brushes for putting blusher on, half eaten tubes of cherry throat sweets. The little phial with its gluey liquid was hidden behind a pair of black lace evening gloves with no fingers.

The diva was pregnant. She knew she ought to throw the bottle away. Once the two little dots on the test paper had turned pink there was no more use for it. But it made her laugh inside to look at this portion of her urine. She felt as if the bottle itself contained the tiny embryo that would be her baby.

Carlos might not be so pleased as she was. The tenor's wife had little use for him in person but she was attached to the place his surname gave her, not only in their home town of Buenos Aires but in international jet-set society. *He* was attached to his daughter. He adored her and could not conceive of life without her.

Mercedes was undaunted by the problems. She grinned into the cheery row of lightbulbs that ran along the top of the mirror. Usually she sighed as she put on her make-up. The lights showed up every hollow, drained away all colour. She didn't like to see the shape of the skeleton beneath her skin so clearly. Tonight she didn't care. She thought of the little shape forming beneath her skin and she exulted.

The first time she'd appeared at the Edinburgh Festival she had a makeshift dressing room beneath an old church. There were a dozen of them, men and women changing on opposite sides of a sheet down the middle of a very dusty basement room, which was usually used to store trestle tables for the church's annual fete. The star of the show had the verger's little office all to herself. Mercedes was in the chorus then, the only Scot in a production full of English people.

It was a very hot summer, hardly a breath of air in the city. Mercedes wandered through the wynds of the old town, wishing she could afford the embroidered T-shirts and purple crushed velvet loon pants on sale in the boutiques. As she inspected the astrological charts and cabbalistic jewellery she thought how useless the hippies' bland white magic was. She needed some black magic, so that the star could dislocate her spine and have to stay in traction for a while, or perhaps be injured in a fire and so hideously disfigured she could never set foot on stage again.

In the end the star got chickenpox. Mercedes was surprised, but regretfully dismissed the idea that her thoughts could possibly have had any connection with the woman's illness. Still, she had to choke back her glee at the idea of those revolting spots all over her face. In her heart she thought it was apt revenge for the star's namby-pamby interpretation of Tosca. It should have been possible to create a stifling, claustrophobic version of the opera; there were so few characters in it anyway. But the star's insipidity diluted any atmosphere and Mercedes usually ended the evening furious with frustration.

Theirs was supposedly the alternative version of Puccini's great opera, though the company bitterly thought of it as the low-rent version. They were touring, staying in commercial hotels where the sheets had not been changed from the previous lorry driver's occupancy and where the breakfast always came limned with hot grease. Even the thought of having to spend money on food during the day couldn't bring Mercedes to eat the wizened bacon and glutinous eggs.

She heard about the star's misfortune when she came into the dusty basement to find the other five girls squabbling behind the sheet about who would take over. Mercedes simply turned on her heel and walked out.

She found the artistic director in the wine bar next door.

'Pinky *can't* do it,' he wailed into his Pinot Grigio. 'I know she's your girlfriend but she's got a voice like a screech owl.'

The company manager, who was also the marketing manager, the administrator and the van driver, looked stubborn. 'I've told her she can,' he said.

Mercedes stood in front of them both. 'I'm going to do it,' she said. 'I'm the only one.'

The van driver looked at her as though he wanted to strangle her.

'She *is* a Scot,' said the artistic director, who had been ogling Mercedes' legs in her mini-skirts for some weeks now – it was one of those years when Britain was actually having a summer. 'That could get us a bit of publicity here.'

The van driver thought of the ticket sales. 'But can she sing?' he asked grudgingly.

When she told her family what happened next they listened with appalled admiration.

'Weren't you just mortified?' said her shy brother, Alan.

'Who dares wins,' said her father unexpectedly.

Mercedes felt that sopranos often sing *Vissi d'Arte* with too much reverence. They get misled by the beautiful melody and the churchy words. *Always in true faith my prayers rose in the holy chapels. Always in true faith I brought flowers to the altars.* From the very beginning Mercedes felt that Tosca was enraged by the thought of having to submit to the slimeball Scarpia.

Standing in the tasteful surroundings of the Edinburgh wine bar, with its discreet green and gold decor, Mercedes for a second wondered how she could go on if she didn't take over this part. Then she felt fury rushing through her veins. She flung down the words *Vissi d'arte, vissi d'amore* (I have lived for art. I have lived for love) as a personal anthem. Rage vibrated in her throat, so powerfully that she had to fight to control her voice. Only when she asked, *Perchè, Signore, perchè?* (Why, oh Lord, why?) did she allow anguish to take her over.

A well-known Scottish poet was in a corner of the bar, spending his Arts Council grant.

'Man, you've got tonsils,' he shouted, lurching drunkenly to his feet and clapping.

It was a reaction that was to recur, in more civilised forms, throughout the Festival. One night Mercedes peered through the wings and saw Claudette Colbert, the famous film star, sitting in the audience, still elegant in spite of her advanced years. Another night it was the writer, Bernard Levin. Mercedes was introduced to him after the show and rather hoped he would try to seduce her, he was such a little imp of a man. The critic remained circumspect. He gave her a rave review the next day, though. Said she was the most intelligent soprano to come along since Callas and potentially as thrilling.

She was the star of the Festival that year. *The Scotsman* said she was Scotland's best hope for international operatic glory since Mary Garden. *The Observer* music critic said he had fallen in love with her. Glasgow's tabloid paper, *The Daily Record*, had the headline TOSCA THE TOWN! and said she had scored a winner for the home team. But Mercedes cared only for the comparison with her beloved Callas, Callas who had started off American and become Greek, who had died in Paris but was mourned all over the world.

Now, fifteen years after her first heady success, the diva prepared to sing in her homeland. It was a bittersweet moment. Her mother had always been dazzled by the foreign triumphs, the first night at La Scala with its crazy number of curtain calls, the trip to New York to storm the Met. But her father, had he lived, would have loved this the most, the Scottish singer bringing the world to her feet in Scotland.

She wished they were both there. They would have been so proud, of her singing at least. Mercedes knew, though, that her relationship with Carlos would not have gone without comment. A married man, no matter how estranged from his wife, was forbidden territory. Her mother, reading the news of the latest Cabinet minister to commit adultery with a porno movie actress, would shake her head.

'I don't know how a woman can break up another woman's marriage like that,' she would sigh.

Her father would look up from *his* paper in disgust. 'They're all keuchs,' he would say.

Sometimes Mercedes felt as if she had moved into another world when she became a singer. It was a wider, richer, freer world than the one she had grown up in, yet sometimes she found herself longing for the old simplicities, wishing she could crawl back into the safety of the world she had grown up in, its certainty.

She would look back and think, *Right was right and wrong was wrong then, and nobody had any difficulty in distinguishing the two.* And then the voice inside would remind her, *Except you,* and she would remember her constant arguments with teachers and even her own classmates. She would remember how bruised she felt inside, the horrid names they called her. *Odd-bod! Odd-bod! Odd-bod!*

Normally she stayed in her dressing room till it was time for her first entrance, but tonight Mercedes felt impelled to go and look at her audience. These were the people she had left behind. She stood high above the stage on the fly floor, looking down from above the battlements of the production's Castel Sant'Angelo. There were the proper-looking businessmen, the politicians, the douce Edinburgh women with their soft dresses and their hard hair, the youngish couples who had left their stripped pine kitchens for an evening of culture. Up in the gods were anxious-looking music students waiting for her to prove to them that the future was possible, that you could be from Scotland and be an artist.

I have lived for art, I have lived for love. Mercedes felt proud. She had sacrificed much for this cold goal. Years of self-discipline, study, travelling, loneliness. A few mistakes, though she tried to be discreet about her indiscretions, the nights in strange cities when she went to bed with strange men, for not very strange reasons.

There had been times when she looked at her nieces and nephews and longed to snatch them away and keep them for herself. There had been times when she wished she could settle for this charming man or that charming place. Times when she wished she were normal.

But she hadn't given up. The diva began to feel her own power. She knew she could move the people in this hall, make the blood tingle along their veins and explode inside their heads. Standing up there above her audience, unseen by them, she raised her arms aloft.

'My God! She's going to jump,' spluttered the stage manager downstairs, spraying Coke all over his best velvet jacket.

'I have lived for art. I have lived for love,' Mercedes declaimed into the rafters. For now her voice was lost in the hubbub of sound below, but in a few minutes, when she sang on stage, none of them would be able to ignore her.

In Questa Reggia

THE DAY THE DIVA FELL IN LOVE was the most exquisite of her life. She had been dubious about doing an open-air concert – they were linked in her mind with fast bucks and fast food. She did not want to be part of a package, in on a deal, on a percentage, even when it involved one of the world's finest tenors. She also remembered the open-air concerts of her youth: the sweaty, lank-haired men; the queues for latrines that smelt like cow sheds; the bodies all jostled up together; the drunken sound systems; the drugged performers. 'It won't be like that,' they told her. But it wasn't till they mentioned fireworks that she agreed.

She wandered a little in the grounds a couple of hours before the concert started. Nobody recognised her as the diva when her hair was messy and she had no make-up on. Most were too busy cutting up Marks and Spencer's quiches and handing out cold chicken legs. Others had game pie and plastic coolers with champagne. The diva looked back up at the elegant neo-classical sweep of the house. She felt at peace.

Both she and the tenor had been staying at the house since the day before. He smiled shyly at her when they were introduced by their host, one of England's aristocrats.

'I admired your Turandot very much,' he said.

The diva was surprised. 'You were there? You should have come backstage to see me.'

Carlos Mazarron inclined his head. 'That was my loss.'

Richard Fortescue-Gardner showed Mercedes all over his house. The tenor came too, though he had seen it. He had already been there for a couple of days. Only half had been restored, very lovingly. As they viewed the cracked Adam ceiling in the ballroom, the mildewing books in the library, they understood that they would be underpinning the restoration of the rest. Mercedes took great pleasure in the thought that she was making herself part of such tradition. She stood in the massive drawing room, watching the stage being rigged. The lawn curved down to the river like the breast of a giantess. Beyond were hills stretching into unfathomable Wiltshire countryside. She wanted to sing superbly.

The programme for the concert was eclectic. The diva was taking a chance. As the climax to the first half she would be singing *In Questa Reggia*, from Puccini's *Turandot*. For all the ecstatic reviews she had received in the role, she was unwilling to sing it too often, not just because of the killing demands it made on the soprano's voice, but because of the strange, venomous brew of emotions it unleashed in her. She thought of herself as a feminist, and it always slightly disappointed her that at the end of the opera the icy power of the Princess was transmuted into something as conventional as love.

Mercedes knew that love was not the whole of life. How could it be when so few people loved or were loved? She was after something more, something harder, something less easy to understand. So when she stood on stage that night, looking out over thousands of faces in their swarming maggoty mass, she felt a cold anger seethe in her. Upwards she looked, to the splendid balance of the house's proportions, but tonight it was not enough for her. She saw only a thicket of preposterous phallic columns. She was at the extreme edge of humanity and she found herself liberated.

Her voice was harsh as she began to tell the tale of Lou-Ling, her dark ancestor. In this palace. In her mind the upturned faces listening to her became separated into men and women. The women's faces came rushing up before her, lifting themselves out of the crowd, burning, flaming in her retina. As she sang she sang for all the women. She felt the long centuries of suffering, of the Princess Lou-Ling and of the proud women who had been raped, killed, often *because* they were proud. She heard Lou-Ling's terrible cry echoing round and round inside her head. She felt vengeance and pride and she was not afraid. *Mai nessun m'avrà!* (No-one will ever possess me!) she sang, and she knew herself to have gone beyond commonsense, beyond civilisation. She knew she would never in her life feel such pure, cold strength again.

There was silence when she ended. Then a surge of applause that sent the rooks cawing up into the air in panic. Mercedes wanted to leave the stage but they kept calling her back. She was dazed when she finally walked off. Carlos Mazarron stood clapping at the side of the stage. He put out a hand to help her down the step. She could see curiosity in his brown eyes.

At the interval he came to the little trailer at the back of the set that was her dressing room. She had wept when she reached it. Now she was simply drained.

'That was ...' He frowned in his effort to find words. '... So fine. I can't tell you what I felt.'

He clasped her hand. He seemed not to know what to say. His hand was warm and dry, the fingers more finely made than Mercedes' own. She looked at him closely, the magnificent boldness of his head, his tentative eyes. She knew he would be kind.

In the second half of the concert Mercedes felt light, free. Mimi. Tosca. Lucia. Desdemona. She could be anybody she wanted, sing anything. In between her own numbers she stood at the side of the stage while Mazarron sang. He was not an intellectual singer, but he had a passion that made him stand out from others. He sang from the heart. It seemed to her, watching him, that greatness in art lay simply in being what you are to a greater degree than other people are what they are. He knew who he was. He was Mazarron as absolutely as Callas was Callas.

Mercedes almost laughed out loud with pleasure as she walked towards him for the drinking song from *La Traviata*. It was often done at concerts as a way of getting audiences to join in. Even the least knowledgable could stamp and sway in time to it. Tonight Mercedes felt it was for her benefit, a way for her to have fun and flirt, be like other people. She leaned her head back against the tenor's shoulder, eyes alight. His arm closed over her own, held her against him. She swayed with him, marvelling at the heat from this other person's body.

They gave encore after encore, so engrossed in their curious courtship, intimate in spite of the thousands of people there, that neither cared how long the concert went on. Mercedes hardly saw the crowd. Her eyes went beyond the lights, beyond them, beyond the magnificent house even. But she saw trees, caught the pungency of the river in her nostrils once as a breeze blew up.

As the orchestra at last began the triumphal finale they ran for the waiting limousine. The tenor gripped her hand in his. Inside the car she could smell their mingled body sweat, her own heavy perfume, his aftershave, the leather of the seats. Up the driveway they sped, to the house. The tenor covered her hands with kisses. 'When we are inside you come with me,' he said. He scrambled from the car, but even in his haste turned to thank the driver. Mercedes liked that.

They practically ran through the throng of glitteringly dressed people. A lady in a silver turban saw them and raised her hands to clap but the tenor gave her his shy smile and put a finger to his lips. She simpered with delight. Mercedes felt breathless. The tenor swept a waiter's tray away as they passed.

They ran up the great mahogany staircase, the tenor with the tray under his arm and a clutch of champagne glasses in his hand, Mercedes carrying the champagne. She felt bubbles rising up inside herself. She felt she would explode with laughter.

Then they were running through a huge bedroom, to the window and out on to the balcony. The music crashed and the champagne cork exploded from the bottle. It foamed over their glasses as the first burst of fireworks erupted into the sky. The tenor's eyes seemed black, his pupils were so dilated.

'You are ...' he sighed fervently, and raised his glass to her. Mercedes found him bewitchingly funny.

The music swelled and soared as a thunderstorm of pink and green and golden rain raged in the sky. They were all caught up together in the turbulence, the noise and light rioting around them, Mercedes and her tenor and all the people down below lifting their faces like children, entranced. Purple hail hissed and there were flashes of turquoise lightning and it rained, rained, rained colour.

The final firework fell and the last flakes of pink light swirled to the ground, tiny atoms in a world of black. The tenor turned quietly to Mercedes.

'That was beautiful,' she said.

'I suppose we must go down now and meet the rich people,' he said. 'They wait for us.'

Mercedes slid her arms round his neck. 'I don't want to,' she said, and kissed him, passionately. This was not her usual approach with men. Mostly she waited for them to pursue her. She had found this to be less confusing for them.

The tenor's eyes closed. She could feel his champagne glass pressed against her side.

'Is this your room?' she asked. He nodded.

'Huh. It's bigger than the one they gave me.'

The tenor laughed. 'It's yours,' he said.

'Good. I want all of it.' And she dragged back the heavy coverlet that draped the bed. They knelt together on the bed, kissing. The tenor gripped her tightly. His shoes left a black mark on the white linen sheet. She pushed his evening jacket back off his shoulders and he unzipped her black shot silk dress and they were kissing the whole time. It was rough and hurried. Mercedes threw the dress off and it landed on the floor with a sigh, like a parachute coming down to land.

'Carlos,' she said, and found her tongue was unwilling to let the name go. 'Carlos.'

He had a broad chest and short, muscular legs. Mercedes unzipped his trousers but she was too shy to look at him. She wriggled against him so that she could press her stomach against his. She didn't know why that always pleased her so much. She felt it was a little like Eskimos rubbing noses. Usually she liked hard, sculpted men, but his stomach was soft and cosy. He was stronger than she would have thought. His movements were very definite and he touched her so urgently that she could feel all her limbs dissolving with heat, as if her whole body had become a stream of molten liquid. Generally she considered it correct bedroom etiquette to reciprocate caresses, to do her share, but this time she simply forgot.

Afterwards she lay in a haze. She could see her black silk underskirt had milky white stains on it and she thought she probably ought to move it out of sight but she didn't. The bed smelt sweet, of perfume and him and her.

'I think this is going to be a long night,' he said.

'I'm starving,' she said, but she could hardly believe her luck and she nearly laughed out loud.

'What's so funny?'

'Nothing.' But her eyes were spangled with laughter. He studied her over the rim of his glass, puzzled. Then he leant forward as if to kiss her. She could taste a warm flow of champagne seeping between her teeth. She could feel the warm flow of her own blood as it moved through her veins, never still. She could hear it pulsing through her ears. She felt that with this man she could do anything.

In the morning she knew that she must be in love. For almost the first time in her life she didn't want to jump out of bed and rush off immediately. She studied the man sleeping beside her, gloated over the harsh nose, soft mouth, the top lip puckered upwards like a Roman statue or a leather bike-boy. She let her hand drift in and out of his chest hair. The heavy lidded eyes dragged open. His instinctive smile was fleeting and replaced almost instantly by an anxious expression. Carlos propped himself up on one elbow.

'You are serious about this, aren't you? It is not a game for me.'

'I'm serious,' she said, but already she was thinking ahead of how she would splash him with water when they had a bath.

They went downstairs together to the breakfast room. Silver chafing dishes with kidneys and kedgeree were laid out on the mahogany sideboard. The lady with the silver turban was dressed in more matutinal style. Her turban was red. She winked at Carlos, gave him a knowing smile. Richard Fortescue-Gardner looked sulky. They had clearly spoiled his triumph the previous evening.

'I say, you might have stayed a little longer last night, you know. A lot of big-wigs were expecting to meet you.'

Muffy, his wife, gave them a roguish wink. 'Oh, you naughty things!' she trilled. 'We were looking for you everywhere. I know what you were up to, Carlos, you beast.' Mercedes grinned at her lover's discomfiture. She could sense the disapproval of the other people in the room but she didn't care. She felt proud that they hadn't been paraded through the drawing room like trophies.

'He's not the beast,' she announced grandly. 'I am."

My Heart Beats only for You

FOR YEARS AND YEARS THE DIVA had found it difficult to understand what people meant when they said they were broody. She had grown up with so many children around her she wasn't sure she would ever completely recover from the experience. Over the years she found herself sounding more and more like her father in her head. *Affectation*, she'd think scathingly, as yet another girlfriend revealed her innermost longings. 'Just your hormones,' she'd say. They always hated her for it.

But when Mercedes fell in love with Carlos she began to feel this ache in the pit of her stomach, or what she thought of as her stomach. It was not. She knew from voice reproduction that her stomach was tucked in behind her ribcage just below her breasts, but like everyone else she mentally located it much further south. She located it, in fact, precisely where her unborn baby was shortly to nestle. But she did not know that yet. All she knew was this pain. It was there and it was real. On autumn days she would find it hard to catch her breath and sometimes she even worried she had a cancer eating away inside her.

Mercedes knew the tenor loved her, not because he said so, though he did. 'I love you, Mercedes,' he'd say, and bury his nose in the underside of her breast. But then every Latin said that, usually after around four minutes of her company. They liked her dark eyes and the haughty way she carried herself.

In the first months she thought of Carlos constantly, but always with a tinge of melancholy, because he was, after all, someone else's. They would meet up in Madrid. She had always felt at home in Spain, perhaps because its men were as absurdly macho as the Scots and usually more polite. The tenor just felt pleased he could speak his own language there.

Always before she had stayed at the Ritz. He had, too. But they would not stay there together. It was too public, and Mercedes associated it with the plush, plump safety of jet-set travel. What she had with Carlos was too raw for that.

They booked instead into a shabby tourist hotel on the Gran Vía. Its reception was one floor up off the street so most people passed by and didn't ever realise it was there. Mercedes and Carlos would lie at siesta time in the rackety double bed, with sun streaming in through the lace curtains, showing up the filth that was encrusted on the windows. You could write your name on the tiles in the bathroom, so each wrote the other's. Mercedes. Carlos. But the towels were white and fluffy and the sheets were pure white cotton.

There in the heat of the afternoon they plotted the next stage of their love. The hot, passionate present in this grubby hotel room was only a prelude. The diva was determined that some time in the future they would sing together. She picked up the telephone and rang her agent. Laura was a chic Italian who terrorised the world's greatest conductors on Mercedes' behalf. This meant that when Mercedes decided to terrorise them too the joint effect was devastating.

'Laura, you haven't cancelled the *Trovatore*?'

'Not yet, but the tenor's pulled out and you mustn't sing with one of Eduardo's pin-up boys.'

'I want to sing with Mazarron. He was wonderful at Melfort House.'

'I heard all about him at Melfort House. I think you went crazy for a little while back there.'

'He excites me,' she said, and ran her hand down the tenor's thigh.

There was a sigh at the other hand of the line. Laura's cool, American-accented voice was world-weary. 'You have him there, don't you?'

Mercedes laughed. 'Don't be silly. Of course not.'

'Mercedes. Just because Callas was an idiot for love, is no need for you to be so, too. He has a daughter, you know. And a wife, of course.'

'Still, he's a magnificent singer. You get him for me, Laura. And Laura …?'

'Yes.'

'Callas was only an idiot for love when she thought her voice was going. I'm not bloody finished yet.'

They did *Il Trovatore* at the Paris Opera that autumn. The tenor had a flat in the city but Mercedes refused to stay there with him. It was a new production and she knew that his wife would fly in for the first night. She did not intend to be humiliated.

Instead she made him stay with her. She rented a huge flat off the Rue St Antoine. Beyond the wrought iron security gates and the concierge's room was a typical Parisian apartment building, elegant and stuffy, with rows of blank windows that looked as if only terrible things or nothing happened in the silent rooms behind them. It must be, she thought, like the flat Maria Callas died in in this city. She lived her last empty years in the Avenue Georges-Mandel, with only stacks of unopened blouses in polythene wrappers for company.

Mercedes soon found that her flat was taken over by the tenor's books. This surprised her a little as he was noted more for the emotion of his singing than its intelligence. He read all sorts of things, modern novels, the history of war, sporting biographies, poetry, and many, many books about the great singers of the past. In bed one night she asked him, which of these artists he admired the most. He laughed out loud.

'Callas, of course, but singers are not who I admire,' he said gleefully. 'Once I was in a little village high in the mountains of Mexico. It was their fiesta, the fiesta of the Virgen de las Flores. They were having their *corrida*. They had only one such bullfight in the whole year. And this matador comes in. He was on horseback, not a picador, but really a matador. He was wearing a red velvet jacket and the hat, you know, like Valentino in *Blood and Sand*?

'It was only a dusty little place. It was nowhere really, but he gave the people everything. He was so courageous and so elegant also, the way he swoop so close to the bull. I have never seen anything like it.'

Mercedes shoved him in the face. 'You and your sport,' she said, climbing astride him. But she knew it was more than sport.

In rehearsals she found it hard to disguise the excitement she felt at working with him. She would see him leaning over the piano, absorbed, and she would want to run, screaming her joy up the centre of the theatre. It maddened her that he seemed so normal on the outside. She wanted everyone to know that he felt passionate about her as she about him. She also wanted no one to know, and so she kept her face as cool and mask-like as she could. Behind her back the other singers whispered she was a bitch. They all, without exception, adored the tenor.

A corrupt industrialist had agreed to sponsor the production so they had longer than usual for rehearsal. They even had time, on occasion, to discuss the opera.

'The troubadour is a total chauvinist,' declared Mercedes. 'It's all right when he can worship Leonora from afar, but as soon as he might have to commit himself he runs back to Mummy.'

The tenor was outraged. 'This is not fair,' he shouted. 'He's not running back for himself. His mother will die.'

'You Latins, you're all the same. Mothers' boys, every one of you. You don't know how to deal with women who're your equal.'

'You ... you ... you feminist!'

'Of course I'm a feminist. I always have been.'

'Children! Children!' Eduardo, the director, insinuated his plump body between theirs. 'You are using up your beautiful voices.'

It seemed to the diva that the troubadour himself was quite a modern figure. He is a poet and a guerrilla fighter, a man who falls in love at first sight yet who honours the most traditional of obligations, that of the son to his mother. Leonora, she found baffling.

Perching at the back of the dress circle with a cup of honey and lemon, Mercedes watched Carlos pore over his part with the pianist. His dark hair curled over his collar at the back. Love at first sight she could understand, though she did not consider that to be the case with her own feelings. She had had a whole tour of a stately home, a music rehearsal and half a concert before she had finally succumbed.

She could understand Leonora rushing into a convent when she thinks she will lose the troubadour. It was not a modern solution but what, after all, was her own singing career but another version of the religious life? She too lived a daily discipline. She had faith that hard work now would bring its reward later. And she had the experience of ecstasy whenever she sang on stage.

No, the question that troubled her was that Leonora wants to die for the troubadour when he has chosen his mother above her. That was love of a purer order than Mercedes could dream of. She huddled over her cup, letting the steam from her drink steal through her nose and eyes. Maybe by the time they reached performance she would understand.

As rehearsals went on she found them peculiarly painful. At first she had thought this opera was about romantic love, but gradually she knew it was not. It was about death. The knowledge of that seeped through everything the diva did. Even trying on her costume – a rich, dark red satin that would normally have lifted her spirits – left her depressed. She looked at it against her white skin and knew that if the blood came spilling out of her body it would be that colour.

When they came to *Di Quella Pira* she simply felt what it was to want to die. The troubador's aria is a great popular piece, a strident call to arms. A trumpeting of testosterone. Carlos was very secure on the high 'C's' at the end. Some tenor inserted them into the aria years ago and they have remained there ever since. He galloped through it to deliver them with all the panache at his disposal, teeth gleaming white against his brown skin. *I was her son before I was your lover. Your suffering cannot hold me back.* Mercedes hated him.

Eduardo saved her. As the tenor finished he came bustling forward, sliding his arm round Carlos' waist.

'Oh ... darling ... you make me go weak at the knees,' he sighed. 'But you know. I think maybe we try it at the original tempo, as Verdi wanted it.'

'The slow version?' asked the tenor suspiciously.

'*Si, si, si,*' said Eduardo briskly. 'You will see. It makes more sense. Then when he says, *Era già figlio,* I was her son ... he is sad about it. It breaks his heart to run off and leave his beloved.'

'There was just a *touche* of the indecent hastes the way you sang it,' drawled Aubrey, the director's assistant.

The tenor scowled. 'What has it got to do with *him?*' he said crossly, as Eduardo steered him back to centre stage. Mercedes felt only relief. At last it had started to become clear to her. *Oh quanto meglior sarìa morir!* How much better it would be to die! These people were rushing towards death. It was as if there were no brakes on them. Ordinary life was too banal to hold them. Only perfection could satisfy them. Mercedes knew she was not like that. She didn't need all the world to be happy. She would settle for just enough of Carlos.

Her certainty was not to remain untested. Two nights before opening he did not return to her flat. She phoned him at his own home, only to be answered by a cultured Latin voice.

'Carlos? Of course. I will get him for you.' The woman's voice was half a tone lower than its natural pitch and carefully modulated.

She sounded like someone who would always be in control of herself. She sounded condescending.

'Why didn't you tell me she was coming today?' hissed Mercedes.

'Yes, I'm sorry. I meant to phone. I've just come back from the airport. Sofia's flight was actually a little early.' The tenor's voice was polite, but distant.

'You bastard,' she said. 'You've done this before.'

'Not like this. I swear it.' He sounded hurt but Mercedes slammed the phone down. She didn't believe him.

She refused to look at him over the next two days as they went over the last details of the production. Often she would glance up and see his brown eyes fixed on her, pleading. *Rat's eyes*, she thought contemptuously, and looked cold. Once, it was his wife's eyes she found looking at her, calculating.

The woman was exquisite. Her suit whispered of cashmere and class. Her legs were long, with the attenuated elegance of an Art Deco figurine. And about as functional, thought the diva crossly. She probably only ever used them for tottering out of limousines and into posh hotels. The diva contemplated her own jeans and sweatshirt with disgust, but she was thinking of how it felt to wrap her legs round the tenor. She was thinking of the power in her thighs, when she tightened them round him.

On the first night she felt ill. Carlos came knocking at the door to wish her luck, but she was throwing up in the toilet at the time and found it easy to banish him. 'Beat it,' was what she actually said. But as soon as she heard his first notes, the sweetness and power of his tone, she knew she would have to relent.

It was easy that night to sing her love. The worst part was controlling the beating of her heart. It felt like a woodpecker hammering away inside her chest. Only, when she came to sing *D'amor sull'ali rosee*, she thought it might burst inside her with pain. In the dark outside the tower where her lover was held captive, she willed her love to him. She sent it winging through the night, beyond the bounds of this chest, these lungs. She willed it backstage, past the young chorus members flirting with each other in the wings. She wanted it to reach him where he stood in the dark, waiting. She knew it would.

In the second of silence that followed the end of the aria, before the crash of applause, she saw in the wings the subdued faces of the chorus. They looked uneasy, and a little wistful. In their world she knew such passion was considered a joke. They thought they were too cool, too much in touch with real life to indulge in such naive excess. And yet, somewhere inside they were like everyone else. That was all they wanted.

It took the diva a long time to reach her dressing room after the show. There were so many hands to shake, even in the corridors. She knew the tenor's flowers as soon as she came into the room. Dark, dark red roses, heavy with perfume, and the white lilies of death. *My heart beats only for you. Without you I am nothing*, read the card.

This time when he knocked on the door she opened immediately. They said nothing at first, simply embraced. The tenor crushed her so hard it hurt. His eyes were distraught.

'I can't live without you, Mercedes,' he said.

Against her better judgement, the diva found herself in tears. She would have said, 'I love you,' but it was a phrase that was impossible to pronounce in a Glaswegian accent.

'Oh Carlos,' she wailed instead.

Laura, her agent, poked her head round the door. 'Oh my God,' she said. She came into the room, shutting the door firmly behind her with her Chanel-suited bottom.

'So, Carlos, you are upsetting my client.'

'No. She is upsetting me.'

'You were both magnificent tonight. I would say this to you anyway, but you know is the truth. I think my mascara is almost as much a mess as yours, Mercedes.'

Mercedes grinned. 'It's not,' she said.

'Darling, if I was you, I would try to look like a normal human being. The wife is just outside.' Laura patted his shoulder. 'She's a killer, that one. I think she must have English blood. She looks as if she's just been to a tea party.'

Sofia glided in as Laura opened the door. From the tip of her blonde chignon to the toe of her calfskin Italian shoes, she was impeccable, irreproachable and irredeemably insufferable.

'Darling,' she said, kissing gloved fingers to her lips. 'You were sensational. I'm sure not even La Callas could have moved me more. As for my angel. Was he not divine?' She clasped his hand in hers. 'You mustn't be too long, my sweet. M. Fabregas insists we travel to the party in his limousine.' The corrupt industrialist expected his status as patron of the arts to be recognised tonight.

'You go on,' said the tenor. 'I can't rush tonight.'

'You must get him organised,' she said offensively to the diva, as if she were his secretary. 'You know, my dear, you have such a strange way of speaking English. Where is it you are from?'

'Scotland.'

'Oh, I see.' But the diva was sure she didn't.

The tenor sighed when she had gone. 'I wanted her to bring Ana, my daughter, but she says she has to be in school.'

'It's a pity. This would be far more of an education for her.'

'She never says it but that's always the threat. That I won't see her again.'

Mercedes walked to the door. Laura was outside with a party of visitors.

'Bugger off, the lot of you,' said the diva. 'We'll see you at the party.' She grinned at Laura's dumbfounded face and swept back in. She locked the door. The tenor looked sad now and she couldn't bear it. She walked towards him, the dark red satin rustling. Her breasts swam like milk against the rich colour. She pushed him back on to the chaise longue. She wondered why she had ever thought you couldn't have it all.

Outside in the corridor people were laughing, calling to each other. A champagne cork went off and the bubbles fizzed up. Someone yelped. There were giggles. The diva kissed her tenor. She would have liked to rip his shirt open but he reminded her it was the theatre's costume. They both stood up then and tossed the heavy fabrics down into the corner.

The diva was free of the national guilt about sex that afflicted many of her countrywomen. With all that the nuns at her school had told her, she had expected to find it complex, at the least. She was surprised to find it was mostly just pleasurable. But now, as she perched herself on his chest, she was afraid she would embarrass herself. It was not simply that her insides had turned to jelly. She wanted him so badly she thought the jelly would start oozing out before they had even started, perhaps spurt and gush in an uncontrollable flow, overwhelm him.

Later she felt as if they had made love time after time, but she knew it must have been only once. He left her and she felt bruised. As she dragged herself up from the sofa she could smell the earthy scent of the dark red roses, the waxy exhalation that came from the lilies. The room reverberated with the scent of her admirers' flowers, the trophies of her triumph. Orchids, freesias, roses, irises. She pulled at the vulvular petals of one of the lilies. She felt only longing.

Up-ended Geisha

CARLOS CAME WITH HER to see the scan. He came with her to Glasgow. For reasons that surprised her, the diva had decided to have her baby in Scotland. She had not lived there since she was at school but in some part of her it seemed to be her home, if she had one. She rented a tenement flat in the city's West End. It was elegant and sunny, with a view across to the hills. When she had grown up in the city she hadn't known anyone who lived in such style. Carlos said it was cold. He said she didn't care if he died from water on the lungs.

The room where the scan was to take place was small and murky. There was a monitor like a portable television set which emitted an eerie grey light. Mercedes lay down on the couch. An icy blue gel was smeared all over her stomach. It was so cold she thought her skin had probably puckered prematurely into old age. 'Listen to this,' said the nurse, handing her a set of headphones. Pounding in her ears was the sound of a heartbeat, but speeded up, a heart beating away crazily like the soundtrack of a silent movie. Mercedes' heart kickstarted into racing in sympathy. *Slow down. Everything will be all right, little baby.*

'There it is,' said the doctor.

Mercedes gazed at the screen. She could see only grey fog, with blobs sometimes of white, sometimes of darker grey. She had no idea which was supposed to be shape, which shadow. The doctor laughed.

'Whatever angle you look at it's always got its fist in the air like a Black Power salute. Baby Power!'

Carlos laughed. 'Oh no. She is going to be like her mother. A feminist.'

Mercedes peered at the fishy little thing she thought she discerned on the screen. She knew her baby would be a fighter.

The loneliest times were when Carlos was away visiting his beloved daughter, Ana. There were still half a dozen of Mercedes' siblings living in the city with their spouses and children and often she would go and have dinner with one or other of them on Sundays. This was usually an ordeal, not because they didn't make her welcome, but because their children were so unfailingly tiresome she would come away wondering if she was right to have this baby.

Tiresomeness could be genetic.

Pregnancy did not agree with the diva. She was past the age for being radiant. As the months went on she began to feel like some great aquatic mammal, stranded out of its own element. She moved slowly. She was used to being light and free in her own body and would wake up appalled at the protuberance that had sprouted on her overnight. In the mornings she would put her feet up and listen to Carlos working with his accompanist. She would hear him sing a beautiful phrase and almost fall in love with him again. Then she would remind herself sternly that this spawn taking over her body was his.

He wasn't there when the birth began, of course. He was off seeing Ana. Mercedes was having dinner with one of the most gruesome of the siblings. There wasn't anything wrong with him in himself but he already had seven children and there was another on the way. Halfway through the roast chicken with Paxo thyme and lemon stuffing, Mercedes began to feel queasy. She put this down to the fact that Eddie, one of the middle children, was trying to beat the family record for shovelling frozen peas into his mouth with the edge of his knife. Gravy was trickling down his chin.

'You look awfully white,' said her brother's wife.

That was when Mercedes felt the beginnings of a contraction. Even underneath the cool satin of her overshirt she could feel the skin of her stomach burning. The baby was pushing out from inside. It would break through the wall of her stomach any minute. She knew it. Yet in another, more rational part of her brain she knew that the baby must be pushing out in the conventional direction. Her pubic bone was vibrating with pain. Up till now it had never occurred to her that she had one.

Mercedes was confident that the contraction was only a false alarm, but the mere suggestion that birth might be imminent sent her brother into a frenzy of preparation for her departure. Given the large number of children in the house Mercedes thought he couldn't possibly be squeamish about the physical aspects of birth. She decided he must want to protect her from his children, who would probably treat her as some kind of interesting, if familiar, scientific experiment.

It seemed to her in the long hours that followed that the pain was something separate from her. In her mind it had a living existence as distinct as that of the baby or herself. It was a malign trick of fate that trapped the three entities together in her body.

In their family, childbirth was not uncommon, but in the continuous recurrences of this seemingly banal event she could remember no mention of pain or humiliation, no feeling from her mother or sisters or sisters-in-law of how demeaning the whole process was. None of them seemed to mind being trussed up like a piece of poultry while some man in a white coat trawled their insides, as if looking for the giblets in a plastic wrapped chicken. And not one of them even mentioned how curious it was to spread your legs and bare your rump in the harshness of daylight. Mercedes felt like an up-ended geisha in a Japanese engraving but without the erotic pleasure to look forward to.

When labour began she knew from a television doctor's latest birth and pregnancy book that the amount of pain she experienced would depend on her own expectations. Her expectations were that she would have an easy time. She came, after all, from a line of women who dropped babies as casually as most teenagers drop litter. So it was something of a shock when she found herself screaming like a beast for hours on end as an unseen torturer applied electrodes to the very core of her being.

It was just at the moment when she felt she would do anything rather than continue to exist and feel this pain, that she discovered within herself the atavistic passions of a killer. She had been left on her own for what seemed like hours as the midwife was sure she was nowhere near delivery. There was a large mirror in the room and she found it hard to recognise herself in the bug-eyed monster who moaned out of the glass at her. *She* didn't have stringy hair like that and she was sure her face wasn't exuding that sickly sweat. She didn't have huge veins standing up on her breasts, nor those obscenely dark nipples that looked like a sex toy from some fetishists' mail order catalogue. Surely this woman wasn't her?

After ten hours of feeling that her body was the epicentre of a series of volcanic eruptions she had had enough. She opened her highly trained lungs and screamed louder than she had ever heard anyone scream before. Not a tenor in the world could have competed with the searing, piercing sound of that high C. It was then that the midwife came back.

'For heaven's sake! Would you stop that racket,' she said. 'It's well seen you're on the stage.'

Had Mercedes not been in the throes of a shivering fit she would have disembowelled the woman.

The light in the room seemed very harsh to her and she was nearly sick from the smells, the hospital disinfectant, the animal sweat seeping out from her skin, the acrid smell when she pushed and released some urine. She was relieved she had chosen to have an enema. She could not have faced further embarrassment. But in a way there was none. The hateful woman, the sounds from the ward seemed as if they were happening some distance away. All she cared about was contained in this hot, rank bubble of pain.

Here inside, her body was rearranging itself. Contractions seemed a polite word for the convulsions that were picking up her insides and hurling them at the walls of her stomach. Her back ached and the lower part of her body had transformed itself into a tunnel. At last she felt a burning sensation deep down inside the tunnel, as if her body tissue had been plugged into an electric socket. In the mirror the wild-eyed woman had a yawning gash where Mercedes knew her vagina was. A red mass of pulp protruded from it. As each attack of pain raked her insides she could see the pulp pulsating. Its slick, sticky surface heaved up and back down again. She felt as if the lips of her vagina had rolled back and slipped into her skin.

Now Mercedes' heart was careering through her chest like a train. She was panting. The train and the tunnel were one. They were pounding, pounding away from her. She wanted to slow them down but there was no way to catch them. The midwife took hold of the red pulp but Mercedes pushed her hand away so that she could feel her baby's head. Then a convulsion gripped her and there was the body and two scrunched-up bandy little legs. The baby bleated and Mercedes let out a war-whoop of joy and triumph. She was sobbing and tears dripped down her face. 'Wah! Wah! Wo-o-o-a-a-ah!' she yelled. She felt demented.

The midwife clucked in disapproval but she laid the bloody, waxy little creature on top of Mercedes as she clamped the cord. The diva had never felt anything so beautiful or so tiny. Her hand was streaked with the sticky fluids smearing the baby's skin. *My daughter*, she thought. *My daughter, Maria Callas McMorine.*

Post-natal Dementia

THE DIVA LOVED THE MET. She would stand on the east side of the Lincoln Center Plaza and look across at its five dizzying arches and feel that when she walked through the smoked glass doors she would be walking into a new world. Here was the jewelchest of violent passions that opera had always been, yet shot through with a modern coolness; a recognition that it was not always necessary to be the victim of emotion or fate. People here were hip and knowledgeable, technocrats, all the things that the diva was not.

She and Carlos had been lent an apartment in the Dakota building by a film director friend of the tenor. Inside it was magnificent, if a little on the heavy side for the diva's taste. The marble floors and mahogany panelling made her think sometimes she was shut up in the vaults of some rich family's mausoleum. She had a feeling of foreboding too when she approached the entrance, but she told herself it was only because she had seen it so often on the television when John Lennon was gunned down there.

The tenor was opening the Met season as Pollione in Bellini's *Norma*. The diva thought of it as *her* opera, her link across the years to the moment when she found Maria Callas and her own vocation. Now, though, at this moment in her life, she knew she could not have done it justice. She would have found it impossible to sing the scene where the Druid priestess contemplates killing her own children. The thought made her shudder. In the past she had made it work by focusing on Norma's desire to save her children from abuse by the Roman enemy. Now the priestess' despair at losing her lover made her seem cheap and trivial to Mercedes.

Her passion for her daughter surprised even the diva herself. She knew Carlos' place in the biological scheme of Maria's conception, but it was as if he had nothing to do with the bond between her and the baby. He wanted the diva to marry him now, but the idea seemed irrelevant. Mercedes would inhale the sweet acridity of the sweat on the baby's head or rub her face against the round little bottom and she would think that there was nothing else but this in the world.

The best times were when the baby woke in the night.

Carlos slept soundly. He rarely stirred when she left their bed at three in the morning to change the baby's nappy. With the orange light of the fire the only illumination in the room, she would peel Maria's clothes off and just let her kick. The baby adored this. She would make soft little gurgling noises and smile. And when Mercedes trilled her lips against her stomach she would make a curious gasping noise that Mercedes knew to be laughter.

It seemed to the diva that there was no amount of love you could lavish on a baby that would be too much. You didn't have to be careful about crowding her or choosing the right moment. You didn't have to frame the words carefully for fear of frightening her off with your extravagance. You could coo and burble any amount of lovetalk at her and make her happy. The worst time of day for Mercedes was morning, when she had to leave Maria with her nanny, Vivien, and go to work. The diva was recording a selection of arias from operas that she did not usually perform. She would walk to the little rehearsal room they were renting near the Met, thinking not of the arias they were still choosing, but of whether she had expressed enough milk for the baby.

The choosing in any case was proving difficult. In the work that suited her voice there was nothing that would express this love of mother for child. She felt as if opera was failing her, as if it had no language for this passion of hers. The nearest approach, it occurred to her one day, was in *Rigoletto*, but that was a father's love and a doomed one, and the music ends when the daughter dies.

The diva could understand Rigoletto's terror for his Gilda. Many afternoons on the way home, instead of being happy that she would soon see Maria, she would be seized by a terrible fear that something had happened to her. She would see flames licking round the Indian head above the entrance to the Dakota building, searing past the ornamental ears of corn and arrowheads, swarming up the walls towards their flat. All around people would be walking quietly up Columbus Avenue, but Mercedes would be listening to the cracking of wood and glass and the roaring, boiling sound of fire charging through the apartment and into the baby's room. She would always start to run.

Carlos thought she was suffering from a form of post-natal dementia.

'Look at you. Why are you like this?' he would say, regarding her sweat-flecked face with amazement. 'You think you're the only one which can look after babies? She's all right.'

He would slide his arms round her waist and attempt to nuzzle her neck, but the diva would slip out from underneath his arms and clasp the baby to her in relief.

'It's all right, my poppet. Mummy's here,' she would croon, ignoring Carlos' disgruntled face.

Even in rehearsal she would find the image of the baby's face floating into her mind. This unsettled her. For years she had been known for her ferocious single-mindedness. Until Carlos she had not really taken part in the giddy round of couplings and uncouplings enjoyed by many in her profession. She had understood why Callas settled for a plump little man who would look after her, who would adore her as a goddess and expect only the cruelty and self-absorption of a goddess in return. The diva had never wished her obsession for her art to be disrupted by muddling thoughts of male shoulders, the contours of a chest, the demanding need of a man's lovemaking. For all that she spent her life portraying the extremes of erotic passion she had thought of these things in her own life, until Carlos, as simply occasional diversions.

Now it was as if a lifetime of following the absolute had led her away from the things she thought important – the music, the craft of it. Instead she was drawn inexorably down this deviant and frighteningly fragile course of maternal love. She admired those women who took the existence of their babies for granted. She saw them all around her, deep in conversation with their friends while their babies' mouths groped for the nipple; clucking at the price of sweetcorn while their toddlers pulled ineffectually at piles of potatoes. It would never be as easy as that for the diva.

One night she looked up from bathing the baby and saw how lonely her tenor was. She was seized by how much she loved him. 'Why don't you invite Ana to stay here for a while?'

He was touched. 'But Sofia will never let me,' he said.

'I'll see to it,' said the diva firmly.

The tenor's wife was often in New York for charity lunches and chi-chi art openings. The diva chose a 57th Street gallery that specialised in Pre-Columbian art. The tenor's wife was said to be something of an authority on this. She had appeared in American *Vogue* straddling a stone Mayan fertility god, which she claimed kept her company while her husband was away. Her thighs, newly toned after a session with her personal trainer, looked ominously serpentine wrapped round the stumpy little legs of the deity.

The diva hoped their tête-à-tête would be a short one. She did not want milk to leak on to her Armani jacket. The tenor's wife was dressed in Claude Montana. The dramatic cut and amplitude of her coat made her look foreign and exotic against the shrunken-limbed, shrunken-skirted women who prowled the gallery with their bloated chequebooks.

'You want everything, don't you? You have my husband. You can't have my child as well.'

'I have everything,' said the diva. 'I have my daughter.'

Sofia looked at her keenly. Then she laughed. She had an air of satisfaction. 'All right,' she said. 'Don't worry. Ana will look after him for you. And now, I have a little favour to ask you in return.'

'Anything.'

'I am the patron of a small charity ...'

'Of course,' said the diva. She would have sung at the Buenos Aires polo and country club if it had got her what she wanted. She'd have sung to the polo ponies.

Ana was adorable, a plump little thing with her father's great brown eyes and a mischievous smile that was all the more devastating for being hidden much of the time. She was a solemn child, whose perfect manners the diva recognised as the product of a previous era. The children she knew now were confident and chatty, sure that everything they had to say was of interest and would be received as such. Ana was diffident, over-respectful, as the diva knew herself to have been.

The little girl loved the baby. She would rush to help when Mercedes went to change her nappy, eagerly pulling talcum powder and zinc cream from the change bag where they were kept.

'Papa, Maria *is* my sister, isn't she?' Mercedes heard her ask one day.

'Of course she is, my darling,' he said.

'She smiles at me, you know, Papa.'

'I think she's a little young for that. It's probably just wind.'

'And she talks to me.'

He laughed out loud. 'She's certainly too young to talk.'

'No, Papa. I *know* she's trying to say something to me,' said the little girl earnestly. 'She thinks she's telling me things but she just doesn't know any words yet.'

Carlos laughed but Mercedes nodded her head as she bent to kiss the baby's stomach. Maria's little arms jerked upwards in that curious way babies have, like insects caught by a sudden buffet of wind. She made a cooing noise, followed by a little yelp. 'Yes, yes, my darling,' said the diva. She agreed with Ana.

They Can Do Anything

THE DIVA WAS THINKING about the death of Maria Callas the night her life fell apart. She was alone in the living room of the apartment, looking out the window but seeing only Callas, dead of heart failure so many years ago. The breakdown of a valve, the powerful physical organ that had supported the magnificent voice for so many years? Or was it deliberate, too many pills perhaps? No music. No love. No life. Left. Had Callas' heart failed her at the thought?

Carlos was on the phone in the study, talking to his agent, deep in dates and rates. Ana ran into the room and tugged at Mercedes' skirt. 'I'm going to help bath the baby,' she said. The diva thought that Callas must have been dead for quite a while before she died. She blurred her brain with pills so that no one would know she wasn't really living. But *she* knew. A disc of her arias was in the player. The diva wanted to hear her sing Marguerite's lament from *Mefistofele*. She had always found it unbearably lucid in its rendition of pain.

'Oh, tell Vivien she can go,' she said. 'I'll be in in a minute.'

It was in that minute that it happened. Vivien had run the bath with hot water, while she turned down the baby's cot and laid out her little nightie. In the Dakota the water came hissing out of the taps as strongly as hot springs gushing up from the ground. It was rich people's water, always boiling, always instantaneous. The nanny knew that a minute for the diva was not exact, that it could stretch, become minutes, tens of minutes. She left the diva to run the cold.

Little Ana was eager to help. She ran through the hot steam without thinking, just liking the sting of it on her face. *Oh my darling, oh my darling, oh my darling Clementine*, she sang as she slipped the baby's clothes off and deposited her nappy in a plastic sack.

Maria gave her gloriously gummy smile. 'Uh, uh,' she grunted, cherub legs flailing.

Ana screamed when she realised she had lowered the baby into blisteringly hot water. She let go of her, paralysed with horror. 'Mama, Papa,' she shouted, and went on shouting when the words had ended. Her terrible cry resonated round the marble bathroom as the steam trickled down the walls.

Mercedes reached her first. She snatched Maria from the bath, heedless that she was plunging her arms into burning water. She felt it slosh over her chest, searing her skin. The baby was gasping. Her beautiful baby. Where were her eyes? These aching slits hardly to be seen in her puffed up flesh? Where was her baby? Where? Where? Where? Where?

In the car on the way to the hospital she watched numbly as Carlos tried to comfort his daughter. Ana was inconsolable. Mercedes wanted to reach out and touch the little girl but she was afraid to release her hold on Maria. She knew that the baby's raw red skin would melt away if she let go of her.

They took Maria from her in the hospital. Mercedes' breast was thumping with pain where the water had burned it. She began to shake uncontrollably when she saw the baby was gone from her. Carlos tentatively took her arm. When she did not push him away he led her to a chair.

'She will be all right,' he said. 'They can do anything these days.'

In the days and nights that followed Mercedes chanted the words to herself like a mantra ... *They can do anything. They can do anything* ... For hours and hours she and Ana sat in the intensive care ward. The little girl never said anything and she never left Mercedes' side. Carlos often left them there together. He offered to give up his performances but Mercedes felt he should go where he could do something. He seemed very far away to her. She wondered if she would need him again.

Other people's children had always seemed selfish, squalling, smelly little beasts to her. Now she found herself watching them in the hospital corridors. She felt relieved when she heard them clattering noisily along to the canteen or arguing about baseball.

'Yankees gonna cream you guys.'

The small Mets fan looked indignant. 'You couldn't cream my sister.'

'Mets are meatheads.'

Sometimes she and Ana went along to the crack unit, with its rows of addicted babies born to addicted mothers. The 'boarder babies', the nurses called them. Their pain had become a social problem to be solved, and therefore had the requisite care programme attached. People who felt guilty about having a lot would come along to help these children born with less than nothing. Mercedes would stand and watch the babies shivering in their cots, as their little bodies struggled to cope with the loss of the drug they had been born with. Around her, bankers and lawyers picked them up and cuddled them, but Mercedes didn't dare to. She just wanted to see babies surviving without the plastic tubes and drips that enmeshed Maria.

Most of the time, though, she sat in intensive care with her anxious little shadow, Ana. Behind the surgical mask all you could see were the child's beseeching eyes. Mercedes knew that the little girl's life would never be the same after this. They sat there day after day and watched the baby under her plastic bubble, talking gently to her to soothe her. There was no longer a delicate curve to her cheek. Her skin was lumpy now, red and mottled like raw mince.

It would be better for Ana, the diva knew, to go away from this, not to see this terrible damage. She was so young. But Mercedes could not deny her request to stay. She needed her there, knew she was the only one who could assuage the child's suffering. It cost her sometimes to make the effort of kindness, but the little girl's gratitude comforted her in return.

For much of the time the baby lay without moving or making a sound, but occasionally she would let out a little whimper and sometimes there would be a rasping noise in her throat as she struggled to breathe. Mercedes was always terrified when she heard it. She thought it must be the death rattle. Fear such as she had never known bombarded her then. It was a physical feeling, as if some intangible force was pounding away at her heart, forcing all the fluids in her body to drain away.

She could not bear the uncertainty of Maria's struggle for life. There in the cot she lay, surrounded by plastic and metal. It was all to make her comfortable, the temperature thermostatically controlled, everything that touched her sterilised. Only when she opened her eyes they seemed dumbfounded with pain, like the eyes of a suffering animal. She looked very alone.

Sometimes it seemed to Mercedes that she even understood this. She would look up and the bludgeoned look would be replaced with some kind of longing, with a kind of pleading. For what, Mercedes was not sure. For release? Or for comfort? After nine days the strain made her bold.

'Please,' she begged the nurse. 'Can't I hold her? Just for a moment?'

The nurse looked down at the baby. She looked sad. 'You might as well,' she said.

Mercedes lifted her daughter away from the coil of equipment and into her arms. She knew then. The baby's skin was warm and sticky with ointment. It felt rough against her hands. Mercedes took her mask off. She tried to smile. Her Maria looked up at her and sighed, as if she had been waiting for this all along. Then she died.

It was a full minute before Mercedes remembered Ana. She beckoned her little companion over.

'See,' she said. 'She's smiling.'

After the funeral Carlos took Ana home to Buenos Aires. It was unthinkable to let the little girl travel home on her own. The flat seemed dreary without them, but it satisfied Mercedes, the silence, the empty rooms. The marble floors stretched out endlessly, a desolate waste. She was entombed here, with her loss. She had never known a time so bereft of sound.

One night, as the city turned to dusk, she climbed up to the roof of the Dakota building. Up here, Tchaikovsky had stood where she stood and looked over the lights of the city. He had thought the whole building belonged to his host and that it was greater than the Czar's palace. She knew this man, knew his was music born of pain, of emptiness inside. Had he not started to compose at fourteen, the year his mother died?

It was time, she thought. She switched on her Walkman to listen to Maria Callas sing *L'altra notte in fondo al mare*, from Boito's *Mefistofele*. She needed to complete a cycle. The sky was electric blue, streaked in the distance with orange, but even as she listened it seemed to grow darker. The introduction to the aria was like great waves of blackness rolling through the twilight towards her. Just as she thought they would engulf her they would sweeten into a peaceful stretch, but always behind was the sound of dark strings, singing of madness and dread.

Callas' voice, when it came, was harsh with grief. The diva had always admired her ability to use the dark tones of the voice. She did not shrink from ugliness if it would express what she felt. The mystery for other singers was that on stage she had never been known to shed tears, but they were always there, in her voice. They were there now as she sang of her baby, drowned in the dark in the sea. There as she cried that, to send her mad, they blamed her.

Then the voice was bleak and lonely. The diva could feel the cold air and the sombre prison. Up here on the roof, with a city spread before her, she knew what it was to be trapped, to have no release from despair. She too wished her spirit to be like the sparrow, to fly, fly away. Callas' mastery of the coloratura was complete. The diva had heard many recordings that sounded stolid in comparison, from great singers who were not flexible enough to let the bird carry the notes away. With Callas you heard the little sparrow fluttering its wings, the soul rising in flight out of the dark wood.

Down below were cars and people and smells, noises that she could not hear. The lights of the city beckoned her but they were blurred. A track of salt ran down her face, scorching her cheek. The diva opened her throat to capture the warblings of the bird but she could not make any sound. All she could hear were her teeth chattering in her head. She did not think that she would ever sing again.

THE
FOUR MARYS

You Make Me Forget Everything

IT'S 3.50 IN THE AFTERNOON and her breasts are bare. This is not the norm for Mariana Scott, who has never so much as sunbathed topless, not even when her husband Crawford begged her to join him on the roof of the villa they'd rented in the Spanish desert.

'Don't be ridiculous. Of course no one can see,' he said, leering suddenly with a lop-sided grin that made him look like Charles Laughton in *The Hunchback of Notre Dame*. 'Except your doting husband, heh, heh, heh.'

'What about that crop-duster plane? It always seems to be zooming in low,' she said crisply, wondering if she'd made a mistake in marrying such an idiot. His humour became less charming by the minute, but maybe it was because she was hot and tired and in need of the siesta that was becoming her favourite part of the holiday.

'Well, give them something to zoom in for,' he said.

She'd shrugged. 'I'll pass ...'

Now she finds her state of semi-nudity to be not just thrilling and terrifying (given that it is in Professor Kalas' office and anyone could just walk in) but empowering. She despises the word, used mostly by ninnyish girls who think the height of female endeavour is to hold on to a man, but oh, she is glorying in the state. To be naked, if only from the waist up, and have the man she loves nuzzle her breasts, breathing her name as if making invocations to his goddess, makes her feel as if she can do anything. She is strong, beautiful, she could make men go to war over her, have them kneel and kiss her feet.

'Oh, Rahman,' she sighs, lingering over his name as if speaking it slowly will prolong this moment. Her fingers trace the fine planes of his cheekbones and nose. How delicate his features are, quite unlike Crawford's rugged looks. Other people find her husband handsome but for her he has become over-fleshy, his face broad as a boxer's, the slightly broken nose proclaiming him for the rugby player he was. That was the attraction probably, this large and powerful man towering over her, promising her adoration, security. He was big, he came from a wealthy family and he earned pots of money in his own right. Of course she thought she was in love with him.

'Are you sure he's the right man?' her father asked. 'You do seem to be falling into biological female patterns of mate selection. Crawford clearly offers both protection against predators and superb hunter-gathering skills.'

'You mean I think he's rich?'

'There seems to be little doubt about that, my dear,' said her father mildly, returning to his newspaper article on human genetics.

Rahman, Rahman is different. Crawford is solid and stolid, his brain as lumbering as his body, but Rahman has a mercury mind, always playful. 'Go to the window,' he whispers now in her ear.

'What, like this? I couldn't.'

'Yes, like this. I want the whole world to see my beautiful Mariana.'

His dark brown eyes stare fixedly at her as if compelling her to obey him. In one part of her brain she can hear her father saying this is pre-ordained animalistic behaviour, but in another she is dissolving and has the irresistible urge to do what he wants. As she moves to the window she sees a micro-smile flit across his face, so fugitive she's not even sure it was there. She stands at the window, looking down at the quadrangle, which is thronging with students and lecturers moving between classes. Rahman's skin brushes against her back, making a ripple of heat shiver up her spine. Down below, people meander along, in animated discussion with their companions, or else they scurry along heads down, bundles of books clamped to their arms. Few look up – and if they did, could they see?

Rahman's hands slide to her waist. 'Oh dear, we will have to move. My next appointment will be here soon. I think that's her down there.'

'You've got a four o'clock? Rahman, you bastard.'

Her eyelashes flutter closed as his tongue makes a silky invasion of her ear.

'It's your fault,' he says. 'You're so damn lovely you make me forget everything.'

Mariana jerks away from him and starts pulling on her bra and top. This is like a bloody French farce.

'Bastard,' she repeats, shaking her head. But once dressed she feels laughter fizzing up inside her as uncontrollably as an oil gusher blowing. He's laughing too, buttoning his shirt up with nimble fingers. She has rarely felt such simple joy.

'When will I see you again?' he asks.

'Never,' she says, and they both start laughing even more.

'Tomorrow.' It's not a question.

'Maybe.' She leaves rapidly, afraid his next appointment will see her here in the law department, where she's not a student. Having an affair when you're married is much too fraught and complicated for her ... She can't wait to see him again.

She heads down the staircase, holding on to the banister to avoid being knocked over by the stream of people coming up. Which of them is going to see him? Is it the dishevelled girl with earphones in? Or the fresh-faced young woman who keeps dropping her papers? Maybe it's the svelte older woman in the fitted black dress who's clipping upstairs in high heels as if she's heading for a cocktail party. Mariana sighs. She wishes she was his four o'clock.

She Will Not Be Meat

OCTOBER 2013

THE ROOM IS STUFFY AND CROWDED and the only place for Mariana to sit is next to Alice, a fellow PhD student she's seen in a couple of previous seminars. She's elegantly slim, the sort of girl who looks as though she should have a double-barrelled name, her long shiny brown hair clearly maintained by an expensive hairdresser. Mariana smiles briefly at her.

'Is this seat taken?'

'No, you're fine.'

Alice cocks her head to look at Mariana. 'Are you the one doing the thesis on Joan Baez?'

'Well, her Mary Hamilton song is in it, yes.'

'I adore that. I played it over and over when I was a teenager – my mother had it in her record collection. It's so beautiful, and her voice is so pure.'

Mariana tries not to sound surprised. 'Not many people our age know that song. I grew up with it.'

'Me too.'

'I was always told it was about a lady-in-waiting to Mary, Queen of Scots. She'd killed her baby because it was born out of wedlock. The story turned out to be total fiction but it's very sad, I think.'

'Mmm ... I know. Mummy banned me from playing it in the end. She said it made her sad, too. I think it reminded her of the past.'

'I hope not,' says Mariana. 'Infanticide and execution.'

'Oh yes, when you put it like that. But she was a child of the

Sixties, who knows what she got up to then?'

'She's still here, though, I take it?'

Alice's laugh is light and silvery. 'Of course, nothing that would get her hung.'

'Unless the Pope got to hear of it,' says Mariana drily.

The other girl's brow puckers. 'The Pope? I see ... oh, I see ... really ... you think she had an abortion? Is that what the song's all about?'

Oh God, what has she said? Think before you speak, Scott. 'It was just a joke. The Pope was against the pill and sex before marriage and all that. That's all I meant.'

'Was it?'

'No, really.'

'I do think it's infanticide, you know, abortion.'

'Good grief, I don't. Look, those women were the first to be able to terminate a pregnancy legally and safely, so yes, I suppose the song might have had that resonance for them, but that's not what I meant. Honestly.'

Alice's silky hair falls over her notebook as she writes in the date at the top of her page. 'Is that part of what you'll be talking about in the thesis?'

'I suppose so. *The Four Marys* ballad has been around for hundreds of years. It's inevitable that it'll mean different things to different generations. That's what inspired me to study it, really. I was arguing with a friend about the names of Mary, Queen of Scots' Four Marys and when I looked it up I discovered the song had changed several times over the centuries. There's no record of Mary having a lady-in-waiting called Mary Hamilton, and they think the original song might have been overlaid with a later woman's story. She killed her baby, too. She was a lady-in-waiting to Catherine the First of Russia and she and Tsar Peter the Great had an affair, so he thought the baby was his and was so angry that she'd got rid of his precious seed that he had her executed. She was decapitated.'

'How awful.'

'Yes, they kept her head as a curiosity in some museum, which may be how the story came back to Scotland. That's the sort of thing I'm going to investigate. The version Joan Baez sang is one where the setting has been changed from Edinburgh to Glasgow, so I've written to her to ask why she chose that one.'

'Wouldn't it be super if she wrote back?'

'Fingers crossed.'

Alice gives a bright smile but Mariana can see she's disturbed. Oh dear, how would *she* know if the woman's precious Mummy had an abortion? If only she'd kept her mouth shut. She'll have to remember in future to keep her theories to herself. People get so touchy about it, even today. Mariana hasn't even told Crawford about her own chequered history in that department, no point in risking it. She leans over and pats Alice's hand, instinctively wanting to comfort her. The other woman looks up, startled, but smiles back.

The door opens and a smartly dressed woman in a tight-fitting black dress comes in, pausing in the doorway as if by her very presence to impose silence on the room.

'Is *this* Professor Douglas?' Mariana's blood runs cold as she realises the woman is the svelte one she passed on the stairs down from Rahman's office. 'I thought that woman was in the law department?'

Alice perks up, ready to gossip. 'No, but she's the wife of one of the professors there. Professor Kalas, do you know him?'

'I met him at a party a while back, at one of those huge flats in the New Town. It even had its own gym in the basement. My husband has a lot of friends who're lawyers. But she wasn't with him that night.'

'No, she's been attached to some project in Canada. McGill University, I think.'

Professor Miriam Douglas stands erect, her petite frame and fine bones giving her the look of a ballet dancer. One of the postgrad students is giving her the usual introduction: leader in her field, glittering record of publications, the semiotics of traditional narrative, blah, blah, blah. All Mariana can take in is that her husband knew his wife was coming at four and got his mistress to pose, bare-breasted, at his window. My God, what on earth will the professor think of her? How could Rahman do that to her? She's going to have to work in this woman's department.

'She's ever so pretty, don't you think?' whispers Alice.

Mariana looks at the woman, dispassionately at first, then in dismay. She's perfectly lovely, the severe black bob as immaculate as a Japanese doll's, the elegance of her cheekbones echoed in the elegant cut of her dress. Why would her husband have an affair with another woman? What is wrong with men? Only when the professor begins to speak does Mariana realise that she's no longer young. The voice is incisive, cutting through the torpor of the room and emphasising the woman's authority.

There's a phrase Crawford's colleagues use of young flesh – 'fresh meat', they call it – and Mariana feels a sense of disgust rising in her gorge. Is that what she is to Rahman? Is he looking only for the silky caress of young skin, the moist elasticity of young limbs? In the foetid heat of the room, its air stale as car exhaust fumes, she feels as if she might faint. She is not meat. She will not be meat.

'Are you all right?' Alice's hand is on her arm.

'It's a little hot. I need to get some fresh air, I think.'

Alice is surprisingly practical, scooping up both their things and popping them into her holdall. 'Come on.' She levers Mariana up by her elbow.

'Do excuse us, Professor,' she says. 'My friend's unwell.'

Professor Douglas halts mid-sentence, a curious smile flitting across her face. She inclines her head imperiously towards Mariana, eyes lizard-cold. 'Of course. It's very hot in here.'

A male student leaps up to open the windows as Alice propels Mariana out of the room. The other students stare at them both.

'Thank goodness,' says Mariana when they reach the corridor. 'That was really kind of you. You should go back inside. You don't want to miss the professor's talk. She really is at the top of her field, isn't she?'

'Who knows?' shrugs Alice. 'It's not mine, anyway. These research seminars are interesting but not always useful, I find.'

Mariana sits down on the staircase. 'Why do they have them in such stuffy rooms? I bet they've had undergraduates in all day.'

'Undoubtedly. Smelly little boys and girls polluting the atmosphere for us.'

She's all right, this Alice, underneath the willy-wallachy exterior.

'Will we get a drink from the machine? You're probably dehydrated after the heat in there.'

They fiddle about for coins and between them manage enough for two tepid coffees. Mariana shoves the window open and sits back down on the stairs, absorbing the cool autumn air.

'He's super looking, don't you think?'

'Her husband?'

'Yes, Professor Kalas.'

'Mmm ...'

Inside the seminar room they can hear tentative questions and the professor's voice, dry and rasping as a cat's tongue, confidently steering the discussion.

'They have an open marriage, you know.'

'What do you mean? How on earth do you know that?'

'Everyone knows it. They're swingers.'

Mariana rubs her temples, wishing she had some paracetamol. Her head feels as if it's about to blow off, like a film she saw about Tchaikovsky, where statues were beheaded and earthbound objects swept up in swirling winds to the sound of the 1812 overture and its booming cannon. Da da da da da da da dum dum. POWWWWWWW. Swingers? Like cheesy suburbanites tossing their car keys into the fruit bowl and disappearing with each other's partners? Her beautiful Rahman?

'Yes,' continues Alice. 'There are others in the department too, you know.'

'They all seem very prim and proper.'

'Don't you believe it. A few glasses of red wine and they're at it like alley cats.'

'Are they on to the wine yet?'

Alice peers into the room. 'Just.'

Mariana leans her head against the banisters. She ought to leave before the seminar finishes but she's paralysed by the storm of emotions going on inside her. As she closes her eyes there's the sound of clicking heels and Professor Douglas comes out.

'My dear, you're still here.'

'Sorry, Professor. I was really looking forward to the talk. I think it was the heat of the room.'

The professor stands directly in front of her, as if contemplating something distasteful. She stares into Mariana's eyes, like a dominatrix, for God's sake. A thin ripple of sweat crawls down Mariana's spine.

'I do hope you feel better soon,' says the professor. Her kohl-lined eyes are malevolent as a cobra ready to strike.

Mariana can hardly breathe. 'Thank you,' she says, staring after the other woman as she heads off down the corridor towards the ladies' room.

'My goodness,' says Alice. 'What was that?'

'I don't know. Nothing.'

'Do you know her?'

Mariana shakes her head.

'Well, she looks as though she knows you.'

'She's probably just miffed that we left in the middle of her talk. Let's go.'

Mariana pulls herself up. She wants out of here before the professor comes back. She feels she's been given a warning.

Confined to a Cage

THERE WAS NO SPACE in this court life of ours, not a minute in the day when you could be free. At home I used to go for long walks across the moors. Mother would warn me to be careful or to take a heavy shawl with me but she never forbade me to go or said it was unbefitting our station.

Not that our station was so elevated. Since my father's death Mother had struggled to provide for our needs. Were it not for our powerful kinsman, we should have been beggars. He had always had a tenderness towards my mother and he allowed us to stay in our own house, paid for my education. How else would a father-less girl reach the heights of the Queen's service? But there was a price to pay for rising so high in the world. Your life belonged to the Queen, not to yourself. At court there was always something to be done: sewing or learning the latest dance or going out riding. I wearied of it sometimes.

One day when the Queen and Mary Beaton were discussing some Italian poem I slipped up to my chamber. I was tired, I don't know why, maybe the heat. I struggled to open the heavy casement but the strain in my arm was worth it when I felt the fresh air upon my face, the sunshine soothing my tired limbs.

I pushed a little morsel of apple into my pet linnet's cage. 'Oh Gabriel, I wish I could let you fly around outside as you should, but what would I do if you didn't return? I would have nothing left then to remind me of home.'

He cocked his little head to one side as if he understood what I was saying and released a storm of notes into the air.

'I agree with you,' I told him. 'Life is not fair. If it were fair, you and I would be out roaming the heath together.'

He jabbed at the fruit with his little beak. The taste must have pleased him for he burst into the sweetest song, his red chest going in and out like a bellows as he sang. I don't know how long I stood there listening to him before I heard voices outside and a tap on the door.

'May we come in?'

God save us, it was the Queen, with one of her women, no doubt. I rushed to open the door, curtseying to the floor as I did so.

'Why, little Hamilton, you have a pet bird,' said the Queen in that charming French accent she and the Four Marys spoke in. She and Mary Fleming swept into the room, the satin of their gowns rustling against the door.

'I nursed him from a fledgling, Ma'am. He had fallen from his mother's nest.'

'Aren't you kind?' She strode to the window and leaned out, gulping a good breath of air before turning to me. 'You are right, Mary Hamilton, why are we indoors on such a day as this? Let the sunshine pour in, let us savour the Lord's good air.'

Her eyes, bright and curious as ever, studied the room, noting the plain checked blanket on the bed, the lack of ornament. 'I must let you have a red satin coverlet I have – you know the one I mean, cousin? And the tapestry of roses I had from France. That would bring some colour into the room, would it not?'

'Aye, it would,' said Mary Fleming, giving me that grin of hers as if she'd always known me. 'I'll make sure Mistress McEwan brings them up.'

I was overwhelmed by the Queen's generosity. How kind she was to those who served her. She sat down on my bed, making a little face as if it wasn't to her liking. Probably too hard for her.

'I can see why you chose to come and listen to the linnet,' she said. 'Our poetry discussion bored you, I fear.'

'I am just a little tired, Ma'am.'

'Ha, look at the child's face. She cannot lie, even to her monarch.'

Mary Fleming smiled. 'She was not alone, cousin. Only you and Mary Beaton find terza rima a compelling subject of conversation.'

'Ouf, I cannot help it if you are all ignoramuses,' said the Queen. She wandered to the open window. 'You have a fine view here, little Hamilton. I have not been in this room before.'

'Yes, Ma'am. Arthur's Seat is very beautiful.'

'Who put you here? Was it Mary Seton? I swear she has not forgiven me for besting her at cards last week – my view overlooks the kitchen garden,' said Mary Fleming, with a comic grimace on that lively face of hers.

'For shame. It is you who is the competitive one,' said the Queen. 'You know you cannot bear to lose. If you were not of royal blood, I'd wager you cheated, my dear Mary.'

Mary Fleming giggled. 'Mary Seton is so pious she'd never conceive that I might give the cards a helping hand.'

The Queen laughed. 'You are shameless. I expect you're shocked at such perfidy, are you not, Mary?'

I shook my head firmly. I had wondered at Mary Fleming's run of luck last week but hearing this only made me love her all the more. Mary Stuart turned to the linnet, pursing her lips as if to join in the bird's song. 'You are like me, little bird. Confined to a cage. You are not free to follow your heart.'

Mary Fleming's laughter was so loud that a nobleman walking in the grounds below looked up at our window. 'You are the freest woman in all Scotland. You can do exactly as you wish, while ordinary women like the little Hamilton and I must obey your every whim. We cannot even choose who we will marry.'

'With that sharp tongue of yours you will never marry.' The Queen's tone was imperious, but the corners of her mouth turned up in amusement.

'Wait and see, cousin.'

'Don't wait too long, *ma chère*, or that old man of yours will not be able to shift his withered shanks in the wedding chamber.'

'Shh.' Mary Fleming looked uneasily in my direction, but I'd have had to be deaf and blind not to know of her elderly suitor, Sir William Maitland of Lethington, the Queen's Secretary of State. It was clear why he would love such a pretty and vivacious young woman as Mary Fleming, but what on God's earth did she see in him? Why, he was forty years old! She was right, though. We women had no freedom in such matters. Even the Queen was being criticised for choosing Henry Darnley to be her husband. I knew when it was my turn that the choice would not be made on a pair of romantic dark eyes or a fine turn of leg. Nor would it be mine.

'Don't sigh, little one,' said the Queen. 'Sometimes we poor women can break free of our chains.' She glanced at her cousin. 'What do you say? Will we venture into the town?'

Mary Fleming bit her lip, uneasy for some reason. 'Oh, Marie,' she said, using the French form of the name, as all Four Marys and their Queen often did. 'You take so many chances. You know the people would not approve if they were to find out.'

'You mean Mr Knox would not approve. Well, I say fiddlesticks to him and all his ilk. Who is the Queen here?'

Her colour was high, her temper too. I could not understand why the two of them were so agitated till my beloved Mary Fleming nodded at me and said, 'The little Hamilton will never pass for a man.'

'For a man?' The shock on my face made the other two burst out laughing.

'You are right, cousin. This little girl shows everything on her face. You will have to be stern if you are to be a *man*.' She said the word as if it were a joke.

'You are one to talk. There were tears in your eyes in front of all the court when you listened to those madrigals last week.'

Something in me stirred. I was shocked but intrigued, too. What an adventure to be a man, if only for an afternoon, though in my head I heard my mother's voice. I hope Queen Mary doesn't try to introduce her fancy French ways here. Somehow I didn't think dressing as a man was the norm for French women.

'What will we wear?'

'Come, we've done this before, when Mary Livingston was with us. Now you really will be one of the Four Marys,' said Mary Fleming.

We went downstairs to the Queen's apartments, where Mary Fleming delved into an ottoman, drawing out several pairs of curious looking loose trousers with a drawstring at the waist.

'What are those?' I asked.

Mary Fleming giggled. 'Don't you know? They're braies, men's undergarments.'

'Oh my God.' I crossed myself, embarrassed to look upon them.

'Come on, try them.' said Mary Stuart. 'They feel good.'

I turned away from her and Mary Fleming, who started to laugh again. 'Look how shy she is.'

'She's young,' said the Queen, 'not an old boiling fowl like you.'

The braies were made of fine lawn and felt soft against my skin. It was a curious feeling, though, to be wearing garments made for a man. I was uneasy, though I must confess it made me tingle inside, too. Was it because I was imagining a quite different body from what lay underneath my own garments?

'She'd best keep her bodice on,' said Mary Fleming. 'No young man I know has a chest like this wee pouter pigeon.'

Mary Stuart didn't wait for us to undress her but threw off her own petticoats. 'No more stiff bones, no more bum roll to irritate you. How sweet does this feel, Mary Hamilton?' She made a fine young man, was taller than many. Her breasts, though finely formed, were not large, and when she put on a saffron shirt such as the common men wear, they disappeared altogether. Mary Fleming stood behind her and pulled out the pins in her hair, releasing a torrent of red, shot through with gold. Such beautiful hair, fit for a queen.

'That won't do,' frowned Mary, rummaging in the ottoman till she found several large caps. 'You'll need one, too,' she said to me, 'though I don't know how we're going to disguise those sparkling eyes.'

'Or that little button nose,' said the Queen.

'*Retroussé*,' corrected her cousin.

'*Bien sûr, retroussé*. It is not a man's nose, I think.' Her own was long and handsome and could have graced a man's face as readily as a woman's.

'Keep your cap pulled down. Both of you.'

The Queen curtseyed. 'Yes, Ma'am.'

Mary Fleming turned to me, her face serious. 'Now remember, Mary, there must be no curtseying when we are outside.'

The long heather-coloured coats that covered our bodies were rough, though not unpleasantly so. I pulled the cap down low over my face, as much to hide my blushes as my hair. Pausing only to collect some coin, the Queen led the way out of the palace, through the great iron gates and into the Canongate. We were nearly run over by a carter heading towards the London road.

No one looked twice at the three of us as we walked up the hill. They must have thought we were the Queen's servants – as two of us were. Mary Stuart was taller than most of the men we passed, her stride confident; Mary Fleming sauntered along, enjoying the sport. I was tentative at first but it was comfortable wearing men's clothes and soon I was striding out as freely as they. I just wished I could have shed my tight bodice, it was so fine to walk in the sunshine without restraint.

A gust of beer and loud laughter came from a tavern we passed. Mary Fleming made a panting noise as if to say she was dying of thirst. The Queen glanced at me.

'Well, little Hamilton, do you think you are bold enough? Could you brave all those men and ask for a beer?'

'I?' I was amazed, but excited too and determined to show them that I had as much courage as anyone. 'Men hold no fears for me.'

'Well, you can't use your usual wiles in there,' pointed out Mary Fleming.

'Yes, no little smiles from under your lashes, no long gazes,' said the Queen. 'Stride, Hamilton. Stride.'

I was about to protest that I did none of those things but I was hot and thirsty and took the coin she held, marching into the tavern with a straight back. The landlord simply nodded without looking at me when I asked for a tankard of ale, employing the deepest tones I could. On the way back I kept my face severe and found that the men around me made way and let me through if I gave no ground. Had they realised I was a woman they would have teased me and tried to block my path so that I would look at them, but it seemed they were not interested in looking at members of their own sex, but saved their gaze for us women.

The cousins cheered when I brought the tankard out to them. Oh, it was the sweetest drink ever I had, cold and thick with foam. We passed it around among us, standing out on the Canongate, with the sun seeping into our skin like honey into bread. The Queen patted my shoulder and Mary Fleming winked at me over the rim of the tankard and I truly felt one of them.

That's not Living

OCTOBER 2013

MARIANA LOOKS WITH DISTASTE at the table centrepiece, wondering when she became allergic to red roses. She always thought it the most romantic thing in the world when her father gave them to her mother on Valentine's Day. Now they look overblown to her, vulgar, clogging up her nostrils with their heavy scent. She'll have a headache before the night's out, she can tell.

'Prosecco?' says a voice in her ear. Fraser's wife, Elizabeth, is splashing expensive wine into a flute for her. With a lifestyle as groomed and smooth as her straightened hair, she's one of those placid women who make Mariana feel chaotic. Will she ever achieve this level of poise?

'Thank you,' she says, accepting the glass, though the first sip tastes sour. She'd better eat something soon. Oh good, the caterer comes in bearing a tray of canapés – tiny mushroom and goat's cheese tartlets, prawns in tempura, miniature stuffed vine leaves. She must be careful. Last time they came here for dinner she was up half the night with indigestion, the food was so rich.

'You're looking very student-y,' says Elizabeth, startling Mariana till she realises she's the only woman there not in a little black dress. Her hostess' fleeting moue of disapproval matches the one she saw on her husband's face earlier, when *he* saw her in the dress. Its wispy layers of smoky grey linen and chiffon were ferociously expensive, so she's not sure why it's so unacceptable.

'Boho chic,' she says firmly, as though that's an end to the matter.

Elizabeth's eyebrows hover somewhere near her fringe. *If she's not careful they'll stick like that.* Mariana resists the temptation to snigger. Since when has her mother's voice invaded her head? Not that she's an unwelcome visitant. Elizabeth is exactly like those snotty girls at school who made Mariana's life misery with their comments about her mended jumpers, her secondhand blazer. Although she is unfailingly polite, there's a touch of condescension about her attitude that makes Mariana itch to stick a cream pie in her face. *Remember what side your bread's buttered.* Yes, all right, Ma.

'How are you enjoying the student life?' asks Fraser's sister, Helen, a miniature clone of Elizabeth, except that her salon-straightened hair is brown and not blonde.

'I love it,' says Mariana. 'My subject is so interesting.'

'*So interesting.*' What is that squawking sound? Is someone making fun of her, echoing her words in a Dalek voice? Mariana eases her head round and makes out a green parrot in a cage in the corner of the room. It's ruffling its feathers as though it's just woken up. That's all she needs. Those stupid birds are always giving people psittacosis.

Helen's eyes drift past her to Crawford. She's always had a thing about him. 'Oh, really?' she says.

'Yes.' Mariana's not going to let her off the hook. 'It's all about the ballad of *The Four Marys*, you know Mary, Queen of Scots' attendants?'

'Mmm ...'

'You maybe know the Joan Baez version?'

'Of course.'

Mariana's pretty sure she doesn't – that Helen's musical education came to a halt at Spandau Ballet. 'Well, of course it's historically inaccurate as none of the Four Marys had an illegitimate baby or was hanged. Mind you, the Queen had a French maidservant who murdered her baby. She and her lover, who was an apothecary to the Queen, were both executed for it.'

'*To the Queen. To the Queen.*' Why doesn't that bloody parrot listen to someone else? It's giving her a headache.

'Oh, is that the sort of thing you get a degree for these days?'

'I have a degree, actually. This is post-graduate work.'

'I should think that would cost a pretty penny in fees,' says their host Fraser, one of Crawford's ex-team mates.

'Chicken feed to Crawford,' says Mariana tartly.

'*Chicken feed. Chicken feed.*'

Crawford gives his big hearty laugh. 'Anything that keeps the little woman happy.'

Fraser puts down his glass of Prosecco and snaps his fingers at the caterer. 'Bring me a Scotch, would you? I've had enough of this, might as well be drinking Irn Bru. How about you, Crawford?'

'Aye. Quickly, before I turn into a girl.'

Helen's silvery laugh trills out. 'You'd need some powerful black magic to manage that, Crawford.'

He grins at her, complacent – and complicit – in her admiration.

'*Highland Park* do you?' asks Fraser, not waiting for Crawford's reply. 'Hey, Rob, how about you?'

The men in the room abandon their glasses and cluster round the whisky bottle. Did they all play rugby together? With their casual closeness they certainly look like a team, but maybe it's just male bonding. Mariana looks for a refill. This is going to be a long night.

'Did you hear about Christine? She got the townhouse *and* the cottage.'

'*The townhouse and the cottage.*' Heavens, the stupid bird's voice grates on her nerves like nails scraping along a blackboard.

'I should think so, too. The number of women he had. Poor Christine was a laughing stock for years. She deserves a bit of compensation.'

'Why on earth do women stay with unfaithful men? I don't understand it,' says a drab woman with a face like cheese strings.

'They're all unfaithful,' says Helen. 'Look at Christine now – it was worth it.'

'I don't think so,' insists the woman. Elizabeth's stare says clearly that she can't imagine this dreary creature even having a man, still less holding on to one. 'No man's worth being humiliated like that.'

'That's not living, is it?' chips in Mariana, enjoying the irritated look on Helen's face. 'Life is about passion, not the price of property.'

'Not the price of property.' The bird shuffles around in its cage, hopping from one foot to another as if preparing to launch into a dance.

'Going to go up eighteen per cent in Edin in the next five years,' says one of the men. 'Good time to invest in a home-to-let or whatever.'

The caterer taps a little triangle. 'Dinner is served, ladies and gentlemen,' she says. Hooray! Thank goodness, no more parrot screeching. Why did no one else appear to notice? Are they all so used to the bird or is it just Edinburgh manners?

They troop through to the dining room, its brilliant rosewood table gleaming with formal place settings – and roses, more of those damn roses. How long before they all suffocate from the scent? Mariana is sat next to Helen on one side and a chap from a big accountancy firm which specialises in handling other firms' bankruptcies on the other. Crawford is opposite Helen, so she'll no doubt focus all her attention on him, leaving Mariana to the tedious accountant.

The food is exactly the kind Mariana hates, posh Sunday dinners. Her heart sinks at the Vichyssoise starter. Whoever heard of cold soup? As for the roast beef – pink? Why, it's positively oozing blood. Mariana likes meat well enough but hates being reminded it's the flesh of dead animals. Crawford attacks his with gusto.

Around her the talk is of money and property, property and money. It's as bad as the damn parrot.

'Johnny and Amanda have split up, did you hear?'

'She's determined to hold on to the Forres Street townhouse.'

'Well, she's done so much to it.'

'He'll want the cash. That new girlfriend of his is very high maintenance.'

'I think they'll get one and a half for it.'

'Oh, easily. Georgie sold her place in Heriot Row and she made a million two.'

'Really?'

'Well, they're like Tardises, those places.'

Out of the corner of her eye, Mariana sees the pudding being brought in. Oh God, îles flottantes, tooth-scouring sugar breasts floating in a sea of sick.

'Excuse me.' She rises from the table, discreetly asks the waitress the way to the ladies' room. Once in the hall she expels a long relieved breath. Why is she finding this so tiresome tonight? She knew what she was getting into when she married Crawford, went to enough boring parties before she finally hooked him, but tonight she wants to take a flamethrower and run amok in that stuffy dining room. Gratefully she locks the bathroom door behind her. The usual beige marble wall tiles. If she didn't know better she'd think they came with a special New Town discount, along with the gilt-framed paintings and woven rugs they all have. Opening the window, she perches on the Philippe Starck bath and gulps in air from outside as she takes out her mobile phone.

'Darling, where are you?' She can barely hear him, he's talking so quietly.

'At some dull dinner party. Where are you?'

'At some dull dinner party.'

'Why didn't you tell me you and your wife were *swingers*?' She spits the word out, aware he probably thinks she's childish but not caring. It's so tawdry. How could he get involved?

'That is not the word I'd use.'

'No, what would you call it then?'

'My wife and I have an open marriage. That is all. I imagine you have a similar arrangement yourself.'

'An open marriage? Of course I don't. Crawford would kill me if he found out.'

'How exciting for you, darling. It raises the stakes that little bit higher, no?'

'Oh God, Rahman. How can you talk like that? It's not a game.'

'Oh, but it is, my darling. All of life is a game.'

'So that's all I am to you, is it? A toy?'

'That's not what I said.'

She wants to touch his skin, see his face. She knows she should go inside to her husband and his friends but she just wants Rahman to put his arms round her, tell her she's the only one for him. Bleakly she stares at the brick wall outside the bathroom. He is the only one for her.

Chosen by a King

THERE WAS A FULL MOON, the night of the banquet, the night I was chosen by a king. Mother says fools and madmen come out on the night of the full moon but Lord Henry is the most goodly looking madman I have seen. Still, he was a fool to pay court to me, when he was consort to a queen. Queen Mary has as warm and giving a spirit as you could wish for, but when you scratch beneath the exterior she is, after all, a monarch, and will brook no flouting of her will. Perhaps it is I who was the mad one.

We were in Dumfries earlier that day. I weary of our travels. Two weeks here, a week there, first chasing the rebel lords who disapproved of the Queen's choice of husband and then just moving about the kingdom so that the people could see their Queen. It is as well she does not have to do the packing herself, for there is so much a royal personage must bring with her – silver plates to eat off and gold drinking vessels, red velvet cushions, Turkey carpets, tapestry wall hangings, books, fur coverlets for the royal bed. Ah, that is something I covet.

I attend only to her garments and that in itself is exhausting enough. She has endless dresses and petticoats, bodices and mantels, stockings and shoes. Such plenty makes her generous – that day she gave me a pair of sleeves for my new violet gown. It's a most beautiful colour, rich as the midnight sky. The sleeves were violet too, inlaid with little seed pearls.

'You must have them,' she said. 'They match perfectly.'

I'm sure she didn't intend to give me her husband, too.

He's such a handsome man, Darnley, with skin like a lassie's and a soft mouth that makes me want to kiss him and kiss him and never stop. But that day in Dumfries the Queen wasn't thinking of him, though they were barely two months married. Her eyes were only for Bothwell, a different sort of man altogether. Some would say manlier, though to me that just means rougher. I prefer Lord Henry and his gentle ways, but the Queen was as one bewitched with Bothwell, though all they were talking about was politics, and how he was to support her against the rebel lords.

She was tired when we arrived at Lochmaben Castle and went straight to her bedchamber to rest before the banquet. Mary Beaton had asked me to sing during the entertainment after dinner, so I went looking for a music room. There was a little chamber with some virginals near the Great Hall, so I slipped in there to practise. *Crow and Pie* was what I would sing, a new ballad that the Queen had expressed a desire to hear. Usually she preferred her songs from the French court but there was something in that one which intrigued her.

'So Magpie has his way with Madame Crow?'

'Yes, Ma'am.'

'Yet the knave will not marry her.'

'No, Ma'am, she has refused him too often.'

She tilted her head to one side. 'Yes, I think 'tis true. Be too haughty with a man and he will strive to bring you down.'

'No man would dare do such with a Queen,' I said, folding away her sleeves and placing them in the chest.

'I wonder,' she said, looking thoughtful. Mary Fleming, who was bringing out a nightgown for her, caught my eye from the other side of the room and we both smiled. When Mary Stuart had that look on her face it meant she was plotting something, though surely there was nothing to plot when she had the bonniest lad in Scotland for her ane self?

I was trying to perfect my singing of the ballad, which has a tricky line in the verse, when he came into the room. I struggled to my feet.

'I am sorry, your grace. Am I not supposed to be here?'

'I would wish you nowhere else,' he said. 'That beautiful voice has enticed me in. Please do not stop on my account.'

Something in the way he smiled made my cheeks burn, but I was determined he should not see my embarrassment and simply inclined my head in the courtly manner with which I had seen Mary Seton acquiesce to the Queen's requests. This made him splutter with laughter.

'Come now, you're too saucy a wench for such stiff ways,' he said.

'Saucy? I?'

'Oh yes, you're just like your predecessor, Mary Livingston. I think I see something of her lightness of manner in you.'

I was dismayed – Mary Livingston had been known in court as 'The Lustie', and that fierce preacher John Knox had accused her of being with child at the time of her wedding, though Mary Fleming said it wasn't true. She was safely married now, and away with her husband in Perthshire, out of scandal's way. She liked the lively life of the court and often came back, but was no longer there all the time. That was how I came to be in the Queen's service.

'I need four true Maries around me,' she had joked – any lady in waiting to the Queen was called a marie.

'I will be true,' I'd said, curtseying, a vow I remembered now when Lord Darnley was being familiar with me.

'I am Mary Hamilton, but I am light neither in thought nor deed,' I told him. 'I strive to keep the Lord's commandments.'

He leaned in close to me. 'I am your Lord. You will then carry out my commandments?'

'Sir, you torment me. It is unkind.'

'God knows, I mean only to be kind to you. Continue your song, Mary Hamilton. I will sit here and worship at the altar of your music.'

There was nothing for it then but to oblige him, and I took a certain pleasure in the lines:

> *She answered me all yn scornyng,*
> *And sayd, The crowe shall byte yow.*

He seemed undaunted by the message I was sending him. 'I thought my wife, the Queen, had a fine voice, but I swear yours is lovelier still.'

When I reached the part where the Magpie offers the Crow a velvet purse and a good gold ring, Lord Darnley burst out laughing.

'How cruel she is to refuse such a generous offer. I swear you would not use a man so.'

'You are mistaken, my lord,' I said, though he had such a charming laugh that I was sore tempted to laugh, too. He must have read that in my eyes, for he tilted my face up by the chin.

'I do not make mistakes about the ladies,' he boasted. I did not doubt him.

That night, I was so nervous about singing in front of the court I could scarce eat of the banquet, though I had never seen such an array of food – the fields and forests must have been plundered for miles around. Haunches of venison, sides of beef, a whole pig turned on the spit, hundreds of brace of wood pigeon. The Queen's French chefs had prepared exquisitely smooth sauces and pastry so light Mary Fleming said you could float to heaven on it, but I could not eat, only pick at a little fish and sip some sweet wine to calm my stomach when the tables were voided.

We had been in larger great halls than Lochmaben, but still, it was dauntingly vast, and I feared my little voice would float off into its high beams or be trapped in the fine tapestry hangings. In the light of the flaming torches all round the walls, the women's silk gowns shimmered with a greater lustre, their eyes gleaming with unwonted softness. People had drunk deep of the Queen's good burgundy wine and were eager to enjoy the entertainment, though personally I think they might not have laughed so hard at the royal fool, Nicola Ambruzzi, had they only drunk cider – all those stupid puns and riddles. But the jugglers were so fast you could scarce follow their flashing hands and the masque welcoming the royal party to Annandale was beautiful, a feast of gold-embroidered costumes and animal masks showing the Queen's daring in the hunt. The dancers represented horses, a hawk, fleeing wildfowl, the terror of the chase embodied in the tiniest of movements. I am sure it was Mary Seton who played the Queen – she is the only woman tall enough to pass for her, though she does not have her upright bearing. Something happens in a room when Mary Stuart is in it and I swear it is not just because we all know she is our monarch.

When the singing started there was a sense of relaxation. Courtly entertainments are very fine but they're like roasted swan, too rich for many, I believe. But a song, why, the poorest cottager can take part in singing. Alas, that means that they can all judge, too. When the Fool announced my name, I almost swooned with nerves.

'The latest marie to come to court,' she cried. 'You can see from those flashing black eyes that the Queen considers she has not enough trouble in her life. She could have had some peace when lustie Mary Livingston married, but that was too dull for our great lady.'

The Queen shook her head but you could see she was amused, and everyone else in the great hall was laughing out loud. Was I so lacking in modesty? What did these people know about me that I did not know about myself? The Fool pirouetted ahead of me, fluttering her eyelashes over her fan and simpering at all the gentlemen we passed.

'Ladies, when Mary Hamilton sings, you had best look to your husbands.'

I wanted to die of shame, but I was angry too. What right had the dwarf to mock me? I had given her no cause to think me anything other than virtuous. That she was in the Queen's employ gave her the right to make fun of her employer, not of a fellow servant.

My fury gave me strength. I strode to the virginals as though *I* was the Queen there, not Mary Stuart. And truth to tell, when I sang, I felt as powerful as her, that my lungs would never run empty, as though I could move everyone who heard me to tears. Few people were familiar with the ballad. A crow is accosted by a magpie but refuses to yield to him, whatever he offers, so he forces her to lie with him. At the end, though, she will not be vanquished by him.

> *Thoughe a knave hathe by me layne,*
> *Yet am I noder dede nor slowe;*
> *I trust to recouer my harte agayne,*
> *And Crystes curse goo wythe yow!*

I sang my defiance at all of them as the crow sings hers to the man who has violated her. I had no fear of my voice failing or of not being heard. I reckoned they could hear me as far as Holyrood. At the end the sound of their clapping was deafening. The Queen herself stood to applaud.

'Again!' she said. 'I would hear of this crow once more. Ladies, she has much to teach us.'

This time when I sang I could see her saying some of the words with me. She was ever a quick study. It made me think, though, if a Queen took courage from the poor crow, then how much more would an ordinary lass like me need in dealing with the men around the court? For a moment my heart failed me, but so many people smiled at me and told me I'd done well that that dark thought faded.

I was exhausted when the evening was done and could barely stand to help the Queen disrobe. She saw how tired I was and called Mary Fleming.

'Cousin, I can see my little marie is too fatigued after her efforts, would you help me instead?'

'She's not yet grown into her strength,' said Mary Fleming. She was as kind as she was lively and I loved her as much as I loved Mary Stuart. 'Run along, little one. You sang well tonight. You deserve your sleep.'

I could barely keep myself from yawning – in front of the Queen! – as I curtseyed and thanked her. The low murmur of their laughter followed me down the stair as I went to my bed-chamber and I thought how lucky I was to be in the service of such a generous Queen.

Barely minutes after falling into bed I was asleep, the bright light of flaming torches dancing behind my eyes. I don't know how long I slept then but I woke in the dark feeling empty. I had had so little to eat that night that my stomach was griping. Pulling my shawl round me I crept downstairs. I knew there would be food left in the big presses in the kitchens. Would it be regarded as stealing if I were to take something from them? I was so hungry that in that moment I did not care.

The kitchen boy was dozing beside the spent fire when I entered. He started up, looking befuddled and a bit shy when he saw it was me. I gave him my best smile.

'Rab, I am so hungry. Could I beg a little piece of pie or some nuts, anything to keep my stomach from aching? I couldn't eat at the banquet.'

He seemed as one in a trance, his eyes never leaving mine. 'You were so beautiful, my lady. In the song, I mean.'

'I will see your master tomorrow and tell him I bade you give me it.'

His pale face shimmered with doubt but another glance from me sent him shrugging to one of the presses, where he slid out a plum pie. 'Here, Mistress Mary, have some of this.'

The plums were so sweet, the pastry as light as Mary Fleming had said, and all of it topped with a creamy custard. I closed my eyes as I took a bite, it was so delicious.

'You have saved my life, Rab,' I told him. 'Go back to sleep. I promise I will make this good in the morning.'

I went outdoors with my treat, breathing deeply of the night air. A pall of woodsmoke lingered in the kitchen garden from the cooking earlier, but it only made the air sweeter. Riding high over everything was the full moon, sending silvery light glancing over the rows of herbs. I ate the pie slowly, savouring every mouthful of the meltingly sweet confection, with its tart fruit and rich sauce. Sighing with pleasure, I licked my fingers clean. I could have eaten it all over again.

I was just about to step back inside when I heard the low sound of a man laughing.

'Oh, Mary Hamilton, do you enjoy all your pleasures so wholeheartedly?'

I recognised the soft tones of Lord Henry, slightly slurred now, as if he had drunk deeply of the wine.

'You startled me,' I said.

'I would not do that for the world, my little turtle dove. I have other things in mind for you.'

'You can forget your other things, my lord. I serve only the Queen.'

His eyes gleamed in the moonlight. 'What a stern little piece you are. A pity, though, that those roguish eyes and rosy lips belie your words.'

'They do not.'

He took a step closer. 'Oh, but they do, my lady.'

There was a weight on my chest, suffocating me, making me

struggle for breath. The King took a step closer. He ran his hand down my hair. 'How pretty you are with your hair loose. I would see all the women of the court with their locks tumbled about them.'

'You would see a lot of things that are not meet.'

His voice was like syrup. 'I would.'

Suddenly I was afraid, not that Lord Henry would force me to do anything, but that he would not have to.

Chinese Whispers

NOVEMBER 2013

INKY BLACK WATER caressing her limbs, enfolding her in its embrace ... Down here the darkness glows, seduces. She slips through the currents, past shoals of tiny fishes, their fins tickling her in the dark. Black fronds of seaweed brush her leg and once her skin is grazed by a barnacled rock, but the water slides over it, smoothing away the pain. On she swims, and on, till at length she becomes aware of a creature gliding beside her. Is it a dolphin? A shark?! No, it's all right, it's a seal, its blunt nose powering through the water, its clumsy body become elegant in its true element.

They journey together through underwater caverns blossoming with exotic plants, onwards past myriad-coloured coral reefs. After a while the water becomes grey and turbulent, snatching them up and depositing them yards on from where they started. All the time the waves are becoming higher and stronger and they struggle to keep going, even her seal companion gasping for breath as the water continually buffets them. Finally they're caught up in a massive barrier of water twelve feet high and are powerless to do anything as it rolls towards the shore. What will happen? Will they die?

As the great wave hangs poised above the shore, they flounder in a maelstrom of foam and green water, bodies pumping in the effort to keep upright. Crash, the cataract of water smashes on to the sand, tossing them on to the beach like worthless jetsam.

Mariana turns to see if her companion has survived but the seal has turned into a baby, his pearly skin wreathed in seaweed and tiny shells, his little legs and arms pistoning as if trying out the world.

A baby! Mariana wakes, sweating. She couldn't be pregnant, could she?

'Eh? Eh? What's the matter?' She must have thrashed about in bed and woken Crawford.

'Nothing. Go back to sleep. I just had a bad dream.'

He grunts and falls back on to the pillow, eyes instantly closed. She looks for a minute at his tousled hair, his chest gently moving up and down. Sighing, she slides out of bed. Although her dressing gown is cosy – her mother-in-law pressed a cashmere mix on her last Christmas when she had hoped for something more glamorous – the rest of the flat seems cold. She heads for the kitchen, where the Aga radiates its comforting heat all night. Tea, she needs tea. As she waits for the kettle to boil she investigates the fridge. Crawford's usual collection of cooked meats takes up half the shelf space, his bacon and eggs the other. Are there no pickles? She rummages around at the back, her cheek grazing a pulpy packet of bacon, groping till her fingers close over a jar. Good, she knew there were some gherkins there.

It's as if she can't get enough vinegar. She sits at the kitchen table, steadily crunching her way through the whole lot. It's six in the morning and she wants to cram her mouth with food, stuff cake and crisps and sun-dried tomatoes (sun-dried tomatoes? she never eats them) down her throat. It's such an odd sensation that for a second the thought she might be pregnant prickles in her again, but no, it's not possible. She's been bleeding for two days. Probably just some weird hormonal urge.

Four hours later, climbing the stairs to her tutor's room at the top of the building, she's feeling a little nauseous. Breakfast of pickles, pâté, strawberry jam and left-over trifle is not the best start to a day she's ever had. The room is small but has a view across the city to Fountainbridge. If it weren't such a warm day she might feel better, but the magnificent vista in front of her does not affect her desire to throw up.

Dr Annie McNeil looks at her over the top of her trendy glasses. 'Looking a bit rough today, Mariana. Are you all right?'

'I feel as if I have a hangover, but I haven't had anything to drink.'

'That's definitely the worst kind of hangover to have,' says the tutor, in her melodious Highland accent. 'Much better to have had the fun first. I'll make you some nice sweet tea.'

Mariana almost manages to smile. 'Did you get the essay all right?'

'Oh yes, most interesting, Maria Danilovna Gamentova, the Russian Mary Hamilton ...'

'This is just a preliminary sketch, really. I'm hoping to get more information. There's a Russian academic working at the University of York who I'm hoping will help me. But do you really think it's possible that a Russian story from nearly a century and a half later could be overlaid on to the original *Four Marys* ballad?'

'Definitely. It's a little like Chinese whispers, you know? You say one thing and it comes out as something else when the next person passes it on.'

'Like singing the wrong words to a pop song? I'm one of the idiots that thought Jimi Hendrix was singing *'Scuse me, while I kiss this guy* instead of *'Scuse me, while I kiss the sky.'*

The tutor laughs. 'I'm the same. For years I sang, *The cattle are blowing the baby away* instead of, *The cattle are lowing, The baby awakes.'* She pours the tea into china mugs decorated with heather and heaps sugar into Mariana's.

'Thanks. You know, I find Gamentova's story really upsetting. I keep dreaming of drowning babies and heads being cut off.'

'Is that why you're looking so peaky? A bit of academic distance, Mariana, that's what you need.'

'I know,' sighs Mariana, 'but it's such a terrifying way to end your life. There's a very touching Russian painting of her on the day of her execution and she looks terrified.'

'She also looks really pretty, if I remember correctly,' says Annie.

'Yes, she has on a white gown, which of course is mentioned in quite a few versions of the ballad of *The Four Marys*.'

Annie goes to the bookshelves and pulls down a thick, leather-bound book, her copy of *Child Ballads*. She leafs through till she finds what she's looking for.

> *I winna put on my robes o black,*
> *Nor yet my robes o brown;*
> *But I'll put on my robes o white,*
> *To shine through Edinbro town.*

The words sound stately and exotically antique, voiced in Annie's Barra accent, though the tutor looks anything but antique in her short skirt and purple tights, her spiky blonde hair.

'The dress is beautiful in the painting,' says Mariana. 'All ruffles and trailing sleeves.'

'Och, don't you wish we could wear frocks like that sometimes?'

'They're lovely but I don't think I'd like to be treated the way women were then.'

'No, though from what you say in the essay, this Russian Mary Hamilton was unlucky. Her crime came at a time when attitudes were changing.'

'Yes, there'd been a more liberal attitude before, but Tsar Peter the Great decided the law should change and that they should distinguish between women who killed their babies because they were too poor to look after them, and the ones who wanted to hide their own sin.' Mariana looks out at the ancient buildings interspersed with lush green trees, the church spire in the distance. 'You know the bit that really upsets me? When she was on the scaffold, he came up and stood beside her, whispering in her ear. He was huge, six-foot eight, and had to stoop to speak to her. She must have thought he was going to reprieve her. Even his wife, the Empress Catherine, didn't want her executed. He'd been her lover and it would have felt like a caress at first – then he told her to commend her soul to God because the sentence was going ahead. That was very cruel.'

'Ugh, that's hideous.'

'He was a very cruel man. Tradition has it that he suspected his son, Alexei, of plotting against him and had him tortured. When the boy confessed ...'

'As you would,' says Annie.

'Well, yes. Anyway, Alexei was knouted – you know, that terrible whip with rawhide thongs and sometimes a metal ring at the end? Whether by accident or design his son died.'

'So the Tsar too was guilty of infanticide,' notes the tutor.

'Yes, not that anyone would dare execute him for it. Mary was decapitated with a sword, then he picked up the head and started kissing and talking to it. Weird beyond belief.'

Annie's nose wrinkles in disgust. 'Gruesome.' She drums her fingers on the book in front of her. 'It's interesting, isn't it, how dark the *Child Ballads* are? Murder, rape, incest, infanticide – not how we define ballads nowadays. They're schmaltzy, songs for lounge lizards and crooners.'

'Chinese whispers again? Constant transformation?'

'This ballad seems to have fascinated Child, all those variations. A lot of them seem to mention dying in a foreign land.' She flicks through the text again. 'Here:

> *And they'll spread my story thro a' the land,*
> *Till it reaches my ain countrie.'*

Mariana buries her face in her mug, letting the hot steam flow over her skin.

'I thought next time I'd look into the story of the lady-in-waiting Mary, Queen of Scots brought from France, who got pregnant by the Queen's apothecary. The two of them were hanged in 1563 for killing the baby. In some ways that seems a more likely source for the ballad than the Russian theory.'

'Maybe. Hard to tell at this distance. It's not necessarily a logical process.'

Mariana laughs out loud. 'What is?'

Blood

'MARY, WILL YOU SING a song for the babby?' said the Queen, rubbing her stomach. 'I think it is a boy I carry, he kicks so lustily.'

We were alone in her bedchamber, where I was dressing her hair before the supper she was to give that night. Mary Seton usually did it as she had a real way with the combs, but she was feeling unwell so I offered. I loved being alone with the Queen. She was so warm and humorous, even when she was tired, like tonight. Sometimes I could even forget I had betrayed her.

I sang a lullaby I used to sing at home to my baby brother, about a woman whose baby was drowned. The baby's soul turned into a selkie and the woman would go down to the sea and sing till she saw him swimming towards her in the water. It was a lovely song, melancholy enough to calm a baby down and send it to sleep, but with so much meaning in the melody that after a few verses I saw tears slide down the Queen's cheek.

'Your voice alone is enough to touch my heart, but when you sing a lullaby like this, I think I may never stop weeping.'

'My mother aye sang it to me and then I sang it to my brother.'

'And one day you will sing it to your own child.'

That I had no wish to think of. The very idea made my stomach fail – my month-blood was late and I was afraid. Surely Fate could not be so cruel as to leave me with child? I had kept out of Lord Henry's way for months, not difficult when he disappeared so often from court, gallivanting off who knew where. One slip, one brief and frustrating encounter and I could be destroyed forever. I was thankful that we had not yet lit the torches and that my face was in shadow. 'The country people believe to this day that seals are the souls of the drowned.'

'That is a fine idea. There is some comfort in knowing that the ones you have lost are not gone forever. Look, Mary, my belly has ceased to jump as if a shoal of fish were swimming in it. He must be asleep.'

'You are very sure it is a boy.'

The Queen laughed but there was little mirth in it. 'There is only one place where my poltroon of a husband resembles a man and that is in the bedchamber. I know he has given me a son, who one day will be the king he could never be.'

I completed the Queen's hair by weaving some pearls through it. Her skin was pale tonight and their creamy lustre softened her look of fatigue. I held the mirror up to her and she smiled. 'It looks well. Thank you. Will you sing again later?'

'Why yes, David and I have been singing together. We have prepared a pretty piece for you.'

Rizzio, the Queen's secretary, had as fine a bass voice as I had ever heard. It was strangely beautiful, to hear such cavernous notes issue forth from this malformed little man, with his ugly face and crooked back. Those who claimed the Queen had lain with him had surely never seen him. Mary Stuart, one of the loveliest women in the realm, pregnant to a dwarfish popinjay like him? The suggestion was monstrous.

Still, he was amusing enough to entertain her and (thanks to the Queen's patronage) as richly dressed as any man in the court. Many a Scots noble envied his velvet clothes, the rich jewels he delighted to strut about in. I cannot say I loved him as the Queen did, but I did take the greatest of pleasure in singing with him. That day we had been in the music room for two hours and the time just flew by. His voice was rich and low, mine high and sweet. Singing with him was like playing blind man's buff. Round the room we'd go, sometimes touching, sometimes flying off, always returning to each other. In person I found David Rizzio cocksure and arrogant, but in music it was as if he was the man I loved.

Not that I loved any man, and especially not him I had lain with. No sooner had he got what he wanted than he was off to the next unwilling girl. There should have been no surprise in that. He had betrayed his own wife, why would he not betray me? The Queen could hardly bring herself to speak his name and I did not blame her. To this day I do not understand how I fell to him. I knew it was sin and I knew it was stupid. But the blood was coursing through my veins like a torrent in full spate and I could not say no to him. If only I had.

Before I left to change my own dress, I went in to check that the supper table was properly set. We were to be in one of the smaller rooms off the Queen's bedchamber. With its crimson and green drapings, the room looked bright and festive, a room designed for the pleasure of the senses. Card tables were waiting in the adjacent chamber, in case the Queen wanted to play later. She and Riccio often stayed up till two in the morning, playing the French game, Cent. Perhaps it reminded her of her youth in the splendid chateâux of the Valois court.

We were an intimate party at supper, Rizzio the most splendidly dressed of us all, in a red damask robe with fur trimming. Although it was Lent, meat was served as the Queen's condition exempted her from abstinence. I'm afraid most of us shared in her dispensation. She looked very beautiful. Tiredness had refined her features and her skin glowed like a pearly shell in water. She leaned back in her chair as if her back hurt her, her belly big with the child she was carrying.

Most of us were silent as the roasted duck was served, savouring the smell of the hot, flavoursome meat. I had just taken a draught of the Queen's good claret, admiring its ruby colour in the light of the torches, when Lord Darnley burst into the room. We were all amazed. He and the Queen had barely spoken for days and he preferred more exciting entertainments than these intimate suppers – most evenings he was to be found in the taverns and whorehouses of the town. Perchance he had been there already, for his colour was heightened and he spoke in a high, nervous tone as if he had been drinking. Most astounding of all was that he had the temerity to put his arm round the Queen's waist. We all exchanged looks at this familiarity but the Queen said nothing.

Moments later, there was another intrusion – Lord Ruthven came clanking into the room. His face was ghastly white under a steel helmet and we could see that he was wearing armour underneath his gown.

'May it please your Majesty to let yonder man Davie come forth of your presence, for he has been overlong here,' he said, his booming voice filling the chamber. We thought he must be delirious. His eyes were staring and it was well known that he was dying. Was he in a fever that he dared to speak so to the Queen? She evidently thought so, for she snapped at him that Rizzio was there at her invitation.

'Have you taken leave of your senses?' she asked him.

Ruthven stood his ground. 'He has offended your honour, your Majesty.'

We all gasped at his impudence. The Queen turned furiously to her husband.

'What have you to do with this enterprise?'

'Nothing,' he said, but he dared not look in her eyes and we none of us believed him.

It all happened very fast, so fast that none but the Queen acted, not even the Captain of her Guard, who was in the chamber. If there were ever any doubt about Mary Stuart's courage, it was disproved that night – she thought faster and more bravely than the men who served her. Rising to her feet she stood in front of Rizzio.

'Leave at once,' she commanded Ruthven, 'or be charged with treason.'

David's face was white with terror and he clung to her skirts like a little child. The Queen's attendants at last realised how grave the situation was and lunged towards Ruthven, but he shouted in a loud voice, 'Lay no hand on me, for I will not be handled.' I think that was a signal to his followers, for the room was suddenly crowded with armed men, blotting out the torchlight. They loomed like giants in the confined space. Only the Queen was undiminished by their presence. She stood erect, as if daring them to touch her.

But there were too many of them. Ruthven hauled at Rizzio, while Darnley's uncle, George Douglas, leaned over and snatched his nephew's dagger, making sure, I think now, that that craven coward was implicated in the deed. One of the men held a loaded pistol to the Queen's belly, which made everyone hesitate. What if it went off in a struggle? It could kill the Queen and the child she carried, the heir to her throne. Douglas struck the first blow, over the Queen's shoulder, the cold blade passing so close to her neck that it almost touched her. They cared naught for her feelings, did not trouble themselves to remove their deeds from her gaze, but stabbed David over and over in the doorway to her chamber. Blood gushed from his wounds, oozing on to the floor like molten wax, and making the murderers slip and slide as they thrust their daggers into his poor body. One must have struck his artery, for a spray of blood plumed into the air and sent droplets flying over the walls. So much blood, blood everywhere. There was I, longing for my month-blood to come, desperate to see it spreading over my linen. But not like that. Not like that.

Amboise

TAKE-OFF, THE MOST DELICIOUS MOMENT, though Mariana could hardly believe it was happening. That Crawford, her unromantic husband, had decided to take her away for Christmas was already surprising, but that he would choose to bring her to the Loire Valley, when he knew she wanted to go there for her studies, was astonishing. Although he uncomplainingly paid her fees, she knew he was not in favour of the changes wrought in his wife by university life. Her attention had wandered away from him and he sensed it.

'For goodness sake, do you have to have your nose stuck in a book *all* the time?' he'd shouted on Saturday night. They were waiting for dinner guests to arrive but Mariana had remembered something she wanted to check for her weekly essay and sneaked back into the bedroom, smiling weakly at the caterers as she went. Crawford came out of their bathroom and caught her. She'd simply shrugged and said, 'I forgot something,' but it put him in a bad mood – until his friends arrived and he'd buried his temper in several bottles of red wine.

As the plane taxied along the runway and slowly, heart-stoppingly lifted into the sky, Mariana relaxed and stopped pondering why Crawford was being so generous, concluding finally that one of his friends had probably told him to give her a romantic trip. *Got to keep the little woman happy* was their mantra. They always said it humorously, as though they were being ironic, but

Mariana knew that was how they really thought. Well, she would make the most of it.

Now she's in a grand hotel on the river in Amboise. Scented candles flicker round the bath and she sips at a glass of champagne. She never has time just to soak like this. As the heat of the water permeates her body she finds herself drifting off, remembering last week and the very different hotel she was in with Rahman, a budget motel on the outskirts of Edinburgh that for the first time in their affair made her feel cheap. Until then they'd gone to his home, an airy Georgian townhouse in the New Town, but now that his wife was back maybe he felt odd about taking her there. The motel was horrible. She took one look at the brown carpet, the functional furniture.

'Here? Really?'

'This is not where I normally ... but how do I know where your husband goes? I don't usually have affairs with married women.'

'Well, I never have affairs full stop. We have to end this. I can't cope with it.'

He slid his arm round her waist, whispered into the back of her neck. 'Can't cope with what? With this?' The tip of his tongue exquisite in her ear. 'With this?' His hand slid down her hips, lower. For one moment she froze. She could simply walk forward, out of his reach. She could turn and head out the door. Instead she stood motionless, allowing him to nuzzle her, to unzip her dress, to propel her gently towards the stiff-sheeted bed. And then ... she closes her eyes, giving herself up to remembered sensation.

'Hallo-o-o.' Crawford is standing in the doorway, flourishing the champagne bottle. 'Top-up?'

'Mmm. This is lovely, Crawford. Thank you.'

He hesitates, perhaps perplexed by her formality. 'Nothing's too good for my best girl.'

She smiles at him over the top of her glass. 'I won't be much longer.'

'Right. Okay. No rush.' He retreats with good grace, though there was a time when she would have invited him into the bath with her and they both know it. Oh dear, this trip must have cost an arm and a leg, she supposes she'd better make it up to him. Slowly she pulls herself out of the water, snuggling into the fluffy cocoon of her bath towel. When she goes back into the bedroom he's lying on the bed reading a political weekly.

'Not more about the indy referendum?' she teases him.

'You can never have too much information.'

'That's a matter for debate, I'd say.'

'You look cute with your hair up like that.'

'Cute? Cute? Is that any way to describe a grown woman?'

'I like cute,' he protests, tentatively reaching out to tug at her towel. 'And I like this,' he says, as the towel slips open. 'You know what? Your boobs are getting bigger.'

'Oh no, are they? I'd better go on a diet.'

'No, I like them like this.' He pulls her towards him and nuzzles her breast.

She keeps her face stern. 'Are you saying they were too small before?'

'No, no. Course not. Come here.'

'I thought we were going for a walk before dinner.'

'We've plenty of time,' he says.

She clambers on top of him, unbuttoning his shirt and lowering her damp skin to his. Outside, a skein of geese flies over the river, their squabbling calls a mere susurration inside the room. In the bathroom the last of the water gurgles away. She and Crawford have always enjoyed each other's bodies, but today is different. She feels guilty, and can't understand why. The thought unnerves her. There's a knot in her stomach, knot in her spine. This is her husband and her body is tensing. She must relax. What does it mean for her? For them? And yet, it's as if she's being disloyal to Rahman.

Closing her eyes, she wills her muscles to go floppy. Crawford is a good man. She must be kind to him. Think of the Loire meandering along below their window, the sound of the trees rustling as the wind lifts their branches. It's calm here, beautiful ...

Afterwards she feels simply relieved. She smiles at her husband, tries not to leap from the bed too eagerly. He looks rumpled, satiated, content to believe the language of the body.

The hotel, it turns out, is minutes away from the royal château. In the early evening darkness, its circular tower looms menacingly above the street, making them feel small. Mariana points up at the long iron balustrade running along the front of the buildings.

'That's where they held mass executions. Mary, Queen of Scots watched them as a young woman,' she says. 'There was a big uprising here and they hanged the rebels outside the castle windows while the royal family were having dinner.'

Crawford frowns. 'Not exactly suitable viewing.'

'No, Mary was only about fifteen or sixteen and it left her with a horror of such things. She always got very upset at bloodshed or when executions were going on, though for herself she was fearless.'

'But most of the ones in Scotland would have been authorised by her, wouldn't they?'

'She still didn't like them. She fainted during the execution of a lord who'd rebelled against her. One of the ladies-in-waiting she brought from France had a baby to her apothecary and because it was regarded as sinful, the two of them killed the baby. They were hung for it but Mary was totally distraught and refused to attend. She took to her bed. She did that a lot, apparently.'

Crawford shuffles his feet in the cold. 'Is that where your old ballad comes from?'

Mariana turns to look at him. 'I didn't think you'd taken in any of what I said about that.'

He grins. 'Not much, really.'

'Enough to come up with a theory of your own. I'm impressed. Yes, it could easily have been the source of the ballad.'

'Just call me Sherlock.'

'Okay, Sherlock.' She tucks her arm in his, touched. 'Let's go and get that fabulous French dinner you promised me.'

As they leave to go back to the hotel and its grand dining room, Mariana turns for a last look at the massive tower, so solid and imposing, crouching like a giant animal above them. The walls are slicked with rain, dark as blood. She shudders at the thought of the cruelty that went on there. Do the cries of the tortured echo down the centuries? Can the dead speak?

Safe from Drowning

MARY STUART WAS in agony. She writhed around, trying to find relief from the pain that gripped her, but couldn't seem to find a position that made her comfortable. For all the yards of blue taffeta and velvet that draped her bed, for all the physicians she could call on, she was no different from any poor woman in the throes of childbirth. I was terrified watching her. Was this what awaited me? How could I hide it? When the time came, there would be no ladies to wait on me, to comfort me. When the time came, none could know.

The Queen's confinement, though, was not like that of the common woman. It began with death, not life – she sent for the relics of Saint Margaret of Dunfermline to help protect her, then spent days deciding how to dispose of her belongings should she die in childbirth. If only she died, then all her goods were to go to her child, but if they should both die, there was an endless list of decisions to be made. The costliest of her jewels were to go to the Scottish crown, but she left us all little bequests – I was to have a beautiful jewel with a cameo of the Queen's head in crystal surrounded by diamonds and rubies and moreover, a string of pearls.

'Our Scots pearls are the finest in Europe and so is my little Hamilton,' she told me.

She left Mary Seton emerald earrings with pendant pearls and a sable neck fur with gold feet and head, while Livingston was willed a French gold enamelled pendant set with the Queen's arms in crystal. Mary Beaton was to have her French and English books, I her music ones. To Mary Fleming she was going to leave an ermine neck fur even more bejewelled than Seton's sable, and a magnificent ruby and diamond necklace.

'Why make me wait, cousin?' teased Mary. 'I like this jewel very well now.' She fastened the clasp round her neck. 'See how it suits me. I warrant you would feel your beauty overshadowed were you to wear it now I have been seen in it.'

'Think you so?' said the Queen. 'We shall see who the gentlemen of the court favour.'

Mary gave an exaggerated sigh and laid the necklace down. 'Well, of course a queen may command affection where we poor mortal beings must rely only on our charms.'

'You will never wear my jewel then, will you?' said the Queen. The two of them found their jest very funny though I confess the rest of us were a little uneasy at such talk. Still, it lightened the Queen's mood for a while. Thinking of her own death had made her sombre, as were the rest of us.

When her pain first started to get really bad we moved her into the smaller chamber to keep her warm – although it was June, it was a dank, cold summer that year.

'We must summon help from the spirits,' declared the Countess of Atholl. She aye had some hare-brained idea. Mother always told me not to meddle with what could not be understood, so it made me anxious when the Countess started raising her arms and making some daft incantation. Then she got one of the other noblewomen to throw herself about, pretending to take the Queen's pain to herself. The Queen was too far gone to care – it certainly didn't lessen her torture.

The new Mary, Carmichael, who had joined us when Mary Beaton married, was trying to stop herself from laughing, but I was shivering –with fear, I suppose. My baby was come of the same long-shanked father and would surely create as much damage in fighting his way from my womb. If the Queen could not bear the pain then how could I? If only the enchantment would work, then she could find some ease. My beloved Mary Fleming saw my tremors and threw a shawl round my shoulders.

'Do not worry,' she said. 'The Queen will be well. Sometimes she seems frail but really she is as strong a woman as you could ever hope to meet. Nothing defeats my cousin, nothing.'

Mary Stuart lay back on the bed, her hair dishevelled, sweat beading her cheek.

'I wish I had ne'er been married,' she said.

'Hush, cousin,' said Mary. 'You will be glad when you give birth to a king.'

The Queen reached out her hand to me. 'Sing, my sweet Mary. Take my mind from this pain, for a few moments at least.'

Truth to tell, I was glad to have such a purpose and sat willingly by her bedside, holding her hand. I began with a beautiful English lullaby taught me by one of the court harpists: *Lullay, myn lyking, my dere son, my sweeting.* I could see the Queen's breathing slow, becoming more regular as her senses were soothed, though her hand rested still on her stomach as though pressing it would stop it hurting. The song is for the King of Kings, our dear Lord Jesus, but I sang it for the Queen's bairn, who would one day be king of Scotland, and for my own, who would be his half-brother.

Half-brother to a king? The thought made me dizzy. I stared at the Queen as I sang, wondering whether she would ever be able to love my baby. How could she, when he would be born of betrayment? She would no longer love me if she knew I had lain with her man. Tears started to my eyes and I faltered for a moment. I wanted to run from the room, hide my shame. Mary Fleming patted my shoulder.

'Your care for the Queen does you honour, Mary, but she will be well presently.'

I bowed my head and went on with the song. Mary Carmichael looked a little queasy. At seventeen she was a year younger than I, though she was a big heifer of a girl and everyone thought she was older. I knew her inelegance pained the Queen and thought it unlikely that Carmichael would stay in her service. Mary Stuart liked everything fine and dainty around her. Though she herself was so tall, my short stature made me a favourite with her. Sometimes I think she thought she was my mother, though she was only five years older than I was.

It was a long night. The Queen called out several times. 'Please God take me, but spare my baby,' she said once. Sometimes she spoke in French and I wasn't sure what she was saying. I was not a scholar like Mary Beaton.

We four Marys each did what we knew best – Mary Seton prayed a lot; I sang; Carmichael sat in the corner, keeping out of the way. Mary Fleming kept our spirits up as best she could. I think we all felt how hard was the lot of women. Our beloved Queen, the most beautiful princess in Europe and one of the most brilliant, was rolling around on the bed, groaning as if she were a seal about to give birth. No, it is not so hard for seals. I saw one down on the seashore once and it took minutes to accomplish what Mary Stuart took a day and a half to do. The animal's tail rocked slowly from side to side and she edged closer to the water. When the baby came it was as if it suddenly just popped up from underneath her. She called to it, surprised, as her blood flowed out and merged with the seawater. The baby splashed into the water, immediately at home there.

The Queen appeared to be spent by the time her son arrived. It was as if he crept out of her body and just dropped on to the bed while she lay back, drained of all energy. She had been right, a lusty boy, whose cries proclaimed him as wilful as his mother.

Mary Fleming put out a hand to touch him, scooping up a thin piece of some strange, almost lacy material from the top of his head. 'Look, Mary,' she said. 'A caul. He will be safe from drowning.'

The Queen crossed herself. 'Thanks be to God.'

A precious gift, indeed. Now she would never fear sending her son across the water to her family in France, never worry if he went out on the loch for some sport. No matter how storm-tossed the waves or high the winds, her baby would be safe.

It was as if the magical protection afforded her son gave her renewed strength. She sat up in bed and asked for her hair to be dressed. She was a woman but she never forgot she was a queen. Her baby would be king and must never have the taint of bastardy attached to him.

'Fetch that wretched husband of mine,' she commanded. 'Let him see his son. And let no man doubt his parentage.'

I brushed her hair while Carmichael, with trembling hands, washed the infant and wrapped him in a fine shawl. I could hardly bear to look when Lord Darnley came in, his handsome face sullen despite the joyful news.

'My Lord, God has given you and me a son, begotten by none but you. Here I protest to God, as I shall answer to him at the great day of Judgement, that this is your son and no other man's son. I am desirous that all here, with ladies and others bear witness.'

Darnley's raised his eyebrows superciliously, as if he doubted her word. That was no way to treat Mary Stuart. Weary though she was, her eyes flashed with contempt.

'He is so much your own son that I fear it will be the worse for him hereafter.'

If there were not so many people in the room, I swear Lord Darnley was angry enough to hit her, woman though she was, and his monarch. Not that he respected that. He thought he should be the king and she merely his consort. Why? Because he carried a different set of baubles between his legs? He would not have made half the king she did, so lazy and spoilt was he, preferring to run with the hounds or go hawking than address the business of the state. I kept my head bowed, afraid that others would read in my eyes how much I hated him.

I was glad when he left the chamber. We made the Queen comfortable – she was very tired and we could see she would be asleep in minutes once she was left in peace. She refused to let her baby be taken away, as was the custom.

'No, he must sleep here with me. I will not let him out of my sight.'

Mary Fleming took the child and laid him in the wooden cradle at the foot of the Queen's bed, kissing his little forehead as she laid him down. I stood and looked at him for a moment. How different would his fate be from my son's, though they sprang from the same father? He would always have wealth and the respect of those around him. He had God's protection. He would be safe. What of my wee bairn, born without a name? With no land or riches, not even a home to live in? What would become of him? What would become of us?

The Four Marys, Linlithgow

CRAWFORD FROWNS AS HE comes into the bedroom and sees eight discarded dresses and five tops strewn over the bed. 'For God's sake, Mariana, there must be something you can get into.'

'What do you mean get into? I'm just trying different looks.'

'Come off it, you know you've been getting a bit porky lately.'

'Porky? Porky?' She knows her voice has risen to a screech.

He coughs in embarrassment. 'Pleasantly plump, then.'

'Oh God.' She flops down on the bed. 'There's nothing pleasant about it. I look awful in everything.'

'Course you don't.'

He stands sideways to the mirror and starts brushing his hair, peering at the effect he's creating.

'Who're you trying to impress?'

'New client.'

'Female, by any chance?'

'Nope.' He rifles through his bedside table, tucking a bundle of notes into his pocket. 'Mariana?'

'Mmm-hmm?'

'Has it occurred to you that you might be pregnant?'

She sits up, surprised. 'No, of course not. You know I have my periods. If anything, I have more than ...'

He glances sharply at her. 'More than you should?'

'Well ...'

'For God's sake, Mariana. You need to go to the doctor and get it checked out.'

Mariana sits up and starts folding away the clothes, not looking at him.

'Don't be so stupid. What if there is something?'

She bites her lip. 'There isn't. I'd know if there *was* something wrong.'

He looks at her in disbelief. 'Eh, reality check here? How would you know? You've suddenly acquired a medical degree, have you?'

Wearily she holds a fluffy jumper up against herself. It might do. The pale aqua colour's pretty and it's baggy enough to distract people from her stomach.

'Mariana, promise me you'll go to the doctor.'

Why doesn't he stop going on about it? Oh God, what if there was something wrong? She could have stomach cancer, or ovarian cysts. She could be like Mary Tudor, who thought she was pregnant but died in agony, clutching her swollen belly.

'Don't shout,' she says, discarding the fluffy jumper. If anything, it draws attention to her stomach.

'Well, you're infuriating.'

She delves into the drawer where she keeps her tops.

He shakes his head. 'Okay, but I'll expect you to make an appointment by the end of the week. All right?'

'I hear you.'

He snorts. 'Right, I'm going. Wish me luck. If I nail this client, I'll definitely get the promotion.'

At last, something she can reply to properly. She smiles at him. 'Yes, good luck. I'll have my fingers crossed all night.'

'That'll keep you out of mischief,' he says.

By the time she finally finds something to wear she's running late and has to text Alice to let her know. She arrives at the pub feeling tired and dishevelled. Alice is already there, with her rich girl's shiny hair and the neat, rich girl's dress, which makes her look like a future queen of England. Why can't Mariana ever look like that, no matter how expensive her clothes are? She needs to learn quickly – if Crawford gets this promotion, they'll start to make serious money and he'll want her to be a credit to him. What will it be like to be really rich? She already feels she can buy anything she wants, and Crawford encourages her spending, so will it be any different?

'I got us a bottle of Prosecco to start off with,' says Alice. 'Did your husband drop you off? You should have told him to come in for a drink.'

'No, I cabbed it. He's got a business dinner this evening.' She looks round the pub. 'He'd probably like this place, all the real ales. He's a bit of a rugger bugger, you know? I hope you don't mind but I think Annie's going to drop in.'

'Your tutor? Of course, it's research for you two, isn't it?'

'My main area of research tonight's going to be alcoholic,' says Mariana. 'I meant to come earlier and have a look round the palace before we met up, but today was a bit chaotic.'

'You look tired,' says Alice. 'Are you all right?'

Is she? Mariana no longer knows. The bleeding feels almost constant now though she's sure it's nothing to worry about. Or is it? Maybe she *should* go to the doctor and get checked out.

'Maybe you're pregnant,' says Annie's voice behind her.

Mariana turns and stands to kiss her. 'Hi, Annie. Yet another person today telling me I'm fat.'

'Not fat, but you have put on weight. You know you have. Hallo, Alice. How are you?'

Alice looks alarmed at what she clearly sees as too personal a remark. 'Have some Prosecco, Annie.'

Mariana takes a deep breath. 'I'm not pregnant, that's for sure. In fact I'm bleeding practically all the time.'

They both look at her, concerned.

'I'm sure there's nothing to worry about, but you shouldn't neglect something like that,' says Alice.

'She's in denial,' says Annie firmly.

In the women's silence, the ordinary sounds of the pub seem magnified, the clinking of glasses, the hiss of beer being poured, the loud laughter from other tables.

'I suppose I am a bit worried,' admits Mariana.

'Alice is right, it's probably nothing to be alarmed about, maybe even something to celebrate. You *could* be pregnant – my cousin had a lot of bleeding and it turned out to be cysts. She went on to have a perfectly healthy baby boy.'

Mariana shudders. 'Well, I'm not going to worry about any of that tonight.' She takes a gulp of her Prosecco, but somehow it tastes sour. Good grief, is she not even going to be able to have a drink? Maybe some food will change her body chemistry. 'Let's go and eat, I'm starving.'

They walk through to the dining room at the back of the pub, past walls full of historic pictures. These are the people and events Mariana has been living with for months – the original Four Marys: Seton, Beaton, Livingston and Fleming. As she lingers to look at them more closely, she has the sensation that the women are whispering to her from across the centuries, drawing her into their world. John Knox is here and a large picture of the execution of Mary, Queen of Scots. What must it be like to know the time of your death? Mariana's not sure she could meet execution with Mary's courage.

The dining room is all dark wood and red velvet, with a comfortingly womb-like atmosphere. As he's showing them to their table, the waiter glances at his watch.

'We have a psychic event in here at nine o'clock. You ladies would be very welcome to stay for it if you're having dinner.'

'How do you have a psychic event?' asks Annie. 'Is it a seance?'

'Not exactly. A group of mediums comes in and they respond mostly to the audience, though you can have a private session if you want to.'

'Sounds like fun,' says Alice.

The waiter nods to her. 'How are you, Miss Alice? Your parents were in a couple of nights ago.'

'Were they? I bet Daddy had the haggis as usual?'

He smiles. 'I believe he did.'

'I didn't realise this was your local,' says Annie. 'I just thought Mariana wanted to come here because of her research.'

'My parents have a farm outside the town. I told Mariana about the pub and she wanted to see it.'

Mariana is studying the menu, wondering what she can eat that's not too rich or spicy. Mull of Kintyre macaroni cheese, maybe.

'Haggis fritters,' she says. 'Someone's got to try them.'

'A bit kamikaze, isn't it?' says Annie. 'What you Lowlanders do with your food. Batter round everything.'

'Correct me if I'm wrong, but didn't you teuchters wrap oats round everything till just a few years ago?'

'Much healthier,' laughs Annie.

As the meal progresses, Mariana feels marginally less queasy. The cosy lighting in the room, the comfort food, the banter with her friends all revive her. 'Will we stay for the seance?' she asks. 'It could be a laugh.'

'Aren't you afraid?' says Annie in a spooky voice. 'Messing with the occult. You're entering the danger zone.'

'You'd have to believe in it to be afraid,' says Alice, with a grin at Mariana.

'Well, if we're staying, we'll need fortifying,' says Annie. 'Let's get a bottle of red.'

For a moment, when the wine is poured, Mariana has the sensation that the glasses are filled with blood. Her gorge rises and she has to take a deep breath to stop herself from being sick, but when she eventually calms down and takes a sip, the taste is warm and soothing.

Waiters are clearing tables and re-arranging them to create an informal space for a stage area. 'Oh look, the entertainment must be about to start,' says Annie, as a group of women come into the restaurant and sit down at the other tables. When the room falls silent the familiar opening chords of Strauss' otherworldly *Also Sprach Zarathustra* fill the room, the ominous drumbeats filling Mariana with an inexplicable sense of dread. God, she's over-sensitive tonight. She *must* go to the doctor tomorrow.

As the music builds to its climax, four black-clad men and women move into the room and stand in front of the audience, slowly raising their arms heavenward to the final majestic organ note.

'Gosh, it's a bit cheesy,' mumbles Alice, embarrassed as always by anything she sees as over the top.

The leader of the group, a large woman whose flowing garments billow out over her curves, extends her arms in welcome, setting her myriad silver bangles jangling.

'Good evening. I am Malena and my fellow mediums are Ossian, Serena and Tristana,' she says in rich, contralto tones. 'Tonight we are going beyond the veil, into the unknown realms of the spirit world. We will not go alone – we need your help to do this. What we ask is that you keep your minds and hearts open and let the spirits in. Do not close yourselves off from this spiritual experience.'

Walking slowly to the front as the other mediums sit down, she raises her hand theatrically to her brow. 'With the help of my spirit guide, Hemetre, handmaiden to a noblewoman in the reign of Queen Nefertiti, I will now go beyond the veil.'

There is complete hush in the room. Malena closes her eyes and raises her head as if seeking inspiration from the heavens. 'Agnes, I'm getting an Agnes.'

An elderly lady tentatively puts her hand up. 'I'm Agnes,' she says.

'I'm getting a Billy. Would that be right, Agnes?'

'Mmm, I don't think so, dear.' The old lady seems apologetic, which makes Mariana want to giggle.

'Perhaps it's Millie?'

'Mmm, no, I'm afraid not.'

'Tilly, it's Tilly.'

'Mmm, I don't know any Tillys.'

Alice has her hand over her mouth to stifle her laughter. 'My God, it's too funny.' She turns to Annie. 'I'd say we can relax, we don't seem to be in the danger zone here.'

Annie rolls her eyes. 'My mother could do a better job. She does have the sight, actually.'

'Really. So you do believe in this stuff?' says Mariana.

'Put it this way, I think there are things we don't understand.'

'Yes, like why people pay good money for this sort of charlatanism,' says Alice.

Annie shrugs. 'People want to believe, I suppose. It's more comfortable for them.'

Ossian, a dark and dramatic young man with thick hair and a thick Fife accent, meets with similar success to Malena. The audience are getting restive when the third medium, Serena, moves to the front of the stage, proclaiming that her spirit guide is a Native American woman whose husband and sons were killed in the Battle of the Little Bighorn.

'Why are they always Native Americans and Egyptians?' asks Mariana. 'And did none of them just have ordinary lives?'

Serena is blonde and slender, her chic black cocktail dress incongruous beside thehippyish garb of her fellow mediums. She says she belongs to a famous family of gipsy fortune tellers, which seems to impress some of her audience.

'Elspeth, the name Elspeth is coming through,' she says.

A thin woman at the next table raises her hand. 'I'm Elspeth.'

'There's a man called Jonathan. He says you've to stop smoking. He can see you on the balcony of your flat at nights.'

The woman looks stunned. She gazes solemnly at Serena but says nothing. The younger woman with her is shocked. 'Oh Mum, you promised you'd give up. After all that chemo, how could you?'

'He says he's with the little one,' continues the medium. 'He'll look after her till you come over to the other side.

'I don't smoke,' says Elspeth. 'And I don't know anyone called Jonathan.'

'What does she mean, *the little one*?' asks her daughter.

'It's not me she's talking about,' insists the woman. 'There must be another Elspeth here.' Her face is pale and tense.

'Does Dad know about this Jonathan?'

'No, because he doesn't exist.'

The medium raises her eyebrows and moves on to another name, leaving the woman staring stolidly ahead, ignoring her daughter's questions.

'Gosh,' says Alice. 'I'm beginning to think you're right, Annie. This is dangerous stuff.'

The final medium, Tristana, comes forward, wearing a long black, mediaeval-looking dress. Her hair is black, her skin preternaturally pale. While the other mediums have tried to communicate with the audience, she simply stands there, looking at them. With her erect bearing and fierce gaze, the effect is electrifying. At last she speaks. 'My spirit guide is Catriona, a woman who was murdered in the massacre of Glencoe.'

'A Scots spirit guide at last,' exclaims Annie.

'She never lies to me.' The voice is low and musical. 'I do not wish any of you to lie to me, either. If you do not wish to accept the truth of what Catriona is saying, please just shake your head.'

She prowls round the limited stage area, dark eyes finally coming to rest on Mariana. 'Catriona would prefer to speak to you in private.'

'Don't fall for that. It's a scam,' whispers Alice. 'A private session costs fifteen quid.'

Tristana fixes Alice with a withering look. There's something compelling about her gaze and Mariana shivers.

'There is no charge,' says the medium. A murmur of surprise ripples round the room.

Her stare is impossible to ignore and reluctantly Mariana gets to her feet. She feels suddenly weak. What can this woman have to say to her? She wants to run away but feels impelled to obey. Alice and Annie look at each other, uneasy as Mariana walks out after the medium.

'She's just following that woman like a zombie,' says Alice.

Annie nods. 'I don't like it. She's not herself just now, but I can't tell what's wrong.'

'No, I can't, either. She seems to have lost that natural sarkiness she had, her feistiness.'

'Has she got problems in her marriage?'

'Not that I know of,' says Alice.

Tristana stalks from the room, long dress swishing, her departure causing a frisson of dismay and perhaps fright in her audience. Mariana follows, mesmerised. As they leave she hears Malena returning to the front to take over the session. Making sure the audience get their money's worth, no doubt.

Offstage Tristana seems less imposing. She leads the way into a small office, sitting down opposite Mariana.

'I don't want to alarm you,' she says.

Mariana waits, unnerved by the intensity of the medium's stare.

'I see you with three children,' she says.

'You're a bit premature,' says Mariana drily. 'I don't have any.'

The other woman's voice is unexpectedly gentle. 'You have two in the spirit world and one inside you.'

One inside her? Mariana gasps. She can't have. That's not possible. Her stomach twists inside her and she closes her eyes in terror. Two in the spirit world? Does she mean the two abortions? How could this woman know? How the hell could she possibly know? She must have been there too, in the clinic. Was she having an abortion herself? Is that it? Mariana leans back in the chair, hardly able to breathe. It's a trick. The woman has seen her medical records. She must have.

'Did you know you had a boy and a girl?'

Mariana feels utterly sick. 'How dare you?' she says.

She was so young, the first time, not even sixteen. Down the woods with Sandy Forrester, twigs digging into her bare bum, him pumping away on top of her, crushing her pelvic bones. It astonished her that such a joyless conjunction could produce anything. Sex astonished her, full stop. It was so sore and messy. She was sure his semen had missed her altogether, there was so much of it on her skin and frosting her pubic hair.

Her mother was furious when he found out, beyond words at first. She drew her hand back and would have slapped Mariana full in the face had she not blocked her. 'Why?' she wailed. 'Why would you want to repeat my mistakes? You've seen what it's done to my life, having your sister too young. Do *you* want to end up on a council estate like me? Like her too, for that matter? I thought you were brighter than that.'

'I didn't think he'd gone inside me.'

'Who was it?' said her mother. 'I'm going to kill him. I wanted you at least to go to university. Oh Mariana, I wanted you to have the chances I never did.'

Seeing her tears, Mariana knew right away what she was going to do. 'I'm not having it, Mum.'

There was a silence before her mother finally responded. 'An abortion?' she said, her voice heavy as lead. 'Yes, that's what we must do. I'll take you. But we won't say anything to your father. It would break his heart.'

On the day of the termination Mariana was pale with fright, her stomach turning over, much as it is now with the medium's revelations. The clinic was a bleakly impersonal yellow colour, the nurses semi-kind.

'It's over in a matter of minutes,' one told her.

Lying on the bed, rigid while cold anaesthetic gel was squirted into the neck of her womb and what looked like a miniature vacuum cleaner was inserted into her, Mariana felt relief. There was no child inside her, only tiny body parts with no neural pathways connected to the brain. It was fine. When it was all over she asked to see what was left.

The nurse blanched. 'You don't want to see that,' she said.

'Actually, I do.'

The other woman stared at her but Mariana refused to be cowed. Eventually the nurse shrugged and brought out a sieve with a handful of pink gelatinous tissue at the bottom. Mariana felt disbelief that the woman had tried to prevent her seeing this tiny amount of matter. There was no baby; those few grams of goo were her freedom.

The second time was harder, though. How could she have been so stupid twice? She was at university by then and thought she was in love. Kenny Macdonald was everything she wanted in a boyfriend. His father was rich, a prominent lawyer in Edinburgh, and *he* was both clever and an athlete. Now she can't remember why the sport was important. Maybe because it gave him – and by extension her – special status. She was the girlfriend of a man who ran for Scotland. She was somebody.

If only he'd married her, maybe things would have turned out differently, but when he heard she was pregnant he wanted nothing more to do with her. She wanted to kill herself. There were months of grief and almost a breakdown. Only the entry of Crawford into her life saved her. He was everything Kenny was and what was more, he loved her – more than she loved him, it turned out.

Now she feels pure rage. This charlatan is trying to tell her that the pink goo at the bottom of a sieve was a *baby*? How could it be? It was *nothing*. It was like the stray bits of innards you get inside poultry. A boy and a girl? *No. No, it was not.*

The medium sighs. 'I'm sorry. I don't want to upset you but I can only pass on what the spirits tell me. Catriona wants you to know that your children who've passed over are both happy on the other side. But she has a message for you. She is afraid for the baby you are carrying. She says you have to leave hatred behind. I don't know what that means but perhaps you do.'

'No, I bloody don't.'

'Well, perhaps you will in time.' Tristana rises, her high-cheekboned face sombre. She pauses for a moment and looks straight at Mariana, who feels as if her every thought is laid bare. 'Please don't ignore what the spirits say. Catriona was very insistent. She lost her baby and doesn't want you to lose yours.'

'I don't have a baby.' Mariana walks to the door. 'Don't you come near me again with your mumbo-jumbo.'

She pauses in the corridor to collect herself. What to say to the others? Taking a deep breath, she walks back into the room.

'Are you all right?' Alice is frowning. Clearly she finds such drama somewhat distasteful.

'I'm fine,' says Mariana. 'What a load of nonsense. She said my mother was trying to get through to me about my pregnancy.'

'Do you think you are pregnant, then?' asks Annie.

'Only one way to find out,' shrugs Mariana. 'Honestly, what a load of hooey.'

The three of them leave together, the subject of fierce discussion among other members of the audience. Mariana demolishes the integrity of the medium most of the way back to Edinburgh, until she realises that Annie's gaze is beginning to be quizzical rather than supportive. The other two women are dropped at their respective flats, leaving her free. She taps on the driver's window.

'Could you drop me off at the twenty-four-hour supermarket, please?'

Once there she walks up and down the brightly-lit aisles, looking for the medical section, and picks up a pregnancy testing kit.

She can't possibly wait till she gets home and, anyway, Crawford
might be back by now. Her whole body is shaking as she heads
into the customer toilets. The light inside is icy blue and diffuse.
Shivering, she tears the package open, struggling to read the small
print. There's a little thumb grip to the test strip and she holds on
to it, hoping the stream of urine she releases will hit the right spot.
Please let her not be pregnant. *Please.*

What will she do if she is? What would her mother think if she
were alive? Mariana can hear her voice echoing in her head: *How
could you be so stupid? You're about to do a doctorate. We've never had
a doctor in the family. And what about your husband?* Oh God, what
if the baby isn't Crawford's? Her hand shakes as she holds the strip
up to the harsh lighting, watching as its colour slowly changes, and
with it her world.

No Place in the World

TANTALLON CASTLE MADE ME SHIVER. It stood high above the Forth, its massive walls louring over us like a malevolent beast as we rode towards it. I was so tired I thought I might slide off my horse. We had been to Kelso and Hume Castle, to Langton and Eyemouth and Dunbar, and the month was not yet out. I know the Scots people needed to see their Queen but did it have to be quite so much?

Mary Seton gave me a sharp look as we advanced towards the great gates. 'You look spent. Does something ail you?'

I was swift to deny it, did not want her questioning me further. The stiff stomacher I wore hid the presence of the baby, which had the forethought to lie high up, almost on my midriff, but I knew people were beginning to talk. Only a few days ago I had walked in on a discussion between Seton and Carmichael.

'She is with child, I know it,' said Seton.

'But who would she have lain with?' said Carmichael.

'I hardly dare think,' said Seton, in her customary dry tones.

She pursed her mouth when I came into the room and they both fell silent, but I saw her studying my belly with those sharp eyes of hers and felt a sharp stab of fear. I pulled my cloak further round me as we entered the castle. It was an icy November day but I am not sure my trembling came from the cold.

As we dismounted I felt the bairn kick inside me and had to clutch on to the saddle to thole the pain.

'My month-bloods,' I told Seton.

'Really?'

I followed the Queen into the castle, staying close to her side. She was kind, despite her own troubles. Her illness of last month had continued into November and she was heartsick. She had lowered herself by pleading with Lord Darnley in front of the whole Privy Council, only for him to equivocate. Then she had ridden fifty miles in a day to visit Bothwell when that boor got injured in a fight. If I were a man, I would have finished him off. I did not like the ugly little runt and doubted of his intentions towards the Queen – yet another arrogant man thinking he was better than women. After such a punishing journey she ended up in convulsions and vomiting blood. We thought she would die. Poor Mary Stuart. For all her learning and wit, she was no judge of men. But then I too knew what it was to follow the passions.

Now I hoped that if she saw my pallor perhaps she would excuse me from her service for now. I just prayed I would have a chamber to myself. Mary Fleming's brow furrowed with concern when she came up to join us.

'You look as if you need to rest, little Hamilton,' she said.

The Queen turned and looked closely at me. 'You are too pale, Mary. Find her a chamber, cousin.'

I curtseyed my thanks and gratefully followed Mary Fleming. She secured a room for me and accompanied me upstairs, carrying a beaker of red wine to warm me. I sat down on the bed while she loosened my cloak. She was very quiet.

'Mary, the Queen and I are afraid you are not well.'

I nearly wept at the kindness of her tone, but I dared not tell her the truth.

'I am well,' I said. 'I fear the horse I am riding is too strong for me. I am weary by the end of a journey.'

'Yes, it is a fatiguing life we live. But you are a young woman ...'

'Young, but not perhaps as strong as Mary Carmichael.'

A smile flitted across her face. 'No, Carmichael has the strength of two. Well, rest now. The Queen too is unwell still, I fear, and wishes to lie down, so you will not be called upon again tonight. Would you like me to have supper sent up to you in your chamber?'

'Just a little broth. I do not think I could eat.'

She patted my hand. 'You would tell me if something was wrong, would you not?'

I nodded, just wishing her to leave now. I was afraid she could read my thoughts, see the dread whirling around inside me. I wept when she had gone, wept for my poor baby and for myself. What would happen to me? What could I do? The bairn kicked again and I wrapped myself in the bed coverings, trying to get warm.

I must have slept for a while because I woke to a knock at the door. One of the servants stood there with broth for me and a warming stone.

'You look pale, ma'am,' she said.

'I am just a little fatigued. Thank you. You are very kind.'

She had a sweet smile, but I wondered if her kindness was simply bought and paid for by the Queen. How would she act if she knew what I had done, if she knew I was with child? Would I be whipped from the court? Shamed in front of all of them? But even as I wondered, I knew that what others thought did not matter. What mattered was what Mary Stuart thought. My greatest sin was not that I had lain with a man but that the man was her husband.

That night as I lay in the dark I knew my time was coming and was afraid. I had seen my mother give birth and knew there was a lot of blood and water. Although I had set aside some linen to protect the bed, I did not know if it would be enough. I spread it out over the blankets and waited. My thoughts were black. I wanted to rip the baby from my womb. How could I look after it when I was in the Queen's service? How could I live if she dismissed me?

My waters, when they broke, were surprisingly meagre. When my mother had her last bairn we had had to stand back from the bed, so much liquid gushed out, but thank the Lord, only a small pool formed on my sheets. The pain came in waves, rushing in like a tide to the shore, then retreating. There was no one to put a damp cloth to my brow or hold my hand when it got too great, but I knew it was just. I had sinned, against God and my Queen, and did not deserve comfort. But when the huge breakers rolled through me and cramps made my body retreat into itself like a sea urchin, I wished I was not alone.

The night was long. I do not know how many hours I suffered. I dared not cry out or gasp too loudly, though I wanted to scream to the heavens. The candle had burnt almost to the end when suddenly it was as if my whole insides were taken over by an earthquake, the pain rumbling through my body and hurling me towards destruction. I began to push harder and harder, trying to expel the demon inside that threatened to annihilate me.

At last it was over. It felt as though my insides were slithering out on to the bed. Trembling, I held the candle up. There was no imp or demon, just a wee bairn, covered in blood and a white grease like molten candlewax. He cried out when I picked him up and I put my hand over his mouth to hush him. A white rope of skin snaked out of his belly like a writhing serpent of hell but I had no knife to cut it and had to wind it round his little body instead, placing the bloody placenta on top. I held him against my skin for a moment. My son, half-brother to a king.

But my poor baby was born with no caul to protect him. He let out another loud cry and I covered his mouth again. 'Ssh, no one must hear you.' Presently there was a knock on the door and I heard the voice of Mary Carmichael. Thank God I had locked my door, for she tested the handle.

'Does something ail you, Mary?'

'No, nothing. I just have the stomach gripes. Go back to bed. I will be well in the morning.'

That sleekit strumpet, sneaking around me, trying to find me out. I would not let her destroy me. A fever seized me then. I snatched the bloody sheets from the bed and wrapped my baby in them, keeping my hand over his mouth so he would be quiet. I had not the time even to wash properly but pulled on my night-gown with my cloak around me. Holding the baby against my chest, I slipped out of my room and tiptoed down the staircase. I froze for a moment when I thought I heard a door open behind me, but I could see no one.

It was pitch black and I nearly tripped and fell several times. The heavy wooden door creaked as I dragged it open, terrifying me. The noise was bound to wake someone up and what would happen then? Out in the cold air I paused. What was I doing? Where would I go? Down below the castle I could hear the waves crashing against the rocks. It was as if the sea was calling me and I must go there, though I knew the descent was sheer and jagged. I stumbled often as I went down, the rocks lacerating my knees, tearing my feet.

The wind's moaning was like a woman keening. When I reached the edge of the water I threw my cloak open and unwrapped the bloody swaddling around my baby. He was cold and still but when I felt his chest there was still the faintest of heartbeats. I wailed aloud, not knowing whether I wanted him quick or dead. He whimpered, a bleat like a lamb's. I held his little face hard against my chest. There was no place in the world for my wee bastard bairn.

I sang to him then as I clutched his cold body to my chest. I told him that his soul would go to the selkies and that one day he would come back to me. I told him that I knew I could have loved him, but the wind snatched my words and bore them away across the surging water and the rain started pounding my face. I held him fast, not able to move. I couldn't leave him.

The Perfect Wife

MARCH 2014

MARIANA CLUTCHES THE PILLOW to her stomach. She has never felt such pain. No matter where she moves her insides are on fire. She writhes about on the bed, trying not to groan, but there's no relief. Oh God. It's agony. Agony. She rolls over on to her stomach. Maybe that will squash the little fucker.

She must not cry. Crawford will be in soon and he won't want to see her face all blotchy. How could she explain it? *I'm upset because I'm having a baby and the man I love has dumped me?* She can't believe Rahman could be so callous. The evening was supposed to be so romantic – dinner in the little country restaurant and then she would tell him, over liqueurs by the log fire. Well, *he* was to have a liqueur. She wouldn't because of the baby. Crawford was away on business and that bitch Miriam was at a conference, so they'd booked a suite upstairs for afterwards.

Things started to go wrong as soon as they started looking at the menu.

'That sounds good, pork in a creamy white wine sauce with mustard mashed potatoes,' she'd said.

He'd looked at her appraisingly. 'Isn't that a little fattening for you at the moment?'

'What do you mean?'

His eyes were cold. 'Don't make me say it, Mariana.'

She felt as though he'd kicked her in the stomach. 'Don't dare say it.'

He raised his eyebrows in that weary way he had, shrugging as if to say she was unreasonable.

'I suggest baked cod loin with roasted vegetables.'

Why did she not just slap his face and walk away at that point? What kept her glued to her chair, mute? She knew why she'd put the weight on, she had no need to feel a greedy, self-indulgent failure, though she did. She should just have come out with it there and then? Instead she'd simply nodded.

'Whatever.'

She had only one glass of wine during the meal and afterwards, when they were by the open fire, she opted for coffee. Time enough to tell him when they were in bed. Not for the first time she began to wonder what his reaction would be. He had no children with Miriam but perhaps that wasn't by choice. Perhaps he secretly longed for a son and would divorce the barren bitch. Then she would move in with him into the elegant townhouse. She loved its spare minimalism but perhaps she would insist on some splashes of colour, just to make it different, just to let him know that she was his wife now.

'You seem distracted.'

'Sorry, just dreaming.'

He looked straight at her with those dark eyes. She felt seen by him.

'That sounds promising,' he said. 'Let's go upstairs.'

Excitement mounting, she rose and followed him up to the room. He slid on to the four-poster bed and stretched out a hand to her, his movements sinuous and graceful. Her eyes not leaving his, she moved towards him, mesmerised by his gaze. This was more than just chemistry. She felt a visceral pull towards him, she was meant to be with him.

He eased her back on to the pillows and pulled her top down with his teeth, burying his head in her breasts and breathing deep of her skin.

'This is the one good thing about all of this. Your breasts are perfect now.'

'Weren't they before?'

'Practically perfect, darling.'

There was no point in thinking about any of it. She leaned back, closing her eyes, hearing him switch the light off and welcoming the submerging darkness. Her clothes slid from her as easily as a snake shedding its skin, him caressing her all the while as he took his own off. Only when she felt his bare skin against hers did she open her eyes, seeking out his.

'I love you, Rahman,' she murmured, sighing with pleasure as he went hard against her.

He said nothing, but nuzzled her with unexpected urgency. Then they were joining, coiling their bodies round each other, sliding together into black unknown forests. There was no Mariana, only her and him dissolving into one being. When it was over she fell back on the bed, luxuriating in the sensation of being wholly alive, of being desired.

Rahman covered her gently with the blankets and laid an arm round her waist.

'Mariana ...'

'Mmm?'

'What do you think of my wife?'

She's a mean cow.

'Well, she's a very brilliant woman.'

'No, do you like her?'

'Oh Rahman, how could I? She has you. Anyway, she's always a bit snippy with me.'

'You could punish her for that.'

His tone was silkily seductive and she frowned in the darkness, uncertain of what he meant.

'I meant, do you like her body?'

Mariana half sat up, but unexpectedly, he pushed her firmly

back down, running his hand down her side.

'Don't you think she has beautiful pert breasts? Wouldn't you like to touch her bottom?'

Sick now, Mariana struggled up. 'How could you say that to me? You know I'm not one of your swingers.'

'Don't be such a prude, darling. Everyone in your department takes part.'

'No, they don't. I know Annie wouldn't do anything like that.'

'Of course not *her*. She's a dried-up Calvinist Highlander, who would want her?'

'She's a Catholic, actually. From Barra.' Mariana's tone was icy.

He slid his hand on to her breast, as always making her nipple stand erect. Maybe this time it was just because she was angry.

'Why are you being like this? I'm offering you something most people will never experience.'

'Rahman, I love you. I want only you.'

He gave a short laugh. 'What a silly little girl you are. Miriam says your husband is very attractive in a rugged sort of way. I bet he would love to take part.'

She switched the bedside light on. 'You sick bastard,' she shouted. 'I'm pregnant. I'm having your baby.'

He stared at her, his face still with shock. When he finally spoke it was in a coldly venomous tone she had never heard him use before. 'You stupid, stupid bitch. I thought you were smart. Have you taken leave of your senses?'

She could hardly breathe. How handsome he was. Was that why she hadn't realised what an ugly person he was? Her face locked into stubbornness.

'It's your baby.'

'Don't be ridiculous. You can't possibly know that.'

'I do.'

He took her nipple between his fingers and twisted hard. 'Then get rid of it.'

She thumped him in the chest. 'I can't, you fucker. It's six months.'

'You imbecile. What on earth did you think the deal was? Did you think I would leave my wife for *you*?'

She was totally winded, gasping as she tried to get the words out. Had she suddenly developed asthma? It was scary, trying to find the breath to speak. She had never felt such shock in her life. When she tried to get off the bed her legs couldn't move.

'Don't you want a child?'

'I have children. Two by my first wife. Why on earth would I want more?'

Her stomach started heaving then and she knew her face had contorted into ugliness.

'Get into the bathroom,' he said. 'Quickly.'

When she made no move he gripped her savagely by the arm and frogmarched her towards the en-suite, shoving her in. He looked at her coldly. His penis seemed almost purple in the dim light. 'You disgust me,' he said.

Now she feels sick the way she did that day, really sick, as though she wants to throw up, vomit up everything in her stomach, including the disgusting creature lodged deep in her body. Living off her. How could she possibly love it? When she thinks of it she thinks of an ad she's seen for toilet cleaner, where the germs are grotesque carbuncles with pustulent skin. That's what's growing inside her.

Poor Crawford, he's so happy. He really thinks it's his. If only he was right. There's no way to find out, though. Those smudgy scan photos can't tell you what colour a baby is. If it's Rahman's, she doesn't know what she'll do. How could she explain that away? A genetic throwback? Oh God, let it be Crawford's. If it is, then she'll be a good wife to him. She'll never betray him again.

She does love him, really. Yes, really she does. Rahman was just an aberration. They'll get their own townhouse, not just a poxy flat. Well, it's not poxy. It's far better than anywhere she ever stayed in. But a townhouse would be better. He has to get the promotion first but no harm in thinking about it. One with a gym so she can lose the baby weight fast. And a state-of-the-art kitchen with black granite worktops, maybe. Pale colours in the bedrooms but some pattern in the public rooms, traditional kilims in dark reds and blues, that sort of thing. Tasteful. The sort of thing rich people have in their homes. Crawford is rich, of course ...

Slowly she gets off the bed. She'd better smarten herself up before he gets home. The blue dress he likes so much, a bit of make-up, some perfume. He'll never know. By the time she hears his key in the front door she at least looks presentable, if not the serene domestic presence she hoped to portray.

'Mariana!' His voice is loud and ebullient. Does that mean he's got the promotion? She rushes out to the hall to greet him. Oh God, his face is hidden by a massive bunch of dark red roses, whose scent instantly makes her feel queasy.

'I got it. We're on our way, girl. Andrew Forrest was gutted, but getting the Maitland contract sealed it for me.'

He sits down heavily on the sofa, pulling her down beside him. 'I couldn't be happier, Mariana. You, the baby, and now this.' His speech is a little slurred. He must have celebrated on the way home. She leans her head against his, arms sliding round the thick girth of his waist. He'll probably be quite fat in a couple of years. The roses are practically in her nose.

'I'm so proud of you,' she says.

She'd better leave the university. Let someone else study the Four Marys. Let someone else have their head filled with the different Mary Hamiltons and their royal lovers, with apothecaries and ladies-in-waiting, with Tsarist Russia. With dead babies. She needs to think of happy things now. She'll wait for a politic moment to tell Crawford but she knows he'll be ecstatic. She'll not just be a good wife to him now, she'll be the perfect wife. So why does she feel as if she's on the way to her own execution?

Shining through Edinburgh Town

THEY CAME FOR ME in the morning. The knocking was so loud that I thought it must be that big heifer Carmichael. She's so clumsy. Then, as if from a long way away, I heard the men's voices.

'That's the third time of knocking. She must be sleeping the sleep of the dead.'

'She will be soon enough.'

'A bonnie lass like that, how could she be so cruel?'

'What's a quine to do if she has no money and no protector?'

'Still ...'

'Wait, sirs,' I said. 'I must dress.'

I heard one of them laugh. 'Let's go in now. That's a good-looking wench,' he said, but the others hushed him.

'Leave her be. The lass has enough to bear.'

There was still blood on my nightgown, even on my skin. I scrubbed at it with a wet cloth but left one little patch – it was all I had of my baby. I had so many dresses, red, pale blue, the beautiful violet silk that I was wearing when Lord Darnley first noticed me, but I picked out a white one. If I was to be dragged through the streets to die, then I would go shining through Edinburgh town.

The men all stared when I opened the door. I could see lust in their eyes and almost begged them to let me go, but I knew they had not the power. I would not demean myself by pleading to them for mercy.

Flanked by two on either side, I walked down the stairs, my head held high, though inside I was terrified. If only I had kept my wits about me the night before ... I had stood by the water's edge, just holding my baby for what must have been hours. At dawn, Mary Seton rose to pray and saw me from her window. As the sky started to turn pearly grey I suddenly realised where I was and put the baby in the water. Maybe if I had kept on holding him I could have persuaded them his death was an accident, but Seton told Carmichael and Carmichael told everyone else. Then there was no doubt, I would be condemned.

They brought me into the presence of the Queen. Her face was ashen, but I could see too that she was angry. Had she discovered that I had lain with her husband? Or was it simply that she was a mother herself and could not forgive? Mary Fleming looked shocked, and sad. She winced when she looked at my white dress and gave me a puzzled look. I suppose she was right. Far better to wear penitential black or brown than to parade myself like this. But I knew I did not want to die as someone else. I was a woman who had caught the eye of a king. They would not forget me.

Mary Stuart stood up. She was so tall she made me feel a child. 'They are saying you lay with my husband.'

I could not look at her. 'Aye, my lady. I regret it bitterly. It is you I love, not him.'

'Who could love him?' she sighed. 'At least we have that in common.'

'It was the work of a moment, a moment of madness.'

She looked at me not unkindly. 'I warrant it was he who importuned you.'

I nodded and bowed my head. 'I wish no one had found out about it,' she said. 'I know you are not a bad woman. But there is nothing I can do for you. I cannot be seen to condone murder.'

Later that month she would keep repeating the same words over and over again, when they asked if she would sanction the murder of her husband. Mary Fleming came to see me in the Tolbooth and told me it all, that the lords wanted rid of Darnley. I did not blame them. I would have put a dagger in him myself. For a few moments' pleasure that selfish, whoreson fool had destroyed my life. I warrant he has destroyed Mary Stuart's life, too. He has made her more enemies than ever she could have dreamed of.

I was glad to be in the Tolbooth, where there was no hope. I did not deserve hope. The very walls there were crumbling. The Queen had ordered it to be demolished but work was slow and too many people were crammed into too small a space, along with rats and every other sort of vermin. It was hateful. It would be better to die than to live like this. My white gown was gradually becoming filthy grey and the people around me stank. I assumed I did, too. None of it mattered. The worst thing was the heavy weight in my stomach where once my baby had been.

Mary Fleming stayed true and came to visit me, ignoring her surroundings, though they must have made her feel sick. One day she brought me paper and chalk, though the only thing I found myself drawing was hundreds and hundreds of little mouths and eyes and noses, all detached from each other and floating on the page as if hundreds of babies had been torn apart, feature by feature.

Another day she brought me some pastries, which she made me eat while I was with her as she knew they would be snatched from me by the other prisoners. They tasted very rich to me after the plain oats I had had to eat in the prison. After she had gone I was violently sick, which earned me a kicking.

'Keep your foul mess inside you,' said one of the other women. 'Murdering whore.'

The next time Mary came she saw the bruises. 'Why have you not paid the turnkey for a room?' she asked.

I had to tell her that I sent my money to my mother and kept only a little for myself. 'I dare not tell her what I have done.'

'Oh Mary, your own mother will love you no matter what.'

'As I loved my wee babby?'

'You would have been a good mother, I know it. You should have had more faith.'

'How could the Queen have let me stay, knowing I betrayed her?'

'Mary Stuart is a very tolerant woman. She was angry at first, but she knows what it is like to love too well.'

When next she came we went into a separate room as usual, but this time she put a large parcel down on the stone flags. 'I have brought you some clothes. This will be your chamber from now on. Here, take off this filthy gown. I will have it washed for you.'

I was hardly able to thank her, I was crying so much. Why was she being so kind to me? Everyone else had only contempt for me, as I had for myself. But I had always loved her and perhaps she knew it. She sat down (as we had so often in different circumstances) to gossip about recent events.

'Twelve thousand pounds she had to borrow,' she said, shaking her head. 'My cousin is reckless, Mary. To christen a babe? Even if he will be a king.'

I thought of my own babe, half-brother to a king. His christening was even more expensive – it would cost a life.

'I wish you had been there. It was the grandest ceremony we have had in Scotland, as fine as any we saw in the French court, though like to be the last we will ever have. The Lord only knows what will happen to my cousin. The lords want to be rid of Darnley, who lies in a fever from the pox. The Queen wants to be rid of Darnley so she can marry Bothwell. The country wants to be rid of all the turmoil.'

'Darnley has the pox?'

Mary Fleming turned to me, her face aghast. 'I am sorry. I did not think.'

I could not stop laughing. 'How fitting. I wish him well of it. Do not worry. I will be gone before ever his itching reaches me.'

She laughed then, relieved that I was still able to jest. 'Oh Mary, you should have seen the beautiful christening font Queen Elizabeth of England sent. Solid gold and inlaid with precious gems. What a struggle they had to put it in place. It was so heavy it took three men. That red-haired shrew must be worried. Mary draws ever closer to her throne. Poor bastard queen, she can never be easy wearing the crown.'

A bastard queen. I had not thought of Queen Elizabeth like that before, but of course, those of us of the true faith believed her father's marriage to Anne Boleyn to be a sham. Look how far the bastard queen had risen, though, and she a woman. Pain twisted my stomach when I wondered what my son could have become.

'I wore pearl drop earrings and a gown of dark blue ormosing taffeta, such fine stuff.'

'What is that?'

'Oh, don't you know it? That special taffeta from the Isle of Ormuz in the Persian Gulf. Mary Beaton has a very fine gown of it in emerald green.'

'Goodness, I warrant John Knox would have an apoplexy at such extravagance.'

'As well, then, that I did not seek the preacher's permission for my finery. You and I both know that beautiful things are necessary to a woman.'

Yes, I knew it. I should have been there in my violet silk, with the sleeves given to me by a queen. I should have feasted on venison and swan, danced the galliard, perhaps even have sung for the royal baby. As the tears started to my eyes, Mary Fleming swiftly changed the subject.

'The food would have astonished you – there was a whole wild boar and great towers built up of delicious little pastries. There was a syllabub strewn with rose petals, twelve roasted peacocks, oysters cooked in almond milk. It was all brought in by men dressed as satyrs with long tails. When they passed the party from the English court they waggled their arses at them. The English thought it was an insult and were black affronted but I am afraid we all thought it was very funny.'

That made me laugh again, as I am sure she intended. She sat with me in the darkening afternoon, telling me the rumours of this lord and that lady, the constant machinations against the Queen, the loathsome pustules that had broken out on Lord Darnley's skin. I felt whole again, for a while. I felt loved.

She came but once more, to bring me my clean white dress. She had married by then, to that old goat, Maitland. Was it my own woes which made me dislike all men now?

'I think it is this one you wish to wear?' she said. Her voice was hushed.

My skin, I think, was as white as the gown. I had not been out in fresh air for over three months, had barely seen a scrap of blue sky from this prison chamber.

'When?' I could not complete the sentence.

'Soon, I fear.'

Her eyes were red, as though she had shed tears lately.

'Has my Queen forgotten me so completely? She pardoned those who murdered her beloved David Rizzio, could she not forgive me?'

'Oh Mary, if she were her own dear self then I know she would. But she is fallen into a sad decline. You mind how she was after Jedburgh? When she fell ill after riding so far to visit Bothwell?'

I nodded. I had had my own troubles then but I remembered. I had not paid as much attention as I might, maybe because women like me did not have the luxury of lying in bed weeping. Mary Stuart was highly strung, we all knew that, but what could be the matter now?

'I think you have not heard about Lord Darnley?' Her voice was gentle and I knew from her tone that something terrible must have happened.

'I hear nothing in here.'

'No.' She looked round at the bare stone walls and floor, the minute sliver of light coming in from the outside. 'No, I see that.'

'He is dead, then?' My knees were shaking though I hardly knew why. It was not as if I would miss him or mourn him.

She looked nervous. 'He was staying in a house called Kirk o' Field, overlooking the Cowgate. There was a huge explosion in the night and the house burned to the ground. But the King and his servant were found in the garden, strangled.'

I studied her face, seeing she was uncomfortable. So the lords had decided to get rid of Darnley once and for all. Perhaps her new husband had been one of them? Rage bubbled up inside me when I thought of it. There was no heat in the blood in their murder, yet they would undoubtedly walk free, while I, who had been at my wits' end in terror for months before my baby was born, was to hang. An unnatural, unfeeling mother, the judge had said, though I do not see how he could be privy to what is natural in a mother.

'And what was the Queen's part in it?'

'None. She was not there that night. She had gone to Bastian's wedding masque. He married Christiana Hogg, on the last day before Lent.'

Bitter Lent, that would lead to no re-birth for me. Bastian was the Queen's favourite valet. Of course she would not miss his wedding masque but would be seen to be there, that others would know she loved him. It could have been so with me had things been different.

'And does she weep for Lord Darnley?'

'She weeps,' said Mary. 'Though not perhaps as much for Lord Darnley as for herself. The lords thought they were helping her, but all they did was drive her into the arms of Bothwell. A king for four weeks.'

That boor, it was what he had always wanted, but I would never call him my king.

'They cry her whore. Some made banners with Bothwell's family crest, the hare, and the Queen as a mermaid – you know they use this word for a woman who is a prostitute? My poor cousin. She has been loved all her life and now she is hated. She is in such a melancholy as I have never seen. I fear for her.

'Rebels have her in their charge. She will never be Queen of Scotland again.' Mary Fleming began crying uncontrollably. 'Last night she was brought to Edinburgh and this morning she stood at the window of the provost's house, with her breasts bare and her hair all hanging down like the mermaid, crying and screaming at the people that she had been betrayed. She cannot help you now, Mary.'

We clung together, Mary Fleming and I, like two women hanging on to the wreckage of a storm-tossed ship. Mary Stuart was not in the room but her presence was there with us. We had laughed so often together, danced, ridden across country like the wind, yet here we all were, struggling to survive the black breakers that threatened to engulf us. I gave Mary Fleming the necklace the Queen had given me and the last of my coin to send to my mother. When she left that day, I knew I would never see her again.

I sat for a long time as the evening turned black, thinking about the sheer courage that Mary Stuart had always shown. Yet she had come to this, half naked and raving in the sight of her people ...

If only I had never left my mother's house. Life there was hard, but it was peaceful. There was nothing to win but your daily bread, nothing to lose. My poor mother. What shame she would feel. How she would weep for me. She would call out my name in her sleep, imagining the rope around my neck, trying to wrestle it off me in her dreams. I knew it. There was no dignity in a hanging, but I vowed then that when my time came I would die like a Queen.

This morning I rose early to prepare myself. I have not eaten for three days – I do not wish the shame of soiling myself from fear as happens to some poor people. Or when the rope bites. I feel tired, but I am young and strong. It is better this way. As I begin combing my hair, I hear a persistent sound from outside, as if the sea is roaring in the distance. So the people have begun to gather, even at this early hour? There is little enough to entertain them, God knows, though I have never known what pleasure there can be in watching a hanging. The Queen felt like that too and often took to her bed afterwards, though I doubt I will be able to do the same.

As I pull the comb through my tangled curls, I remember the times when I was a wee girl, when my mother brushed my hair for me at night. She always sang little lullabies to calm me down for sleep. Quietly I hum to myself, letting my breathing get deeper and slower. I dress my hair as well as I can. It does not reach Mary Seton's standards but it is pretty. Now for my white gown. I slide it over my body, relishing the caress of the silken fabric, grateful that Mary Fleming has allowed me to look my best. People might think I am vain, but I know that to look well will give me courage.

Outside, the waves of sound are getting louder, as if the sea is advancing towards the land. I find myself weeping, but these tears will be my last. I must die like a Queen – my baby would have been half-brother to a king. If only I had been braver ... I wonder, will I see him on the far shore when this is all over? Will he forgive me?

When the knock comes on the door, I am ready. The guards are gentler than I expected. I think I see pity in their eyes. They walk on either side of me, their boots thudding on the flagstones. The walk seems very long and I have to force my legs forward. How can I be so weak? I almost fall when I try to climb the stairs but they each put an arm under me and help me up. They stop at a heavy wooden door. One of them looks into my face.

'Are you ready?'

I take a long breath. Yes, I nod. They part the doors and I walk through, on to the execution platform at the side of the Tolbooth. The tumult all around is overwhelming, a huge breaker of sound that washes over me and almost knocks me down. I walk forward, and individual voices in the crowd start to filter through to me.

'She's a bonny wee thing, is she no'?'

'She's nothing more than a bairn herself. That's no' right.'

'Her wee babby is dead. That's no' right, either.'

I raise my head, trying not to shiver in the cold. The fragrant smell of roasting pork comes wafting towards me, making my mouth water and my stomach gripe with hunger – some enterprising vendor is roasting a whole pig and selling it off in small portions. Others are selling wine and cider, hot sausages. It is the best food I have ever smelt in my life.

There is a festive air among the people, as if seeing another person lose their life will make them feel more alive. They jostle for a good position, laughing and joking, some holding hands or standing with their arms around each other. They have many days to live. I have only minutes.

I am glad there is no one I know in the crowd. My poor mother … I wish she might never find out, though I know she will. What will my sisters think of me? Will they despise me?

I try not to think of what will happen to me, my face turning blue, my tongue lolling out, my body jerking on the rope. While I am alive I will be dignified. I gaze over the crowd. A sliver of blue has appeared to break the monotonous grey of the sky. The hangman is reading out my sentence but it is as if the words are in a foreign language. I cannot tell what he is saying.

The crowd is silent. I have nothing left to wish for, nothing left to mourn. Nothing to say. The hangman steps forward and leads me to a small ladder, but my legs seem not to work and the steps are too high for me. He puts out a hand to help me and I walk up, my head high and my back as straight as I can make it. I smile my thanks to him. He looks away. He is a decent man.

As the noose is put around my neck I look out over the crowd. Another great crashing wave of sound breaks over me as they roar, in approval? Excitement? The ladder is kicked away and I swing forward into nothingness. My neck burns with the rope. I cannot breathe. The blue sliver of sky has gone and all is grey. I strain to hear the sound of the selkie's song, but oh, I am so far from the sea …

He'd Never Come back to Me

MAY 2014

'DOING ANYTHING SPECIAL TODAY?' says Crawford, struggling with his cufflinks, an accessory Mariana had never actually seen anyone wear until she met him and his friends.

'I'm getting a bit stir-crazy in the house. I might go out for a drive somewhere.'

Crawford looks alarmed. 'For God's sake, Mariana, you can't go driving so close to your time.'

'I've got weeks to go.'

'Have you asked the doctor?'

No. She hasn't gone near the doctor and she isn't going to. This whole thing is bad enough without having some man she hardly knows interfering with her life. 'Freebirthing' they call it nowadays, she read it in *The Guardian*. Women have been having babies for centuries without medical intervention, so why shouldn't she?

'Women can drive right up to the birth. My sister took the kids to school the morning before she had her last one.'

'Look, babe, we don't want to take any chances. Anyway, I wouldn't call your sister the perfect role model, would you?'

When did he adopt this habit of calling her 'babe'? And why hasn't she noticed it before? She sighs, wishing she'd never given up her university course. Her brain's atrophying, withering into a tight, gnarled-up old walnut.

'Emma's a perfectly good role model,' she says, aware that she never goes to see her sister and has no desire to. Too many children in too small a space. Horrible housing estate. No, thank you. She has better things to do with her time.

But what are they?

'Why don't you go to Jenner's and buy yourself something nice to wear for the boss' dinner party next week?'

Is he a total imbecile? Why would she go and spend a lot of money on something when she's this big? If only she could be one of those women who somehow instruct their babies to hide themselves somewhere about their persons. Like Elizabeth, the wife of Crawford's colleague, Fraser. Mariana is convinced she had words with the baby. *Now don't dare loiter about my stomach and spoil the line of my dresses. I need you to make yourself scarce.* Even at eight months you could barely tell she was pregnant. Mariana's had a bigger stomach than that just from stuffing herself with chocolate.

'Maybe I'll just slump on the sofa and watch daytime television. I'm pretty tired.'

'Good idea,' he says, giving her a sunny smile now that she's seeing things his way.

She *is* tired, but not physically. Bored is what she is, really, though why should she be? She has everything she's supposed to crave, hasn't she? A rich husband, a beautiful home, a baby coming. She doesn't even have to do the housework. They have a cleaner for that now, thank goodness. Once Crawford's gone she flips through the paper to see if there's anything she wants to watch. Cookery programmes, property programmes, house makeovers. Clearly all designed for those aspiring to the next level up of the middle classes. Just like her, till she got there.

You haven't got your doctorate. Her mother's voice again, nagging in her ear. But she's right, why did she give up her course? It was really interesting work, she could have made something good from her research. She loved meeting new people, new ideas. To hell with it, she picks up the phone.

'Hi Annie, it's Mariana here.'

The tutor's voice is warm. 'Lovely to hear from you. How are you?'

'Fed up, really. I think I was a bit premature giving up the doctorate.'

'I meant how's the pregnancy coming?'

'Oh, I feel fine. But it's very dull being at home, doing nothing.'

'Well, your fees are paid up till the end of the year. There's nothing to stop you coming back.'

'You'd have me back?'

'Of course. I didn't want you to give up. Plenty of women carry on studying when they're pregnant.'

'I know. I was just trying to please Crawford, I think. He's quite old-fashioned.'

'Most men are, if you ask me.'

They both laugh. Mariana feels better immediately, picturing Annie's top-floor room, her spiky blonde hair and Doc Marten boots. It will be so good to get back to doing something that's for *her*. So she had an affair? So what? She can't go on beating herself up about it forever.

'You still had an essay to finish when you left, why don't you complete that and give me a ring? Say next week some time?'

'Thursday. I'll definitely have it done by Thursday.'

'Okay, come at four and we'll go to the pub afterwards. I'll drink enough red wine for both of us.'

'Deal. See you then.'

Yessss. Crawford's not going to like it but she'll go round the twist if she just stays at home all the time. She'll get round him. He's not a difficult person to manage, if one person can ever be said to manage another. He has simple needs, straightforward ambitions. He loves her, doesn't like trouble, of course she manages him. Doesn't she?

She's elated now. She will go out. Fuck it, why shouldn't she drive? The seaside, that's where she'll go. The coast is not even forty minutes away, maybe she'll see good breakers. It's the perfect day for them, bright blue skies and a high wind that lifts all the bits of paper littering the square and sends them scudding along the street like out-of-season leaves.

The seatbelt feels uncomfortably tight and she moves it so it's sitting under her bump. As she moves off, the music of the last CD she played fills the car – of course, Joan Baez's version of *Mary Hamilton*. The singer's voice, so pure, so poignant, pierces her to the core.

> *I put him in a tiny boat*
> *And cast it out to sea*
> *That he might sink or he might swim*
> *But he'd never come back to me.*

If only she could put *this* baby in a tiny boat and never see it again. How stupid she's been, ignoring the signs, but then could she really have gone through a third abortion? Even before the nurse in the clinic told her it was too late, she had misgivings. Three would be proof of stupidity of the highest order. How on earth did that medium in Linlithgow know about the ones she'd had before? Did she just take a guess? Mariana can hardly bear to think about it. If the medium's right, then her two children are up there, watching everything she does. They will see what she's done with her life since getting rid of them – is it really enough to justify their not having the chance to live? It doesn't amount to much, does it? A 'good' marriage, a few posh holidays, a degree and a half?

Oh God, *if* the medium's right, her two children will see her giving birth to the one that's coming. Would that make them angry? Maybe they'll haunt her, become the Furies flying at her heels, pursuing her for revenge. And what if the baby isn't Crawford's? What if it's Rahman's? There would be no way back from that, no *managing* Crawford if that happened. It would be the end of the marriage, she knows it.

With a cold chill of fear she realises she cannot imagine having this baby.

She would have to make herself love it if it was Crawford's. Is that possible, can you make yourself love someone? And is it fair, anyway? What a way for a child to grow up, sensing, as it undoubtedly would, that the mother who was supposed to love it had to force herself to do it. If the baby was Rahman's, things would be simple – she would hate it.

As she manoeuvres on to the City Bypass the car feels crowded, as if there is no room for her to breathe. All these dead people pushing into her head. And Rahman, how will she ever get him out of her mind? His long, lean body, the dark eyes that she thought were so romantic, how did she not realise that they were the eyes of a predator? *For such a clever woman you can be awfully stupid sometimes. Not an ounce of common sense.* Her mother's voice again. Her own voice.

Her Joan Baez album is re-playing and she fast forwards to the *Mary Hamilton* track again. Inexplicably after such a fine start to the day, the sky seems to be turning dark. All the better, maybe there's a storm coming. She comes off the bypass at Musselburgh and heads east along the coast. The baby inside her feels like a stone. Weighing her down. She's watched Baez sing this so many times on YouTube, the immobile face, the high Mexican cheekbones, the heartbreaking story that she seems to embody rather than sing. How many young girls over the centuries have fallen into the same predicament? But things are different now – she should have prevented this, she's not a stupid woman. People would have no sadness for her now, as they do for the Mary Hamilton of the ballad, only blame – though thankfully, at least no one would execute her. If only it were as simple as finding a tiny boat and casting the baby out to sea. She wants to rip it from her belly, wishes it had never existed.

Rain is pelting the windscreen now and she has the wipers on at full speed. There's a farm track somewhere around here – she'll head down there and watch the waves. She wishes she'd eaten more at breakfast time, but she felt a bit sick. Now her stomach is aching and she's exhausted. The car bounces over the rutted track, jarring her spine, and she's relieved to reach the little piece of wasteground at the end. Please God she'll be able to get out of here, she doesn't want to be stuck in mud and have to call the AA.

She parks the car and switches the engine off. Outside the sky is pearly grey, threatening. Waves are pounding on the shore, sending great flumes of foam into the air as they hit the rocks. A solitary seal bobs up in the water, buffeted around mercilessly till it sees sense and dives beneath the waves. To the east she can see the ruins of a castle –is it Tantallon? – and in the distance is the squat, unbreachable citadel of the Bass Rock. Out there she knows there are thousands of gannets, puffins, razorbills, cormorants, guillemots – all spraying white guano over the rock – but from here it looks a bastion of solid black, an impacted tooth bearing no sign of the turmoil of volcanic activity that formed it.

The sea is roiling and roaring outside when she suddenly feels an overwhelming urge to pass water. Then it's as if there's an explosion inside her and what seems like pints of liquid come gushing out, flooding the car seat and soaking into the back of her dress. For fuck's sake, her waters have broken. Out here in the middle of nowhere. What on earth can she do? She delves for her mobile, but there's no signal. Oh God, this can't be happening. She mustn't panic, must keep calm.

It's okay, she doesn't want a doctor here anyway.

She tips the seat back and waits. She's cold in her summery dress. Clouds are building up in the sky ahead, massing to create a spiral of black in the greyness. Outside, the wind is rising, gently rocking the car and rippling through the sea grass at the edge of the beach. Outside, the clouds start scudding towards her till it feels as if the whole sky is going to come in on her.

For a long time she closes her eyes against the pain, waves of pain that threaten to engulf her, to smash her into nothingness. She is no longer there, has become purely the aching in her body. As the hours go by, the windscreen is blotted with rain and the sea becomes a blur of grey and white, creating Turner-esque smudges of colour. She can no longer distinguish individual waves – the sea is transformed into a forest of foam. Panting, she tries to control the pain, but her spine feels as if it's going to crack and the nerve endings under her skin crackle. She can smell her own sweat and the crude animal pungency of birth. Will it never end? She screams, knowing the sound will be lost in the raging of the wind and the sea.

The baby, when it comes, slides out in a rush and flops on to the floor of the car, where it opens its mouth wide and starts to wail.

'Shut up. Shut up, shut up, shut up,' Mariana hisses. It's a disgusting little creature, covered in some white gluey substance. Oh God, she'll have it stuck to her for the rest of her life. Thick dark hair sprouts from its head. It looks like a goblin, with its round black eyes gleaming out of its round little face. Heart pounding, Mariana inches forward on the seat to look at it. Oh God, it's a girl and its skin is brown. Maybe it's a trick of the light but its lips look almost purple. It's Rahman's, Rahman's. She stares down at it, nauseous.

'I can't do this. I can't,' she howls.

She wants to pummel its horrid little face in, choke the life out of its body. She could do it. No one's here, no one could even see in if they *were* here, the windscreen is so streaked with rain. She could take it by the spine and shake it to death, put her hand over its bawling mouth and suffocate it.

She mustn't panic. Inside this stinking car her world could come to an end. She's not ready, can't do this. Crawford will never accept another man's baby. He'll divorce her and then she won't be able to afford to go on at the university. Where will she go? Where will she end up? In some sink estate like her feckless sister?

She won't do it. She is not Mary Hamilton, some young, helpless girl who had no choices. She stares down at the yowling creature that came out of her body. Shivering, she swings her legs out of the car, over the thing's head, then realises that it's still attached to her, by the revolting wormlike tubing of the umbilical cord. How on earth can she cut it away, get the thing off her? Maybe she has nail scissors in her make-up bag. It's freezing and within minutes of her opening the car door her thin dress is saturated with water. Out in the bay the storm continues unabated. She has never known winds to rage for so long.

No, nothing so tiny could survive in this.

Slowly, she leans over and rummages in her handbag. Her hands fumble in the cold but she finds them. It takes her a long time to cut through the cord, the tubing is so thick and the scissors so tiny, her fingers so blue with the cold. Crawford will be angry at her, but he need never find out that the baby wasn't his. They'll wrap it up at the hospital and he won't want to see it. He'll be too busy comforting his brave wife, who walked for miles to get help.

Mariana shuts the car door, leaving the key in the ignition. It will take a long time to walk back to the road. She starts to sing to shut out the noise of the thing crying. *Yestreen the queen had four Marys, The nicht she'll ha'e but three,* but she can't remember the words any more. Mud splashes her bare legs as she ploughs doggedly up the track. The car is freezing and probably still wet from her waters breaking. All she has to do is keep walking. She should be relieved but as the rain batters her face and the wind sears her skin, it is as if she is the one who has died.

Acknowledgements

My thanks go to Marina Warner, who is as warm and generous as she is erudite; to Dr Katherine Campbell of Edinburgh University's School of Scottish Studies (whose staff in no way resemble the fictional staff of *The Four Marys*); to Emma Grossmith, who has given me her friendship as well as greater musical understanding; to Mary and David, who were the novellas' first readers; to the members of the Scotia Writers' group for their invaluable comments and support, particularly Ray Evans and John Savage; to Zoë, who continues to give me literary support; and to Sara Hunt of Saraband, who stuck her neck out to publish uncomfortable stories in an under-used form.

Jean Rafferty is an acclaimed award-winning journalist based in Glasgow. Her first novel, *Myra, Beyond Saddleworth* (2012), was shortlisted for the Gordon Burn Prize. Jean is Chair of the Scottish PEN's Writers in Prison Committee.